The Ingenious
Gentleman and Poet
Federico García Lorca
Ascends to Hell

The Ingenious Gentleman and Poet Federico García Lorca Ascends to Hell

CARLOS ROJAS

TRANSLATED BY EDITH GROSSMAN

YALE UNIVERSITY PRESS ■ NEW HAVEN & LONDON

A MARGELLOS
WORLD REPUBLIC OF LETTERS BOOK

The Margellos World Republic of Letters is dedicated to making literary works from around the globe available in English through translation. It brings to the English-speaking world the work of leading poets, novelists, essayists, philosophers, and playwrights from Europe, Latin America, Africa, Asia, and the Middle East to stimulate international discourse and creative exchange.

Published with assistance from the foundation established in memory of Amasa Stone Mather of the Class of 1907, Yale College.

Library of Congress Cataloging-in-Publication Data

Rojas, Carlos, 1928–. [Ingenioso hidalgo y poeta Federico García Lorca asciende a los infiernos. English]

The ingenious gentleman and poet Federico García Lorca ascends to hell / Carlos Rojas ; translated by Edith Grossman.

   p.   cm.

"A Margellos World Republic of Letters book."

ISBN 978-0-300-16776-4 (cloth : alk. paper)

1. García Lorca, Federico, 1898–1936—Fiction. I. Grossman, Edith, 1936–. II. Title.

PQ6633.05941513 2013

863'.64—dc23   2012033920

10 9 8 7 6 5 4 3 2 1

Further information appears on page 204.

For Marina and Sandro Vasari, with the gratitude of C.R.

CONTENTS

The road to this translation of Carlos Rojas's *The Ingenious Gentleman and Poet Federico García Lorca Ascends to Hell* was a circuitous one. I first read the novel about thirty years ago, not long after its 1980 publication in Spanish. I was a fairly new translator then, and I kept thinking how wonderful it would be to translate the book and bring it to the attention of an English-speaking readership. As it turned out, I had to wait three decades for that hope to become a reality, but it did, finally, thanks to the Margellos World Republic of Letters and Yale University Press. During all that time I never forgot this extraordinary novel: its breathtaking originality, devastating evocation of historical figures, and sharp-eyed re-creation of the period preceding the Spanish Civil War. The constant explosive violence led to the murder in 1936, soon after the right-wing military coup that started the war, of Federico García Lorca, one of Spain's leading poets and playwrights. He became Spain's best-known martyr, a victim of history run amok.

Rojas has many talents, but one of his great gifts as a novelist is his seamless blending of a meticulously researched historical background (all the characters, with the exception of Sandro and Marina Vasari, are based on actual people) with a highly inventive view of the possibilities of fiction. The novel is filled with figures who walk off the stage of history and into the pages of the book: Antonio Machado, the exceptional poet of the generation just before Lorca's; Rafael Alberti, Lorca's contemporary and fellow member of the Generation of 1927; Salvador Dalí, the great surrealist painter; José Antonio Primo de Rivera, founder of the Falange, the Spanish imitation of

Mussolini's Fascist Party. I've cited only a very few of the literary, artistic, and political personalities who populate this variation on the life of García Lorca and the catastrophe of Spain.

Rojas's debt to Cervantes, the forebear of European fiction, is deep, and it is clearly acknowledged: "ingenious gentleman" is the phrase Cervantes used to describe his protagonist in the title of his genre-defining work. It was in Part Two of *Don Quixote*, published in 1615, ten years after Part One, and just a year after the appearance of an anonymous, bogus continuation of the knight's adventures—what has come to be known as the "false *Quixote*"—that Cervantes took a kind of metaphysical leap through the novelistic looking glass he himself had created and gave obviously fictional characters (Quixote and Sancho) the presence and dimensionality of those other personages who *seem* to be real and are intended to help create verisimilitude, the appearance of truth that was, for Cervantes, the goal of fiction. Since the landscape of *Don Quixote* evokes a contemporary reality and a good number of historically factual people and events, it doesn't require much for the reader to suspend disbelief and accept the actuality of the nobles, peasants, innkeepers, servants, friars, travelers, soldiers, ladies, and outlaws the knight and his squire encounter on their travels. In one of the uncommon inns that stud this seventeenth-century countryside, two gentlemen are reading and discussing the sham continuation, but the "real" Quixote and Sancho, who know, remarkably, of the existence of Part One, which recounts their adventures, overhear their conversation and disabuse them of the false *Quixote*'s authenticity. The profound ambiguity created here is the legitimate forerunner not only of Rojas's novelistic creation but of most, if not all, of the experimental fiction in our own time.

In *The Ingenious Gentleman* we encounter a unique vision of hell and eternity; heaven doesn't enter into the equation, unless it's the reward of total unconsciousness and loss of self-awareness that may be the outcome of each damned soul's impending trial. In the theaters of the damned lining a corridor that ascends the spiral, we discover two alternative endings to García Lorca's life. These variations are physically embodied as aged versions of the younger poet (Lorca was thirty-eight when he was killed), who materialize in his theater and assert their reality. In the second decade of the twentieth century, Luigi Pirandello (*Six Characters in Search of an Author*) and Miguel de Unamuno (*Mist*) walked this path as well, giving imagined characters the status of those who imagine them, but I think Rojas's foray into hyperspeculation is more extensive and closer to the Cervantean imagination. He novelizes himself and slowly becomes a significant presence in the action. The creation of a fictionalized version of the real author also has its roots in *Don Quixote*, where Cervantes's prologue to Part One involves an imagined version of himself and a friend who helps him write the dreaded, obligatory introduction to the novel. Rojas's alter ego (C.R. in *The Ingenious Gentleman*) isn't more solid than the characters in the novel and, in fact, almost begins to blur as Marina and Sandro Vasari come to the realization that they are his creation.

In a recent e-mail, Carlos Rojas described his book in a characteristically enigmatic manner. His remarks foreshadow the fiction you are about to read and are a kind of preview of his sharp, direct style and stunning imagination:

> In death's eternal curvature of space time there is no absolute certainty. In the small hours of either August 18th or August 19th, 1936, a fascist firing squad shot Federico García Lorca between the villages of Viznar and Alfacar, some six miles northwest of Granada. . . .
>
> Needless to add, the proven mortal remains of any of the three Lorcas have never been disinterred in the historical present. Moreover, toward the end of the book, two new characters vainly try to decline its authorship with fictitious arguments. Meanwhile, an unusual hoarfrost and menacing hailstorm as-

sail Atlanta, Georgia, of all places. François Villon, another
poet who lived five centuries before Lorca and also vanished
from earth without a trace, would have said that poetry, or for
that matter narratives, are but lost snows that once covered a
vanished past.

You are about to discover a wonderful writer who will take you to
places you've never imagined in ways you never dreamed possible.
Enjoy the trip.

EDITH GROSSMAN
New York

*The Ingenious
Gentleman and Poet
Federico García Lorca
Ascends to Hell*

THE SPIRAL

I thought the dead were blind, like the ghost of that Gypsy girl in one of my poems, who peered into the cistern in the garden and didn't see things when they were looking at her.

I was wrong. For the dead everything is unanimous presence at a perpetually unreachable distance. All you lived, all you thought, any chimera fantasized on earth becomes at once possible and inaccessible in hell. It's enough to evoke an event or a dream for it to be immediately represented, with perfect precision, in this almost darkened theater where I suffer alone, perhaps for eternity.

Imagine a solitude that is perhaps interminable in a large orchestra section I share with no one. Through two transoms on the tapestry-covered walls comes a very cold light, between amber and alabaster. It barely outlines the backs of the empty seats, covered in turn in ash-colored velvet. With time and in this almost total gloom, I grew accustomed to making out the stage with its long arch and deep proscenium. There the front curtain and backdrop are always raised or perhaps do not exist. On the boards—real boards—the absent becomes present when my desire conjures up mirages of memories, readings, or reveries. If I were to tell you everything I have seen again, and you could hear me, you'd believe that we who are dead are mad.

Right now I see, because I wanted to, the aurora borealis over the Edem Mills lake, lighting up schools of red fish at the bottom of a stand of bulrushes snowy with minute white snails, just as I contemplated it in the summer of 1928 or 1929, in mid-August. I see that caveman, the same one who painted the bison at Altamira and in our world was the Nazi sculptor Arno Breker, after Jules Verne found him in the middle of one of his novels and at the center of the earth. Still in the brilliance of the aurora that sets the night and the fish ablaze with its most fiery red, I see Julius Caesar (a Julius Caesar whom I always imagined resembling Ignacio Sánchez Mejías) reciting unrhymed couplets of satanic pride: "I'd rather be first in a village / than second in Rome."

In the same mix of resuscitated memories, visions of other reveries of mine appear at the edge of the lake and in the middle of the stage. I see Achilles the swift-footed, a pederast too for love of Patrocles. Centuries before Caesar was conceived and in some reading of my adolescence, I learned what he said to Ulysses when he went down to visit him in hell: "Don't try to console me for my death. It's better to serve a beggar than rule over all the dead."

Only now, dead and in this theater, do I understand Caesar's source when he plagiarized that unrhymed couplet after deforming it to the bombastic measure of his pride. In the final analysis, I suppose that power on earth is always reduced to this: to plagiarism. In other words, which are those of the learned men of the Royal Academy of the Castilian Language, to the subjugation of free men into slaves or the abduction of other men's servants to make them one's own. Nothing more but nothing less either. Know this.

With a voice that comes from the obscure roots of a scream and from this corner of eternity, I would like to shriek at you the despair of Achilles in the kingdom of shades. To tell you in a shout, even though you might not be able to hear me, that it is better to be the lowest of men, a beggar, a hangman's apprentice, a lackey, or an all-powerful despot, than to be king of the dead. A monarch preceding time, light, space, and silence itself, an absolute sovereign as eternal as the void, the master and creator of hell, who must reign over all the dead even though we don't know his name and his face.

Any instant of my fleeting, precipitate life, any of the moments now present and impossible on the stage in this theater, is better than immortality in hell. Even if the dead have nothing and aren't anyone, I'd give everything to really relive the simplest or most terrible of those hours that have fled, even the moment of my own death at the hands of my fellow men. To tread again with my own footsteps, the measure of my liberty for I could take them or not, the rainbow on the asphalt of Manhattan after the last summer rains, while the street burns in long gleaming striations that resemble agate in the twilight. Dazzling streams at the feet of the line of unemployed waiting for Al Capone's charity soup at Saint Patrick's refectory. To return to the Café Alameda, where I saw Ignacio Sánchez Mejías for the first time on earth, before people and pride separated us. To hear him say again: "Do you know what Pepe-Hillo replied, when he was fat, old, and suffering from gout and they advised him to abandon bullfighting? I'LL LEAVE HERE ON MY OWN TWO FEET, THROUGH THE MAIN GATE, HOLDING MY GUTS IN MY HANDS."

The magic of free will in hell incarnates those memories on stage. Still, the flashes from the past are always painted, not live. If I go up on the boards, so often confused by their apparent veracity, they vanish immediately at my approach. As a fata morgana flees before you tread on it, or vampires turn to ash at dawn. The proscenium and set are empty beneath the arch and raised curtains. The light from the transoms, which recalls amber or alabaster, illuminates only my shadow on stage. The useless shadow of a dead man, alone in eternity with the mirage of his memories.

In reality there was no encounter between Ulysses and Achilles in Hades either. A blind man merely dreamed it for us. Death is a solitary confinement where each of the dead has an empty theater along the spiral of hell. That is the tragedy of immortality before the spectacle of what has been lived: not ever being able to share it with anyone, as if I were the only man who has lived in vain on earth. Or just the opposite, as if I were the only dead man in the world. Imagine Robinson Crusoe on his island, or better yet, imagine him on the head of a pin, suddenly realizing that in the middle of the night and the universe he is completely alone, as if he were the guilty conscience of all creation. That is the fate of each of us.

You who are alive, who caress the back of a cat or a woman and see the sparks from the stroke of your hand, you fear death because you think it means the loss of consciousness. This may be the greatest irony of human reason in the void of an irrational firmament. You will never be able to imagine the martyrdom of living eternally awake. All I want now is to renounce immortality. To sleep at last and to sleep forever, free of words, memories, even dreams. "Now I shall go to sleep," said Byron in his agony, as he turned to the side his profile worthy of a Roman coin on a cot in Misolonghi, where he died in vain for the freedom of Greece. DORMEZ read the stone on a mass grave of those guillotined in the name of reason and the rights of man.

Vanity of vanities of a species that has not always been human and perhaps is destined to cease being human! Chosen from a time before all times, to be transformed the day after tomorrow into the fish in the Edem Mills lake lit by the aurora borealis in the Vermont night! You are condemned to be immortal. To endure awake, insomniac, and alone forever because this void where you dissolve and come to an end does not exist. It has never existed and this is the greatest irony of our fate! Know this!

"Death terrifies me," I once told Rafael Alberti and María Teresa León, I don't know if it was years or centuries ago. The three of us were standing in a field of flowering teasel before the Castle of Maqueda. In their luminous youth, in the sun of a resplendent Sunday, they both seemed to have come from a Florentine altarpiece. Alberti shook that profile of his, which like Byron's you would say had been minted into imperial sesterces. He replied that he could not decide when he thought about which would be the greater of two horrors, the uncertainty of our fate in death or its interminable eternity. I interrupted him and said that whatever might happen to me after I was dead, whether it was nothingness, the lucid bliss anticipated by

Fray Luis de León, or a medieval hell, didn't matter to me. My panic, my absolute terror was simply the loss of my self: the inevitable renunciation of all I had been and who I had been until then. I never could have imagined, as perhaps no one in the world ever has, that death was in fact a sentence to be precisely who we were, fully conscious of ourselves, through all of time and perhaps beyond days and centuries.

That night, thinking perhaps about Rafael and María Teresa in the middle of the field, I wrote one of my sonnets of dark love. I learned afterward that it was interpreted as a poem of love for a man, because in my country nothing and no one has ever been judged correctly. In reality it was the expression of my old terror, just as I had stated it before the Castle of Maqueda. Desperation at the certainty I felt then that one day I would cease to be who I was among my fellow humans. In the long run, the poem was about irrevocable love though the loved one was me: that poor creature with his burning consciousness, like a match lit at the center of the world, condemned to disappear and be negated. That is what I believed then, though in hell I laugh when I remember it.

And I laugh at and am ashamed of the poem, which like others of mine I could recite from memory. It said that if the coolness of linen and ivy ruled the mortal body, the one that would be snatched from me along with life, my profile would become the long unashamed silence of a crocodile on the sands of eternity. Its irrational expression, the only one adequate to the senselessness of my human fate, withdrew into apparently more intelligible forms in the final tercets. Rhyming *llama* (flame) with *retama* (flowering broom), I declared that my kisses numb with cold would not be made of fire in death but of dry, frozen broom. Free of meters and unities (with a touch of fairly insincere resignation), I foretold that I would be invisible, divided between glacial branches and grieving dahlias.

In reality, hell is a desert very different from the one sketched in that sonnet. It is a spiral, perhaps interminable, in which each of the dead has an empty theater with its curtains raised. I can leave mine whenever I choose through the paneled door that opens with a touch of my hand at one end of the auditorium. Outside, a corridor about ten paces wide slopes upward, which I have walked to the point of exhaustion and which forms part of an arc whose radius I cannot imagine, for the slope of the ground, though real, is almost unnoticeable. From the gradient curve I deduced that an infinite number of turns followed one another around the same center. On the walls of the corridor the transoms of the theater are repeated, fairly far apart but equidistant. The same chrysoberyl light, emanating from I don't know where, keeps the orchestra section and the covered passage in identical semidarkness.

At times I stopped to think about the dimensions of hell. It must grow indefinitely, in constantly opening turns, adding new theaters for each new arrival. And it probably won't close until the last human being comes here, and by then the spiral will be the size of the universe. Don't ask me why or how I've come up with this calculation. I never went past adding on my fingers or multiplying next to the sign of X, but I'd swear I had the dimensions of hell right. Concluded and closed off, it would be as high and vast as the firmament. You could even say that then it would represent another firmament, invisible and parallel to our skies and constellations, empty of humans.

Like the transoms in the passage, the theaters on this spiral are equidistant. Farther along the corridor, a few hundred paces from my orchestra, is another identical one with the same stage opened at the back. I was there on several occasions but never could detect anyone in the auditorium, before I became certain that each of the dead is invisible to the eyes of all the others in hell. Whoever is there, for I sense that someone is being punished in that place, probably doesn't evoke his life or his dreams too frequently, for the boards, beyond the proscenium and above the orchestra, are always empty. Even though we cannot see one another, perhaps by virtue of the design that subjects us to this solitude, the visions of our memories or the memories of our illusions are in fact visible when presented on stage.

The next theater, a replica of the previous one and of mine, just as one tear duplicates another, does serve as the setting for representations. Someone consumes eternity there, devoting himself to strange memories. Through the uncurtained arch, behind the proscenium, a northern city appears. One of those Baltic cities redolent of salt and sun, its light so brilliant and unreal it hurts your eyes beneath the lazy flight of seagulls. Towers, windows, trees, and clouds gleam like precious stones at the heart of a delirium. The houses have red tile roofs onto which discouraged gulls descend, shrieking, while in the distance a flock of storks flies south. On a frozen pond, children wearing caps of scarlet wool glide in ice skates. Gentlemen stroll in top hats along the shore, monocles attached to their lapels, escorting blonde, white-skinned women with blue eyes, their hands hidden in fur muffs. Lights begin to go on in garrets under sloping roofs. Sleepy goblins unwillingly rush to hide under beds and at the bottoms of cedar chests. In large cases of carved wood displaying cornucopias and gilded inlays, all the clocks strike the same hour, while a smiling old man roasts chestnuts at the fireplace in a drawing room. In another room, a lank-haired, extremely thin student in a frock coat and spats cuts out paper dolls with a tailor's scissors for a little girl, while the scent of elderberry fills the air. Behind the windows of a shop, a cobbler polishes a pair of boots and sings as he works. His is a sad, languid melody that tells of the loves of roots formed by the mandrake in southern lands where men don't believe in Satan. In the distance a herd of reindeer passes, their horns twisted, their lips pink with cold, their fur covered in frost. In a cabin two hunters warm their frozen hands over a pot where eucalyptus seeds are boiling. The brilliance of many snows has darkened their faces, and they wear sheepskin jackets with curved knives hanging from the waist. In a tavern at the port, fishermen with green eyes and black beards drink dark beer. They are broad shouldered though somewhat hunchbacked, and long scars crisscross their palms. The mounted head of a polar bear looks at them from the wall with its pink glass eyes. In the same living retable an elf in a nightshirt that is too long climbs the stairs of a bell tower, while the back of his shirt trails along the treads and risers of the steps. He carries a lit candle in one hand and a gold umbrella in the other. Brushes and brooms on his shoulder, a chimney sweep crosses the street paved with polished round stones. He is dressed all in black, and his very high top hat of German patent leather is pulled around his ears, like Raskolnikov before his crimes. He passes in front of a bronze statue of a king and queen whose endless shadow extends across the ice to the center of the lake. The monarchs are wrapped in ermine beneath the ruff of their collars and hold scepters in hands crossed on their chests, like the recumbent figures of other sovereigns lying on their tombs. Gulls rest on their shoulders and the wind from the Baltic whips their impassive faces, while evening descends across an amber sky.

Now everything suddenly changes on stage. The city has been transformed into an Italian villa, perhaps from the Renaissance. Next to a large window, a gentleman contemplates the dusk and sips distractedly from a glass of port. His trimmed, graying beard gives him a certain similarity to a figure by Veronese in *The Wedding Feast at Cana*. Perhaps to Aretino, who looks up to the heavens after the miracle is complete. In a darkened leather baroque chair with carved armrests sits an old woman in mourning who may be his mother, to judge by their vague resemblance. Through lace cuffs one can catch glimpses of her tiny white hands, furrowed with blue veins. In her right hand she squeezes a Mechelen handkerchief as she reprimands the nobleman in a German I don't understand. The same salmon-pink late afternoon shines through the windows of a painter's studio where a cardinal is posing. His mouth has the implacable expression of one who has seen the ghosts of poisoned popes slipping at Advent through the labyrinths of the Vatican rose garden. Very soon, in the semidarkness, his habits will flame like embers enlivened by a gale, while his dark eyes glitter beneath his brows. Around a solid marble table, the kind they say Blasco Ibáñez once had, thirteen velvet-clad councilors conspire in quiet voices. They have identical hands and faces, like thirteen twins. A perspiring rider gallops down the steep street, spurring his horse. At the door of an inn, a plump hussy, her breasts bare, calls to him by name and laughs, arms akimbo. As he passes he lashes her face with his whip, not stopping. A landscape of vineyards opens behind the city. The vines climb the slopes of the hills, cut into terraces of earth as red as cinnabar. Farther away blackbirds fly over a pine grove that perfumes the air with resin and honey. Yellow bees alight on the beds where fennel, thyme, bergamot mint, and pennyroyal all flower. A cloud of martins screeches and a snake slithers into the heather. Slow-moving white oxen, their haunches spattered with dark scabs, the inner corner of their eyes black with flies, come along the path pulling a wagonload of hay. They are led by a drowsy, barefoot boy, his torso bare, who sings a tune in an Italian I don't understand either. On the square a squad of soldiers parades to the roll of drums, as Milanese and Vatican standards wave. Muskets at the shoulder, a dagger at the waist, gored breeches, polished helmets, breastplates gleaming, mercenary beards and smiles, the troop opens before the church. At the open main door a naked woman appears, her flesh as fair as if exposed for the first time to the light of heaven. She has the gaze of one possessed who perhaps has forgotten her own visions or was blinded when she contemplated them. Her deep black hair falls over her breasts and back while the soldiers present their arms to her, their harquebuses raised to the sun of an afternoon as luminous as on Corpus Christi. The crowd presses as she passes and roars in a frenzy: "*Viva, viva la ragione nuda e chiara!*"—Long live naked fair reason!

Whoever pays here for the sin of being born or, for that matter, of dying, deserves to be my brother in hell. I sense this at first and then deduce it, based on the illusions he invokes on the stage of his theater. It is written, however, that we who are dead will not see or hear one another in the orchestra sections along this spiral. I called to him so often in vain, among the empty seats, as the gentlemen in top hats, the sleepy goblins, the monarchs with ruffs at the neck, the vines on the terraces, the clouds of blackbirds, or the squadron of *condottieri* moved across the stage! "Who are you? Where are you from? What were you called among men?" My voice sounds enlarged by an echo, which gives it the tone of a baritone cantor, but no one hears me and no one answers. Only silence descends and remains.

On the other hand, I wouldn't like to see or speak with the damned sinner in the following theater. That is, the third after mine, ascending along the curve of the spiral. I realize now that I always locate the place exactly, as if I wanted to exorcize it. Just as the savage, when time was still young, painted his monsters in caves to imprison them. This theater fascinates and terrifies me for reasons I would never dare explain to myself, not even in hell. It is identical to the others, but as soon as I set foot in it I am overcome by the cold of frozen cemeteries. At the front of the stage the same scene always appears: a landscape of groves of pine, oak, and poplar where rockrose, which I recognize immediately, blooms. It is the Risco de la Nava, near Cuelgamuros, between the Portera del Cura and the Cerro de San Juan. The Mujer Muerta and the Pedriza must be close by. The panorama has not changed very much since the days of my adolescence or early youth. And it probably hasn't changed a great deal since another time, when Philip II chose the spot for El Escorial, between the peaks of the Abantos and the one they call his seat in the rock, past Cervunal and the Machotas. Only the forests have grown a little denser as the years passed over the mountains. The greatest change, the only one to my eyes, is the biggest cross I've ever seen in my life, defying the heavens on Risco de la Nava.

At the four angles of the gigantic pedestal stand four statues of the

Evangelists. Their grandiose bad taste stuns the spirit. I suppose the women at the base of the cross are the theological virtues. They too injure the stone and the landscape with their pompous vulgarity. The monument presides over an underground basilica that, evoked by whoever evokes it in this theater, seems as large as hell itself. Above the bronze door a Pietà no less sacrilegious than the Evangelists in its aberrant conception, becomes a crude parody of Buonarroti's. In view of religious sculptures like these, and perhaps to defend myself against their oppressive coarseness, I thought of my ode to the Blessed Sacrament of the Altar, which I dedicated to Manuel de Falla, not anticipating how much it would offend him. In it I spoke of seeing Christ alive in the monstrance, pierced by his Father with a burning nail, beating like a frog's heart on a slide in a laboratory.

The basilica opens into the rock through a portico that precedes an atrium followed by two angels with swords (*Swords Like Lips*), apparent guardians of a bronze gate. This divides the construction, as if after finishing it they were afraid they had made it larger than Saint Peter's in Rome, or than hell itself. The central nave, with its barrel vault, is preceded by a trail of martyrs and soldiers. Six chapels are sheltered there, with a single altar, a triptych painted on leather, and alabaster statues. Part of the vault is successful, for it allows you to see the living rock, contradicting the vile grandiosity of the rest. Great Flemish tapestries hang from the walls. Incredibly, they all represent the Apocalypse.

Here is the throne, where a man of jasper and sardonyx sits, encircled by a celestial halo as green as newly washed emeralds. Here, also surrounding the throne, are the twenty-four chairs where the twenty-four ancients sit, dressed in white and crowned in gold. Here are the seven lamps that burn before the man of sardonyx and jasper and are the seven Spirits of God, as the Illuminated Evangelist would say. Here is the sea of glass that Saint John would see before the throne, not knowing it was identical to other seas, not yet painted, of Patinir and Dalí. Here are the four beasts recently ap-

peared at the sea and facing the throne. Here is one that resembles a
lion, another a wild calf, another a man, and another a flying eagle.
Here is each monster with six wings, and six eyes on the wings. Here
are the eyes that do not rest day or night, saying: Holy, holy, holy
Lord God Almighty, which was, and is, and is to come. Here are the
ancients throwing their crowns at the feet of the man of jasper and
sardonyx, saying in turn: Thou art worthy, O Lord, to receive glory
and honor and power, for thou hast created all things, and by thy
will they must be and were created.

The truth is I don't know if the man who imagines this basilica
and landscape on stage is still alive or has died. It is possible that our
memories precede us into the theaters of hell shortly before our own
descent into death. In any case, he existed or wanted to exist only to
raise this temple to the exact measure of his pride. An arrogance so
vast that, as I said, it almost rivals in appearance the interminable
extent of this spiral. Whoever it is who suffers or soon will suffer
here, eternally reanimating the same obsessive memories, he fills
me with both fear and compassion. He terrifies me because I, who
imagined so many creatures in my verses, am incapable of imagin-
ing a being like him. And yet I feel compassion, because in spite of
his immense self-importance, he never really lived even if he still
lives.

No, the beasts' eyes never closed before the sea of the Apocalypse. I read that verse when I was fifteen years old and never could
forget it. Even now, in hell itself, I can repeat it word for word: "And
the four beasts had each of them six wings about him, and they were
full of eyes within; and they had no repose either day or night,
saying: Holy, holy, holy." No one noticed, but I was thinking of that
passage from Saint John when I wrote one of my most quoted
romances: the one I called the Ballad of the Summoned One. Like
the eyes of the four beasts at the end of the world (one of them a
man, remember), the eyes of Amargo and his horse never close. His
restless insomnia takes them through Dalinian landscapes of metal-

lic mountains, where playing cards turn into frost. When they finally announce his death, after two months, he finds peace, lies down, and sleeps serenely, concluding his time on earth. The truth made him free, as Saint John would have said, but Amargo pays for his freedom with his life. His motionless shadow on the whitewashed wall of the bedroom concludes the poem.

It goes without saying that in retrospect, recalling that ballad, I realize I had foretold my destiny in reverse. If Amargo's wakefulness, unnoticed by his fate, recalls the endless insomnia of hell, death is not repose or forgetting but the eternal presence of what you have lived in the world and in your soul. You might say that the poet's obligation is to invent the past that men forget, and foresee the inverted image of all the future, on earth and on this spiral.

("Do you know what Pepe-Hillo replied when he was fat, old, and suffering from gout, and they advised him to abandon bullfighting? I'LL LEAVE HERE ON MY OWN TWO FEET, THROUGH THE MAIN GATE, HOLDING MY GUTS IN MY HANDS.") I thought again of the monsters at the end of the world, full of eyes before the sea of the infinite, the ones the aged virgin Saint John had seen, when Sánchez Mejías died. It was the year of Our Lord 1934 and once again, when I evoke it, I understand how clear the signs were then of the great tragedy awaiting our people and how blind we were not to be aware of them. We always take note of our imminent fate too late, in the world and in this prison of empty orchestra sections and theaters populated by the memory of ghosts.

Forty bullfighters were seriously wounded that year. Twelve, one a month, died at various points around the Iberian Bullring. Ignacio Sánchez Mejías had already retired twice from bullfighting, always for the same reason: "At my age, a man doesn't appear in public in pink stockings without looking ridiculous." Two more times he had renounced his decision and returned to the arena. He was rich and aging, very old for the bulls at forty-three, his age on the afternoon he was gored. At the beginning of August he appeared in La Coruña with Belmonte and Ortega. When Belmonte entered the ring for the kill, he had an Ayala bull, and the sword pierced the back of the animal's neck, pulling out of the bullfighter's hand. Incredibly, the bull leaped to the seats and fell, his horns in the neck of a spectator, slashing him open from ear to ear. Not yet twenty, he died in the infirmary, unconscious and bleeding. At the end of the fight, a telegram came from Madrid announcing the sudden death of one of Ortega's brothers. Ortega left by car, accompanied by his cousin and Dominguín, his agent. They were still in Galicia when they had an accident and Paco Caballero, Ortega's relative, died immediately. The bullfighter, overwhelmed by so much misfortune, refused to participate in the event scheduled in Manzanares on the eleventh. The night before, in Zaragoza, where he had just arrived after fighting in Huesca, Sánchez Mejías agreed to replace Ortega, against the advice of his entire crew. The following afternoon they thought he was too fatigued to face more Ayala bulls without running serious risks. The Gypsy toreadors in his crew kept silent about their reasons, at once more terrible and more inevitable. For the past two or three weeks, Ignacio had smelled to them like a dead man. The stink of putrefaction and withered violets that non-Gypsies never could detect was intolerable in small rooms, like the ones in hotels. The flamencos had to make an effort not to tell Sánchez Mejías about it.

They say Ignacio was exhausted when he arrived in Manzanares after countless hours of traveling on roads ablaze with light and past fields of cicadas. He appeared with Armillita and Corrochano on the afternoon he was gored, when the first bull was his: another Ayala animal, dark and powerful, named Granadino. Sitting on the base of the barrier, the bullfighter made a contrary, suicidal pass. Urged on by the crowd, he tried to repeat it. That was when Granadino gored him in the left thigh and threw him over the barrier. Still conscious, he asked to be taken to Madrid. He had seen the town's infirmary before the bullfight and thought it was poorly staffed and inadequate. Still, they had to care for him first in Manzanares and bandage the wound, which was bleeding profusely. Perhaps the wound would not have been fatal if it had been treated correctly at the bullring. Nonetheless, from that moment on misfortunes ensued in frantic disarray. On the way to Madrid the car broke down and no one wanted to take Ignacio in his for fear he would stain it with blood. It took forever—hours and hours—to repair the damage and get the vehicle going again. In the meantime, it was necessary to change Sánchez Mejías's dressings because they were beginning to rot in the hellish heat. When they finally reached Madrid and Dr. Segovia's clinic, he hadn't lost consciousness, but a very high fever made him delirious. He shouted for his son and for me. That man who did not seem to have been born of woman but simply carved out of oak had become a child. He howled, asking us to play Simon says and corner tag with him.

I refused to go into the clinic or the room I would call iridescent with death throes in the most painful of my poems. I didn't leave the sidewalk, where I spent long hours asking every visitor how Ignacio was. They replied that he was getting worse by the hour and was losing hope. They looked away, not daring to meet my eyes because my attitude irritated them. They believed that only an irrational fear, the supposed panic of an effeminate man in the face of death, kept me from crossing the threshold of the building. I would have liked to shout at them right there, in the middle of the street, Gide's declaration of principles: *Je ne suis une tapette! Je suis un péderaste!* (Know I'm not a fairy! I'm a pederast!) Death didn't terrify me so much that I thought it was contagious. I was never that irrational, though I didn't recognize the logic of the universe and don't accept the senselessness of hell. In fact, there was no one who demonstrated greater courage than I did in my poem when I faced Ignacio's destiny. If there was, he left no evidence of his manhood, for the response Alberti dedicated to him compares unfavorably to mine. Simply put, I didn't have the heart to watch Ignacio suffer. To see how gangrene inevitably destroyed him until he was reduced to someone he had never been before: a dead man.

Ignacio himself must have believed in his delirium that I refused to see him because of a homosexual's weaknesses. In dreams his eyes would appear to reproach me for that. They were always very large and open in those nightmares of mine, his gaze fixed and hard in his virile, sensitive face, as broad between the temples as it was long. Under his porphyry forehead, which baldness enlarged in his last years, those motionless eyes denounced and pursued me. Even though I knew I was dreaming, I couldn't wake up or escape his vengeful hounding that reproved me for my absence and the crime of being born homosexual, as he could have blamed me for having been conceived a perfect man.

Constantly pursued by those eyes, between sleep and waking I must have imagined the main lines of my elegy before he actually died. Like the eyes of the apocalyptic monsters, fixed eternally before the man of sardonyx and jasper, I thought Ignacio's would not close at the moment of the final goring. I told myself he would keep them open after he was dead and no one ought to cover them with handkerchiefs. Eternity would transform him into a dark minotaur, beast and victim combined into identical sacrifices. None of those machos, the ones whose bones resonate like footsteps or flints, would dare to see himself in his unmoving gaze in the middle of the funeral chapel, as I, for very different reasons, did not have the courage to see him in his agony.

It was ironic that Ignacio, the most valiant bullfighter who ever lived, would reprimand me for unmanly cowardice. Yes, ironic, since in other circumstances he had meekly and shamefully humiliated himself before me. We all saw him at the festival in Córdoba, holding the muleta, down on one knee in front of a bull as gigantic as one of the stone bulls in Guisando, while with his other hand he smacked the animal's snout to make it charge. If it had, he would have been run through because the tips of its horns were scratching

his chest. His temerity was not completely blind, for he knew the
bulls of that herd too well to fear an attack. Still, if he'd had a
presentiment, he would not have abstained from testing fate because in his immense daring, Ignacio was immune to fear.

I'm referring to the physical, for he very well might have felt
moral fear. Two or three years before his death, he and La Argentinita had been lovers for almost ten. I was very fond of La Argentinita, who played the Butterfly in my first, very booed piece for the
theater in two acts and a prologue. And I would have to dedicate my
elegy for Ignacio to her, although at the time none of us could have
foretold that. La Argentinita always had the unequivocal affection
for me, like a mother's or a sister's, that some women feel for men
like me. A dancer acclaimed throughout Europe, she agreed to
appear in that distant play by a kid barely twenty years old and never
blamed me for its failure. I was never forgetful about gratitude,
though I was about rancor, and I always remembered her courtesy.
Afterward, when my poems and other plays of mine made me well
known, she celebrated them and told me she had always believed in
my talent and the success that fate would bring me. From the
beginning she confided to me her affair with Sánchez Mejías, to
whom she held on immediately and irrevocably, though she had
loved and enjoyed other men before him. She knew Ignacio would
not leave his Gypsy wife, sister of the Gallos, who was both resigned
and jealous, or his farm in Pino Montano, or his son, who, to the
consternation of his father, insisted on being a bullfighter. ("If a
broken body has to come into my house, let it be mine and not my
son's," Argentinita confessed that Ignacio had said to her.) Only
now, in this spiral of hell, do I understand how those words of his
were transformed into other lines in my elegy, without my being
able to see it, when I state in the poem that no one knows his body,
not the stone where he lies, not the black satin where he is destroyed. Even if he left his wife, his son, and his country house,
Argentinita went on, shaking her head, Ignacio would go back to

them, just as he returned to the bullring after his retirements. "It's his destiny, you know? He can't avoid it, and perhaps it's also written that he'll die in the arena."

If there were an invisible book of his life that would precede it point by point before it was lived, it would also have a footnote about other loves, this time incidental. Ignacio had an affair with a foreign woman, married and with children, whose name I forgot even though I introduced them myself. La Argentinita, who was never jealous of Ignacio's wife, was carried away now by resentment, suspicions, and rancor. She called or came to see me almost every day to tell me, in almost identical words, her desperation. I ran from Madrid to Granada, to my parents' house, to avoid her. Or rather, I imposed a truce and escaped the city for the same reasons I didn't want to go to Ignacio in his agony: because I could never bear my own impotence in the face of other people's sorrow. When I returned, on a very quiet Sunday morning, I was with some friends in a café on the Gran Vía when Ignacio happened to come in. He stopped at our table, spreading his legs wide and planting his feet firmly on the floor, his overcoat open and his arms crossed behind his back beneath his Herculean shoulders, his hat pushed back on his bald head of quartz and feldspar, and no one asked him to sit down. He looked contemptuously at my companions, young Gypsies and unripe flamenco singers, very affected and not rich in talent.

"When did you get back from Granada?" he asked me.

"About ten days ago," I lied, because it was only five.

"Why are you so hard to see? You promised to let me know when you got back."

"Well, I didn't."

"What reason do you have for avoiding me?"

"You know better than anyone." I lowered my voice without taking away its coldness or severity. "You acted like a thug with someone I've always loved. This foreigner has her husband and you had La Argentinita."

"That's no reason for you to avoid me as if I were a leper. Can we talk in private?"

"I have nothing to say to you, Ignacio, and it would be better if we didn't see each other again."

He had been recognized in the café and people were looking at us. He knew he was being observed by the curiosity and evil-minded gossip of strangers, as if he were a circus clown, but he couldn't move. Incapable of leaving or of taking a seat when one wasn't offered, the man who kneeled in front of bulls and slapped them to incite them to attack was rooted to the floor and submitted to that contempt in the presence of strangers and my Gypsy adolescents. I looked straight into his eyes. He lowered his, and his shoulders seemed to collapse beneath the coat tailored in London. My attendants, the flamenco boys, began to smile and exchange poisonous whispers.

"Where are you going now?" he asked in a thin voice, biting his lips.

"I was going to have lunch."

"With your friends?"

"With them, in the usual restaurant."

"I'll go with you," he murmured.

"Nobody invited you."

Ignacio slowly began to stoop as if he were looking for a crack in the floor to hide his vanquished eyes. He knew how much I had always admired him and respected his valor in the ring and his talent in the theater. He met the bulls from the base of the barrier, as they left the bullpen, and wrote mad short pieces for the stage. For some time and without ever asking him about it, I had been convinced that his surrealist works and his bullfighting were part of a single magnificent, almost suicidal effort to give meaning to his life and make himself known to the universe. In a kind of symmetrical irony, when I saw him subjugated in that way, I detested my unexpected strength and absurd cruelty. And yet I couldn't renounce either one, once they had been revealed, without ceasing to be myself.

"The restaurant is a public place," he finally muttered. "I can go there to have coffee, if I want to."

I refrained from answering and he left, dragging his feet, not looking at me. He left the way he came, though now his shoulders were bent, his hands still clasped behind his back beneath his open overcoat. I had almost forgotten about La Argentinita and my indignation at her suffering, but I thought about the many women Ignacio had loved. He wasn't drawn to them by lust, pride, or even love, though he thought he was in love with all of them at the same time. The bed, the bullring, and the theater were stage sets or benchmarks where he tried to augment and play the part of the authentic Ignacio Sánchez Mejías. An Ignacio Sánchez Mejías who constantly overflowed the person the universe condemned him to be. I would think about Ignacio and the synthesis of his biographical sketch that I was doing then, when on the eve of the war and my own death, Don José Ortega y Gasset came to talk to me during an intermission at the Club Anfístora. "The man is always more than the man," he said about I don't know who, his long ivory cigarette holder that looked as if it belonged to Marlene Dietrich, the Pall Mall lit at the end, held between those teeth of his that were so incredibly young for his age. "No," I replied. "But some men make the effort. Ignacio Sánchez Mejías was one, and soon it will be two years since his deadly goring in the Manzanares arena."

As soon as I sat down in the restaurant with my two apprentice flamenco singers, Ignacio came in alone. He went to a corner table and sat with his back to the wall. He stayed there for eternities, bending over a glass of sherry or manzanilla as if waiting for the wall to split and fall on his back. From time to time he glanced at me surreptitiously and then became lost in thought again, contemplating the tablecloth. They hadn't finished their garlic soup when I rudely dismissed the Gypsies. They left without embarrassment or surprise because my lavishness made them servile. They were my version of the dark vice as opposed to the love that could not say its name, which in those days I didn't feel for anyone. I had met them in my only period of plenty and squandered the rights to my theater pieces on them so they would kiss me on the sly. Afterward I hated myself for hating them.

When I was alone, I looked at Ignacio openly. You could almost see his skull beneath the skin, just as Freud's cranium was visible in the charcoal sketch Dalí made of him. ("A perfect example of the Spanish fanatic," Freud very accurately said of Dalí.) Sánchez Mejías's was broad across the forehead, the cheekbones, and the temples. Obstinacy had hardened his jaws and pressed his lips against his teeth. Inadvertently I must have guessed then that the two of us, Ignacio and I, would die soon with all our blood spilled on the ground. Almost ten years earlier and in an indirect way, I made one of my characters in the "Sleepwalking Ballad" foretell my destiny. He asks the father of his dead lover to let him die in his bed, the metal one with linen sheets, when he arrives with stab wounds, pursued by the Civil Guard. The transaction cannot be concluded in the poem, just as I failed to be aware of my inevitable fate. Yet the poet's senses and instinct must have perceived whatever reason and conscience did not elucidate, because I suddenly surprised myself by beckoning to Ignacio with my hand. He looked at me without seeing me, as if he could not credit my intentions or my very existence. Finally he stood up, urged on by my impatience, and staggered to the table. You might say he wasn't certain whether this was happening to him or to someone who was his living facsimile in soul and appearance. Once again, as in the café, everyone was looking at us. They had recognized Ignacio, when he hadn't managed to identify himself, but at that point I didn't care about the attention of

strangers. Life was truly becoming a lie, and knowing you were being observed was as appropriate to the circumstances as the audience in a theater might have been. I embraced his shoulders and
offered him the menu, looking into his eyes. They were very dark
and wide open, with silver threads flashing near the iris.

"Go on, man," I murmured, "tell me what you're going to eat and
how the bulls will be this summer."

In your theater, the one you were assigned to in hell, your last day in
Madrid appears and is staged when you recall it. Everything comes
back to life exactly as it was, as it happened to you on that Thursday,
July 16, 1936, the eve of the outbreak of the war in Africa. The
previous night you had a dream that was another man's painting. At
the bottom of the composition, which seemed to be conceived in
glass and the glass secured on a wooden panel, slept Raphael's Paris
unnoticed by the three Graces. Beside him you saw an open shell,
which you had once contemplated in Port Lligat beside some magi-
cal sea of the kind painted by Dalí, in the days when you dedicated
an ode to him. It was half white and half ocher and scarlet in its
hollow, surrounded by an edge gilded by the sun. ("It's called *Crepidula onyx*, which is its exact, technical name in Latin," Dalí had
told you during one of the last summers of your friendship, for he
liked to collect useless information. "In the tropical Pacific, it's
known as the onyx slipper snail.") On the other side of the onyx
slipper snail, flanking it with Paris, was a white Bally shoe. A white,
low-cut shoe you recognized immediately because it was yours.
Your friend Carlillo Morla, the Chilean diplomat, made you buy it
because he was sick of seeing you wear those clumsy buckled shoes
he called the house slippers of Queen Juana the Mad. Above the
onyx slipper snail, in the middle of the glass that was a painting,
hung an enormous, mother-of-pearl shell. Hanging or perhaps held
over the void that was a vortex of red and gold cobras was an amputated naked woman's torso holding an apple. It was undoubtedly

part of the body of one of Raphael's Graces, though Raphael had not painted that monstrosity. Neither had Dalí, even though a mountain or cliff, with smooth slopes and metallic peaks, appeared to the right of the carcass to remind me of Port Lligat. Above that rocky terrain appeared a gigantic ape, squatting as if overcome by a burden that was invisible or omitted in the dream. Though almost as tall as the headlands themselves, one would say he was carved out of tiger's eye because of his yellow transparency. His eyes, on the other hand, were round and turquoise blue. Just in the center of the titanic, mother-of-pearl shell, you saw another that was perhaps a cut panel or the drying incision in a very old tree. You might also have thought it was the fossilized gaze of a man who preceded this species of ours, which has not always been human and perhaps is condemned to cease being human. It was indigo on its exterior that was similar to bark, and the color of dry resin underneath. In the middle of the transverse cut, it became dark and blue again as if revealing the hidden pupil of the metalized eye. A stub of the dream remained, which now erupts at the highest part of the stage, above the sleeping image of Paris. It was another spiral, that of a shell as gigantic as the ape on the cliffs, a great red curve in the rear followed by another that was gray like parchments with a good number of palimpsests. Joined to those curves were those of another of Raphael's Graces, her arms opened to press them against her naked body, seen from the back. Of the third divinity, all you could see, as you see it here, was her torso severed at the height of her breasts. That living bust leaned over the forearm of her companion, or perhaps erupted from the divided exterior of the singular shell, or from a fold opened with a knife between its red and gray ramps.

When you awoke after so many strange dreams, you thought everything that would happen to you that day had already occurred, including the memory of your nightmare. More than thinking it you felt it, in a kind of presentiment. When the two of you went into details, yours was not the sensation you imagined in Ignacio and he then confirmed, that he had been someone else as he approached your table on that winter Sunday in the restaurant on the Gran Vía. No, yours was the certainty that each of your acts and words on that Thursday, July 16, 1936, had been carried out and spoken on another identical day long ago. And still you hesitate and ask yourself whether you really lived those hours twice or foresaw, in the most irrational part of your spirit, that their representation preceded you in hell. It is very possible that our memories anticipate us on the stages of this spiral and that what is remembered appears here before we experience it on earth. In short, you are unable to decide whether the man in the third theater along the ramp of the corridor is alive or has died. Seeing the basilica on his stage, you suspected at times that perhaps memories precede us into eternity just before death. Perhaps it is appropriate to amplify that suspicion and wonder whether each of us might not have our private seating ready in this universe long before we are conceived in the other one.

In any event and as now appears punctually on stage, the doorbell rang in your apartment on Calle de Alcalá while you were still in your robe and slippers, preparing your first café con leche. You weren't surprised and didn't try to guess who it could be, because in an oblique way you were afraid to find out. It was an old actor, out of work and overwhelmed by every plausible and unimaginable misfortune, who the night before had almost anticipated his request for a loan. You invited him to a breakfast of coffee, biscuits, and toast and jelly, which you both ate standing up in your office beside the balcony. As you requested in one of your poems, at your death those windows should be left wide open to let in the wind so you can be buried afterward in a weathervane. On the sidewalks peddlers hawked sea crabs and river crabs, butter from Astorga and cheese from Miraflores. The sun poured in, spilling along the light marquetry and the blanket from Momostenango that covered the sofa.

"You couldn't add up my troubles. Not even I could count them all without forgetting some of the most important ones."

" . . . "

He hesitated for an instant, not knowing where to put the empty cup. You were going to take it so he could return to his complaints, but he anticipated you and placed it on the stone floor of the balcony, at the threshold and next to the blinds and white shutters. He licked the marmalade from his fingers and continued his plaint of praise and academic questions.

"You're still young, but very deservedly famous. You have a natural talent that no one can deny without offending you. That's why I dare to ask your opinion, thinking about my life today, yesterday, and the day before yesterday. Tell me, why are we born?"

" . . . "

"I'll tell you why. It must be to die, though the justice of that escapes me. In any case, it couldn't be only to suffer, which turned out to be my fate. Summing up a life as unfortunate as mine, I have to conclude that my passage through the world is a mistake, because the Great Architect can't construct a life so badly no matter how insignificant it may be. What do you think?"

" . . . "

"I'd say I'm here by mistake and should have been born in another time. In another period in the life of my family, which on both sides is constantly enriched with famous actors and actresses. Did you know a great-grandmother of mine was the sister of the great Máiquez?"

" . . . "

"Yes, sir. Isidro Máiquez himself, who was booing one afternoon at the bullfight and met his match in the matador Costillares, who yelled at him: 'Señor Máiquez, Señor Máiquez! This isn't the theater! Here you die for real!' I'll bet you already knew the story."

" . . . "

"In our family we've passed it from generation to generation since the time of my great-grandmother. Of course she premiered Don Leandro Fernández de Moratín's *New Comedy* in the role of the young Mariquita. She also played Medioculo in *The Oil Lamp's Fandango*, though this does not do us as much honor since it was a simple farce. I should have been born at that time and married my great-grandmother, in the days of *The Comedy* and *The Fandango*, of Máiquez and Costillares, of Goya and Moratín. I'd bet my life wouldn't have been so unfortunate then, the bad Greek tragedy it is now. You, so brilliant a young man, perhaps can answer two questions that seem to me to be Siamese twins. Why do we come into the world and why do we do it at one, irrevocable time?"

"..."

The doorbell sounded again with three long rings, which you recognized immediately. It was Rafael Martínez Nadal, who had promised to pick you up precisely at one so you could have lunch together. I don't know what ailment had covered his high skull with scabs, but it had been shaved with a razor and smeared with sulfur. Now his hair had begun to grow back, dark and curly on his elongated head with the tiny ears of a small-eared lamb. He waited patiently, leafing through a book on the sofa, while you gave a few pesetas and a letter of introduction for Lola Membrives to the great-grandson of the woman who played Medioculo. You wrote the note on a sheet of paper, sitting at your desk and looking at Picasso's drawing of a labyrinth for Balzac's "The Unknown Masterpiece." The actor left, saying goodbye very ceremoniously, and Rafael continued to wait while you shaved and dressed. On the street, the two of you were greeted by a sun as bright as quicklime, and only then did you remember that you had closed the balcony and left the empty cup outside.

"I had lunch for the last time with Ignacio Sánchez Mejías in this restaurant the year he died. At this same table," you said as soon as you both had sat down. "I have a feeling we won't come back here together either."

"Soon it will be two years since the tragedy," he agreed, intentionally ignoring your presentiments. "Still, at times one would think Ignacio hasn't died, that the goring in the bullring in Manzanares hasn't happened yet, even though it inevitably will happen. I'm not sure if I'm clear."

"I understand completely. On one hand I'd swear we'll never have lunch again, here or anywhere else." Andalusian after all, you touched the wood of the table beneath the cloth. "On the other, I'm certain that everything that happens this morning has happened before in this same place."

He was going to respond, as he is about to do now in this theater, but you were interrupted by the maître d' and a couple with the air of recently married provincials. The maître d' was bringing the menus and the young people wanted to know, *encore une fois*, whether you're the poet who wrote "The Unfaithful Wife." They asked for an autograph and you signed in your delicate hand with very tall capitals, which in eternity looks to you vulgar and absurdly precious. They left, extremely moved, after shaking your hand and telling you they were teachers. Martínez Nadal ordered lunch, smiling and claiming that soon your friends wouldn't be able to walk down the street with you because women would contend for your feet in order to kiss them, which is what happened to Joselito in Sevilla. You replied that a woman also yelled at Joselito on the eve of his death: "I hope a bull kills you tomorrow in Talavera!" The gods promptly granted her wish. Rafael fell silent, shaking his head, because they were beginning to serve the meal. You ate almost nothing, for that day you were indifferent to everything except your own fate, which you feared was sealed.

"Rafael, what's going to happen here? If a war comes, I won't survive it."

"This country was always on the brink of chaos. The attraction of the abyss is part of our national character, the exact opposite of what happened with the ancient Egyptians, who, they say, abhorred a vacuum. Eventually everything is fixed with pins and glue. Blood won't run in the river this time either."

He lied to keep you from despair. He was as convinced as you that a feast day of crime was approaching. The only difference between you was his deep certainty that whatever happened, he would survive the slaughter.

"Our time is short and the uncertainty consumes me," you went on somewhat irrelevantly. "A little while before they arrested him, I had supper one night with José Antonio Primo de Rivera." Rafael almost dropped the fish forks as he looked at you, not believing what he was hearing. "Don't be so surprised. That wasn't the first time we got together in secret. Since it didn't suit either of us to be seen together, we always went to some godforsaken inn in a taxi with the curtains closed."

"But why? For God's sake!"

"Oh, no reason! To talk about literature. He knows Ronsard by heart and is very lucid about French poetry from any period. Still, on that day he couldn't say very much. We ate without looking at each other until I exclaimed in a loud voice: 'If there's a war in Spain, neither of us will see the end of it. We'll both be shot as soon as it begins.'" With no transition you took hold of Martínez Nadal's arm at the edge of the table. "Rafael, I don't want to be killed like a dog. Rafael, I could hide in your mother's house, couldn't I?"

He looked at you, astonished at your fear, his eyes sad and stupefied between those tiny ears and beneath the stubble of his sheeplike hair at the top of his forehead.

"Yes, of course you could hide in my mother's house. But who would want you dead? You're only a poet."

"That's exactly what José Antonio Primo de Rivera said. I told him that's why they would kill me, for having written verses. Not for being queer and on the side of poor people. Of course good poor people, you understand. I added that this country is a republic of killers from all classes and that Spaniards exterminate one another like rats at the first opportunity history offers them. They'd shoot me for writing verses and for being incapable of defending myself. Just for that, yes sir. 'Come and look here,' I said to José Antonio Primo de Rivera, using one of the expressions I learned in Havana. 'Do you know that days before the death of Ignacio Sánchez Mejías, the Gypsies in his crew said he reeked of death? If they came in here now, they'd be terrified of the stink of our mortal remains.'"

"Don't raise your voice. Try to calm down."

"I'm very calm. Confident enough to refer to my posthumous glory as if it were someone else's. Many years after I'm shot dead, they'll still be writing books asking why I was murdered. At least I won't leave this world without knowing that." Suddenly, changeable and inconsistent, you went back to your pleading. "Rafael, do you really think your mother will hide me in her house?"

"I'm sure of it. If you like, let's go there this afternoon."

"Yes, let's go, the sooner the better! I'll lock myself in with your mother and sister and not go out until the storm of hatred and crime that's approaching passes. Let's go, ask for the bill. It's possible that even hours are precious these days." Suddenly you slapped the table with the palm of your hand and gave an anguished cry. People sitting near you turned to look. "But, Rafael, what am I saying? Have I lost my mind? I can't hide in your mother's house. I have to go to Granada this afternoon. The day after tomorrow, July 18, is my saint's day and my father's too. We always spend it at home, at the Huerta de San Vicente. I can't miss it. The place will be filled with jasmines and morning glories."

"Now you're being imprudent," he said as he paid the bill, including a tip, which he folded under the cruets. "If anything happens and you're so frightened, you'd be safer in Madrid than in Granada. Many people there who've never read a book can't forgive you for being so famous and for liking men. They'll never be able to understand either one, and they'll find the first more irritating."

"How can you talk this way if you've never been in Granada?"

"It doesn't matter, I can imagine it."

"Well, I'm going anyway, and now it's in God's hands. Why did you pay for lunch? I wanted to. We may not see each other again and you're sure to survive me. Let's have coffee at Puerta de Hierro. Let me buy you a brandy or as many brandies as you want."

He wanted two, and you drank down those Fundadors in a couple of swallows. Martínez Nadal looked at you almost furtively. Part of your panic and especially your uncertainty seemed to infect him. In his expressions you read increasingly clear grief or foreboding. Or perhaps you thought you read them, because you always made of your friends and the world not only a reflection but an extension of yourself and your changes of mood. But on that day and in that café near the Puerta de Hierro, you didn't need to force your imagination to see a collective image of your uneasiness all around you. It was high summer, but people filled the streets of Madrid day and night. No one decided to leave before the war broke out. Assault Guard trucks came from University City and drove down Princesa. Some newsboys shouted headlines about the cessation of the last debate in Parliament. Rafael bought one and you trembled as you read it. The State of Emergency had been extended and the angry controversy over the assassination of Calvo Sotelo continued. Gil Robles said the Popular Front government was one of shame, mud, and blood, and very soon would also be one of hunger and poverty. Barcia replied in the name of the Council.

"Rafael, do you remember the original of the unpublished play of mine, the one I call *The Public*? I lent it to you last week."

"Why would I forget it? Do you think I've lost it?"

"Of course not! Good Lord, don't get angry with me this afternoon!"

"I'm not angry; but I don't want you to think badly of me even for an instant."

"How would I think badly of you when I want to confess a certainty I didn't even dare tell myself?"

"What the devil are you trying to say to me?"

"It's about *The Public*, my play that you have in your house."

"I'm sorry, but I haven't read it yet."

"It doesn't matter. I haven't looked at it either, not for years; but I'm convinced it transcends our time. I moved writing for the theater, mine included, naturally, ahead by several generations. Perhaps entire centuries, though it may be hard for you to believe. Once I read the piece to the Morlas and they were horrified. Imagine, the Morlas, who are so fond of me, and as courteous as benevolent vicuñas! Bebé almost cried with rage as she listened to me. Afterward she said it was all nothing but sheer nonsense and blasphemies. Carlillo scolded me in his fashion, which was more diplomatic, but the man was livid. 'You can't publish that, let alone stage it,' he wailed between deep Chilean sighs. 'You'd better burn the thing and forget it.' Then I realized I had written my masterpiece. You know, the eternal misunderstood masterpiece that to other people's eyes is always a labyrinth."

"That's what it must be, if you say so," he agreed in an exhausted voice. "I'll read *The Public* right away."

"You don't have to read it. The plays of mine that are staged are full of easy concessions. People are astonished and pleased by them because everything else is even worse. In other words, it boils down to pure rubbish. Still, I know how easy it is for me to write them. I feel a little like Zorrilla, scandalized by his ability to rhyme clichés. And a little like Polycrates, frightened by his good luck. *The Public* is different. I had to demand everything of myself, absolutely everything, and climb down to the center of my being on the ladder into my soul to achieve a play that's so authentic."

"All right, all right," Martínez Nadal interrupted impatiently. "I told you I'd read it."

"And I'm telling you again that you shouldn't. Don't be offended but today you won't understand *The Public* either. Just as I didn't really understand it myself, to tell you the truth."

"Why did you lend it to me then?"

"To ask you for a favor that's bigger and much less useless than your reading it."

"Fine, go ahead."

Rafael Martínez Nadal looked at you, intrigued. Up to that point your panic had made him feel irritated and impatient. Suddenly and in spite of himself, he listened to you intently, hanging on your words. Gradually it was growing dark, to the chirping of sparrows and the shouting of newsboys.

"If anything happens to me in this war that's at our door, swear you'll destroy the original of *The Public* right away."

"I'm not swearing anything!"

"Give me your word, then."

"I won't give you that either. Why do you want to burn it if it's your masterpiece?"

"Precisely for that reason, because only I could suspect the importance of what I've written. If I die, *The Public* has no reason to exist for other people."

"All I promise is to return it unread when you get back from Granada."

You yielded in silence, partly because of a sudden weariness and partly because *The Public* suddenly seemed like someone else's work. As if contrary to everything you had just been saying, you were the only person on earth incapable of understanding it. Again you were overcome by the feeling of having lived that day before, in the identical, uncertain frame of mind. Not long afterward, in a taxi that took the two of you to Cook's to buy your train ticket, you couldn't stop talking about another play you had in mind. You called it *The Destruction of Sodom*, and even though you hadn't written a single word of the work, in which the Bible impinged on surrealism, you described entire scenes in complete detail. Lot opened the final act with his invitation to the two angels of the Lord. The righteous man's house would be on one side of the square in Sodom, and in a

Pompeian gallery and portico ("Pompeii as seen by Giotto, Rafael"), Lot would offer his feast to the two beautiful men, Jehovah's incognito archangels. The sides of the stage would be cut on a bias, a little walled garden would appear where the patriarch's two virgin daughters would lament the indifference of the men in the city. Gradually the populace of queers would gather before the portico, hungering for perverse pleasures and shouting for the strangers. "Where are the men which came in to thee this night? Bring them out unto us, that we may know them." And Lot: "I pray you, brethren, do not so wickedly. Behold now, I have two daughters which have not known man; let me, I pray you, bring them out unto you, and do ye to them as is good in your eyes: only unto these men do nothing; for therefore came they under the shadow of my roof." Deaf to his pleas, the mob of deviants would assault the gallery. Lot and the angels would flee then to the house, barring the door as the crowd, increasingly inflamed, pounded on it with their fists. From the house would come the screams of the terrified father. "I shall give you my daughters! I shall give you my daughters so that you may know them and conceive in them! Use them, all of you, and heal your sickness before the One Whose Name Must Not Be Spoken destroys this city as punishment for your sins!" The chorus of roars would be in counterpoint to the lament of the virgins, deluded by lust, in a contrast of tones and timbres dictated by the same desire. ("As in the revivals of black evangelists I saw in a Harlem church. You can't imagine the upsurge, the storm of songs whirling in the air and descending like a rain of whips and lightning flashes on the backs of the congregation.") Unexpectedly the doors would open wide and through the opening the angels would come out, radiant in their beauty. But their gaze would blind like that of the Hydra, because the Lord transformed it into the thunderbolt of His wrath and His punishment in the city of queers. Their eyes burned by the stare of the prodigious creatures, the degenerates would run away shrieking and roll on the ground in the square (" . . . something like Chirico's squares, in his aseptic metaphysical paintings"), howling in terror and pain. Lot would take his daughters by the hand and flee to the mountains along the path through the desert. Behind him it would rain fire and brimstone, and Adonai, He Whose Name Must Not Be Spoken, would burn the pederasts alive after blinding them. You added as a kind of final couplet, for this was the singular lesson taught by the fate of Sodom, that the invention of incest ironically followed the city's condemnation and punishment. Alone with Lot and agreed on between themselves, the virgins would resolve to end their virginity with the help of their own father, for want of another man. They would make Lot drunk twice in a row and each daughter would lie with the patriarch who had sired her on each of those nights. Lot would sow his seed in both and from the elder's lineage would come the Moabites. The younger would give birth to Ben-ammi, father of the house of the Ammonites (*"Rideau"*).

"Rafael, Rafael, I have a wonderful idea! I don't know why I didn't think of it earlier!"

"What are you trying to do? Demolish Madrid with burning sulfur? Maybe it's the fate we all deserve."

"No, no, how awful! I'm not the God of the Old Testament. I'm only an ambiguous creature and a terrified poet. Rafael, come with me to Granada!"

"But, when?"

"Right now. We'll buy two sleeping-car tickets instead of one. Case closed."

"You're out of your mind. Why would I go to Granada? And why this afternoon, for God's sake?"

"Because I'm inviting you. I'll pay for everything, including the ticket, naturally. You've never been to Granada and it's high time you saw it. Besides, I need you. I have the feeling that if you're with me, you'll change my destiny and make me invulnerable."

"You're out of your mind! You think the world owes you every-thing, as if you were the sorcerer's apprentice." Little by little, Martínez Nadal was growing irritated with you, but you didn't become angry or restrain yourself. You were only overcome by an infinite fatigue, because even his reaction to your proposal had been seen earlier. "I'm going to decide to take a trip right away because you order me to! Just like that, just the way it sounds, and only to please you. I don't know what to call it!"

The taxi stopped in front of Cook's, on one shore of the Gran Vía. You paid the fare while Martínez Nadal continued his oration. He spoke now just to hear his own voice, and you didn't listen. You once believed or believed again that this was the world, or at least the country: a chorus of lunatics talking to one another and never hearing anything.

"It's all right, man, it's fine. It doesn't matter," you lied. "We'll go to the Huerta de San Vicente another time. Forgive me if I've offended you in any way."

You took his arm and you both went into Cook's. When you gave your name so they'd extend a very British welcome, the open-mouthed clerk looked you up and down. Were you the poet? We're all poets in our own way. He was referring to the poet and playwright, the one who wrote *Yerma*. Damn, what a play! He had seen it three times! We're all playwrights in our dreams. Did you ever stop to think about that? No, it hadn't occurred to him, but he persisted in his questioning. Were you or were you not the poet of "The Unfaithful Wife" and the author of *Yerma*? No, you were only your brother's brother. Rafael Martínez Nadal laughed, looking aside, leaning his elbows on the counter. He had reconciled with the sorcerer's apprentice almost without realizing it. Now more than ever he reminded you of a sheep about to change into a man. You thought about old verses of yours, scrawled in New York just as you left that black church service ("Go down, Moses! Go down, Moses!"). You bore witness there to the effort in each metamorphosis. The interminable attempt of the horse to be a dog, of the dog to change into a swallow, of the swallow to become a bee. And finally, closing the dance of life, of the bee to transform into a horse. This was the idea of the poem, though you had forgotten the verses, if you ever knew them by heart. The boy in Cook's did not come out of his distressed astonishment. "Excuse me, I'm afraid I don't understand. Are you the brother of your brother?" Without answering you said goodbye, sweeping the air with a gesture. Outside you saw the same taxi that had taken you from Puerta de Hierro to Cook's (or from Cook's to this theater in hell), its flag lowered. You climbed in and gave your address, Alcalá, 102.

You never learned how to pack. When you went to the Huerta de San Vicente from Madrid, you tended to travel with your hands in your pockets. This time you were resigned to dragging a suitcase to avoid a scandalized uproar from Rafael Martínez Nadal. He took charge of collecting your things, while you told him yes, you see, so much running around the world the past few years and you'd put old shoes with new shirts. Or you'd go with a toothbrush in the breast pocket of your jacket. A red brush, with hard bristles, like the orchid George Carpentier always wore in his lapel. You know. At the door of your house, beside the sidewalk on Alcalá, stood the same taxi. Stopped at the edge of traffic, it wasn't waiting for the two of you or anyone else. One might say it had come miraculously from a space without time to take you to an ineluctable destiny. Like the gondola Gustave Aschenbach, or von Aschenbach, takes when he arrives in Venice. When he is unaware that his days are numbered and that before he dies he will experience love, always incomprehensible, for a seraphic adolescent. Though you confessed nothing to Rafael, you would have sworn that the taxi and its driver were strangers in Madrid and had never appeared in any company, registry, or union. Just like Aschenbach's gondola, yes, with its nameless rower ("I'm only the brother of my brother"), or with a name the other gondoliers never learned. "The gentleman will pay," that brutal-looking, distant creature had said to Aschenbach when he asked to be taken to the Lido. Nevertheless, as soon as they arrived, man and boat surprisingly disappeared, as if they had slipped away through the air and not the turbid waters of the canal. Gustave Aschenbach or von Aschenbach could not pay for the service, though his debt, incomprehensible to implacable creditors, still stood.

"Rafael . . . "

"What's on your mind now?"

"I forgot the cup on the balcony again when I was in the house."

"Sweet Jesus! What are you talking about? I don't understand a word!"

"An empty coffee cup. It was left on the balcony when you came by. Then I was distracted while I said goodbye to that actor who boasted of being a descendant of Máiquez by way of a sister, and I forgot about it again a second time until now."

"You're incomprehensible." The small-eared sheep smiled in the back of the taxi. "Simply incomprehensible."

"Why is that?"

"On one hand, you predict a war and say it will devour you as soon as it begins. On the other, you worry about a cup left on the balcony of your apartment."

"It's all tragically joined," you answered, surprising yourself. "Rafael, these streets and the countryside around Madrid will fill with corpses covered in their own blood. This city will be shelled and bombarded until many of its neighborhoods crumble into ruins. Yet I sense too that the cup will remain intact, on my balcony, through all the catastrophes."

Martínez Nadal was silent now. You imagined him deep in thought, trying to imagine your words without understanding them, assailed by another man's imaginings. In the meantime, the afternoon fled up among the roofs, as in some paintings by Pissarro. Thinking about your dream the night before, you wondered whether by chance everything we thought alive were actually printed. In other words, did we really exist as beings doomed to die, or were we conscious images in someone else's painting? You rejected the idea, shaking your dark head that, behind your back, people said looked like a farmhand's. Everyone's destiny was as inexorable and irrevocable as the course of the river, its sources hidden beyond nothingness, which for want of another name people called time. But in paintings, as in dreams, its water and the hours did not flow by. Everything was immobilized on canvases, Van Gogh's hurricanes, Monet's water lilies, and Velázquez's exceedingly slow ladies-in-waiting.

And at that instant, in a kind of sudden revelation, you thought you understood hell.

It couldn't be anything but the previous night's dream, which you also foresaw as your last. Until your death, anticipated with a cold, almost inhuman lucidity, you would sleep blind and in pitch darkness. But you would not forget that nightmare, the sum of all you had lived and dreamed, and at the same time a very accurate foreboding (that, at least, is what you believed then) of endless hell, which would be nothing but the interminable presence of incomprehensible images, surrounding you and settling inside you forever. There, in you and with you, the shell opened with a barber's razor, the goddess cut off from her breasts down, and the appeal adhering to the shell with its long red and gray turns. The fossilized eye of a species earlier than our own, turned into the blue heart of another mother-of-pearl shell. The gigantic yellow ape, its eyes like turquoises, squatting under a transparent burden before cliffs cut by a pickax. The hacked torso of the nude, apple in hand, which even in the dream you attributed to another of the Graces. The white Bally shoe and the onyx slipper snail, lost at the bottom of your nightmare and watching over Paris's rest.

Evidently you were wrong. No one, except the dead, can ever understand hell. This is the only eternal truth and, at the same time, the most idle gossip.

You believed everything was a fleeting part of this kingdom, reduced here to a simple memory, which you can witness on the stage in your theater whenever you please. Perhaps we can deduce an obvious lesson, like the ones in the moral texts of your parents' little schools, and with similar consequences. All of you imagine death, like life itself, as the creation of your dreams. You make man the measure of all things, including eternity. Bluntly, he is not the proportion or scale of anything. His dream of hell is merely a phantom, one of his shades, on this spiral that is the other universe.

When you reached the station, you got out of the taxi, Rafael carrying your suitcase. He was astonished that the driver drove away without waiting to be paid. You weren't surprised. It was written that the gentleman would pay in any case and that man, who had waited for the two of you so patiently at the door to Cook's and in front of your house, had fulfilled his ordained role in your destiny. You still lacked time and space for your sacrifice. You lacked them with nothing left over for you to be killed or your martyrdom repeated, for the dual sensation of a steadily diminishing period of time remaining, and events already experienced, acquired greater intensity on the platforms. With almost oppressive detachment, exhausted by the burden like the gigantic ape in your nightmare, you made an effort to correct all that had been written.

"Rafael, you really won't decide to come to Granada with me?"

"Really, I decided right now," he said with a smile. "Would the gentleman care for anything else?"

"Nothing else, I ought to make the rest of the trip alone, if I'm obliged to undertake it at all."

"As you probably realize, I couldn't reply in any other way."

"And I couldn't fail to ask this time, though it may seem incredible to you."

"All right, man, all right. Let's not make another Roman tragedy."

Your sleeper was at the end of the platform, two or three cars behind the locomotive. In the station, as on the streets filled with peddlers, Madrid rejuvenated and became provincial in a way Granada never was. You were pleased to confirm it, in spite of your state of mind. You definitely had not lost your capacity for observation, which had brought you to Góngora's many years before Dámaso

Alonso attempted to reveal it to you. Seeing clearly was thinking clearly at any moment, as Ortega said in his first book. Along the platform a man dressed in khaki pushed his two-wheeled cart filled with grenadine drinks, sodas, candied almonds, chocolates in tins painted with the canals of Amsterdam at dawn and the bell tower of San Giovanni, in Montepulciano, the one whose clock had been stopped at exactly 12:00 ever since a day in 1452 when Leonardo was born in Vinci. *Granadina*, grenadine, you thought in a parenthesis as you looked at those reds like the recently liquefied blood of San Gennaro, was also the flamenco song of Granada. The one you tried to express as a long sad onomatopoeia of the course of its rivers in one of your early poems. But *granada*, the pomegranate, was also the fruit of the shades in the kingdom of the dead, the one Ascalaphus saw Persephone eat, when Hades abducted her to his domain in the heart of eternity and the center of the earth.

At the end of the platform, Madrid retraced its steps until it returned to the time of vaudeville, outdoor festivals on the eve of a holiday, vernacular operettas, and pasodobles in La Bombilla for the banderilleros and flashy girls of another day. ("Did you know a great-grandmother of mine was the sister of the great Máiquez?") Peasant women in incredible long skirts and kerchiefs tied beneath the chin in a tight square knot ran, laughing and shrieking, toward a train waiting for them patiently. Their livelier husbands, rustics in their Sunday best though it was Thursday, button caps pulled slightly to the left, ironed handkerchiefs around their necks, and tight trousers, followed them. The women had empty straw baskets on their arms, in which they may have carried a capon or a speckled hen. The men grasped walking sticks as slender as reeds, similar to the ones barkers used at raffles, which they wielded in the air with many flourishes of their dark wrists.

A sense of imperative symmetry, as those people passed by, obliged you to evoke the first time you saw Madrid. It was in the years before the European war and in a time as distant now as the Rome of

Scipio Aemilianus. Your parents took you and your brother and sisters in a delayed fulfillment of an almost forgotten promise. As if you were figures in a daguerreotype, you all appeared in Retiro Park on another morning in an uncertain, early summer. The girls almost shivering in their white dresses with big yellow ribbons in their hair. Your brother and you in knit ties with large knots and one-button jackets fastened almost in the middle of your chests. They showed you the statue of *The Fallen Angel*, the only monument to the devil in the world, as your father said emphatically, when Machaquito and Vicente Pastor passed by in an open hackney carriage. You recognized them right away because you had seen them a few times in the bullring in Granada and many more times in the illustrations in *La Esfera* and *Mundo Gráfico*. Machaco had the dull air of a Cordoban impresario or a bookkeeper who had suddenly become wealthy. Beside him, like a giant, his body, arms, and face long, his broad smile, and protuberant bluish jaw, the very Madrilenian Vicente Pastor, the Kid in the Smock. There was no trace or memory left of the workman's smock he had worn to his first amateur bullfight. Still, upon seeing him dressed in his Panama hat and high buttoned boots, his tight vest, trousers, and short jacket, a white silk handkerchief around his neck, a watch chain with three loops across his chest, and a full-blown carnation in his lapel, you were overcome by the certainty that even in your earliest childhood you knew, clearly and powerfully. One day, you told yourself, after many years you would remember the carriage driving the bullfighter through the park. Until then your memory of him in the Madrilenian morning, including *The Fallen Angel*, would lie dormant, preparing for the appointed hour. When that came, it would be returned to you, as the stereotype plate is revealed in the developing tray, to give meaning and fulfillment to a time as irrevocable and irreversible as the water in rivers.

And now Vicente Pastor was returning. The relic of your memory of him suddenly glimmered and identified with the good-looking men in traditional dress, with their starched handkerchiefs, tight trousers, and caps pulled down on one side. One was also the Kid in the Smock with the peasant women in their Gypsy skirts, baskets still warm and redolent of speckled hens on their arms. Everything shuffled together and confused to give you the image of the other Madrid, the one of sea and river crabs hawked in the streets along with cheeses from Miraflores and cakes from Astorga, just as you saw it that morning in your childhood and were witnessing it again now, complete and alive, almost as a loan. The death throes of the Madrid of bullfighters in open carriages and flashy men and women at open-air festivals were coinciding with yours. That entire world, heir to Goya's cartoons for tapestries through various avatars, would end forever as soon as the streets and fields filled with dead bodies, as you had just predicted to Rafael Martínez Nadal.

In the Retiro they were exhibiting old French impressionists. All of you stopped in front of Monet's *La Gare Saint Lazare.* Your father shook his head, a scornful smile spread to his jaws, and he asked what the devil that blur was. He understood perfectly well that after centuries painters cannot paint as Murillo did in his time. He also had known Moreno Carbonero, the great artist of Málaga, and he understood and appreciated art. This was why, this was precisely why, he grew increasingly sure of himself, he denounced these frauds by impostors who did not know what to do to attract attention. Your brother and you answered immediately, expressing much more admiration for the painting than the two of you felt. Even though he was normally ill-tempered and did not tolerate arguments, he took almost no notice of your dissent. He merely shrugged his shoulders, which the years had not bent, taking into account your innocence as well as your ignorance. The girls were silent, and as if she were talking only to them, in a quiet, unhurried voice, your mother began to tell them that Monet did not intend to represent the world of surfaces, contours, and volumes (she was on the point of adding, "the world that, after all, we don't see but imagine so we can understand one another," but didn't dare to in order not to enrage your father, who so far was listening to her with the same studied indifference he used when listening to you), but the other world, the one that light and shadows transform constantly. "His intention, like Velázquez's in the *Meninas* we saw yesterday in the Prado, was to capture a fleeting instant: one of the unnoticed, evolving moments that come, pass, fade, and together constitute our brief lives. To create this painting, constantly fluid and in transition, Monet used very short, thick brushstrokes that stand out perfectly in the picture, the kind we pointed out to you in *Las Meninas*. Needless to say," your mother concluded, "the similarity is not accidental, if we keep in mind that both Velázquez and Monet were trying to represent a pause in time. Velázquez, the instant in which the lady-in-waiting offers the princess a vase, and Monet the arrival of the train puffing smoke at the far end of the Saint-Lazare station."

You listened to her until that point (the point being staged now, with the ghosts of all of you like actors in this theater in hell). Then you stopped hearing her in order to observe your own personal revelation before the painting. As had happened before, when your family crossed paths with Vicente Pastor beside *The Fallen Angel*, you told yourself you ought to treasure the moment, with *La Gare Saint Lazare* in the background, because on another occasion in your life its true significance would be revealed to you. Again in the station in Madrid and at the end of the Andalucía express, you knew the moment foreseen twenty-four or twenty-five years earlier had arrived. Like water in water, the memory of the painting by Monet merged into the present reality, in which you weren't listening to Rafael just as in the Retiro you stopped hearing your mother as she attempted to explain to all of you the secret intentions of impressionism before your father's sarcastic smile. Smoke with smoke, platforms with platforms, iron horses with iron horses, everything intermingled with everything. So tight was the weave of the living and the painted that you didn't know with certainty if you were entering a station or a picture. Suddenly, like a note in the margin of that experience, you repeated everything your mother had said in the Retiro. Monet tried to capture a fleeting instant in *La Gare Saint Lazare*, one of the transitory, marvelous seconds whose passage we are almost never aware of in our lives. He painted an ordinary train entering Paris and performed a miracle achieved previously only by Velázquez. In other words, he stopped time so that men could take delight in the silent miracle, assuming they weren't blind to his painting as your father was. Now his painted moment and your lived moment were one, when your arrival in and departure from Madrid were confused into a single instant at both ends of a quarter of a century that was also the time of your self-aware life.

The rest was foreseeable and you made an effort to shorten it, though you would be overcome again by the certainty of having experienced everything before in some unknown dimension of time or of your soul. Rafael Martínez Nadal insisted on carrying your suitcase into your compartment and lifting it onto the luggage net above some faded photographs of the Rhine in Basel and the Loire as it passed through Amboise, which crowned the seats upholstered in open, embroidered dahlias. You walked with him to the platform to say goodbye from the step of the car, when you saw that man in the passageway and were overcome by terror.

Leaning out one of the windows, his back almost turned to you, he looked absentmindedly at the platform. You recognized his corpulence, his firm jaws that gave him a faint resemblance to pictures of your father in his youth, his camel driver's shoulders, and that hair as black and kinky as an African's. Being a right-wing deputy, he attended meetings wearing a butcher's smock identical to Vicente Pastor's in his early amateur bullfights. In his speeches he took God's name in vain, with the same arrogant indifference he brought to taking a taxi in Granada to go to Madrid, though afterward he tried to avoid paying, hiding somewhere or other. At one of the dinners you and José Antonio Primo de Rivera would go to, also in secret, you referred to the calluses on his hands, which he would show to the Party to prove that a weather-beaten worker could be loyal to Law, Order, and the Indivisible Fatherland. José Antonio Primo de Rivera would laugh heartily. "He's just a tamed worker!" he exclaimed. "Nothing but a tamed worker! When Gil Robles gets tired of exhibiting him, he'll sell him to a provincial circus."

"Go now, Rafael," you said to Martínez Nadal on the platform. "Don't wait for the train to leave."

"Don't be impatient. All in good time. I'm in no hurry."

"You'll do me a huge favor if you leave right now."

"Why so much urgency and mystery? You're like a conspirator."

"Do you see that man? The husky one, with the big jaws, looking out the window. He's a deputy from Granada and a bad character. Under no circumstances do I want to talk to him. As soon as you leave, I'll go into my compartment and close the curtains. Please leave before he sees us."

"All right, all right. I'll go if you insist." Wearily he shook his sheep's head again. "You're the most fearful, superstitious creature I've ever known."

"Whatever you say; but go now. I beg you. He can turn around at any moment."

"Who is that man, after all? A ghost, the bête noire of your sleepless nights, or simply a messenger of fate?"

"I just told you, a right-wing deputy for Granada." You hesitated and summoned all your courage to say his name, which for reasons as yet unknown brought terror to your soul. "His name is Ramón Ruiz Alonso."

With a shrug to express his ignorance or his indifference, Rafael Martínez Nadal said goodbye with a handshake. You saw him walk down the platform, not turning around even once, far removed from any presentiment that your final encounter was ending here. With no nostalgia and no sadness, because your uneasiness mixed an unexpected coldness into your spirit, you watched him until he was lost in a turbulent crowd of hurrying people running toward the

Andalucía express. Then, in your compartment, you closed the door to the passageway and closed the curtains. In the shadows Basel grew dark, and a yellowish-gray Loire ran through Amboise, where you thought Leonardo had been buried. In one of his notes he described the river water we touch as the last of the water that has gone and the first of the water to come. In his opinion, that's what the present was like. No need to even say he was wrong, just as you were mistaken when you supposed the dead were blind. If the days of our lives were like river water, each river would be a circle bound to empty into its own headwaters. Each drop identical to all the rest and each hour the same as one lived earlier. Through you Monet's train began to fuse with the Andalucía train. One was coming into the Gare Saint-Lazare, the other slowly leaving Madrid to carry you to an irrevocable death you had already experienced earlier.

Through the window pane, passing faster and faster, were tracks, crossties, switch rails, sand traps, walls, sidings, ballast, tenders, cars, platforms, and sidetracks. They pass now across the stage in this theater, where memories return to you intact the life you've lived. Each man carries hell inside him, because hell is absolute memory. Those rivers turned into circles, which were your lives, return at any point from their water to the exorcism of desire. Night was falling, as it falls now on stage, as the train moved away from Madrid. The first lights cross the windowpane as they were being lit at dusk in 1936. You felt fatigued and drowsy at the end of that interminable day, the last of your days in Madrid. You stood to close the curtains, as you had closed the ones on the door to the passageway. As your image stands now in the theater to close them. The entire representation is identical to what happened, down to the last and most insignificant detail, as it was so many other times when you relived that final trip to the land where you were born and your inevitable death.

Suddenly, and in a manner as unforeseen as it was unexpected, something on the stage differs from what occurred! One might say you take an eternity, if one can speak of eternity in hell, to close the curtains. You would swear that in the reality of the past you closed them quickly in order to lie down on the bed in your compartment and forget everything, absolutely everything, Ruiz Alonso and Martínez Nadal, Monet and Vicente Pastor, Aschenbach's gondolier and the taxi driver always waiting for you, Sánchez Mejías and Primo de Rivera, Sodom and the church in Harlem, *The Public* and *Yerma*, *The Fallen Angel* and the Huerta de San Vicente, the empty cup on the closed balcony and the great-grandson of Medioculo, the onyx slipper snail in your dreams and your admirer in Cook's. Now, however, your standing image pauses, his back to the door to the passageway, while hell prints an unexpected and terrible message on the windowpane. There, in large, bright letters that never appeared before on the windows of the express, four golden, gleaming words: PREPARE FOR YOUR TRIAL.

THE ARREST

PREPARE FOR YOUR TRIAL.

I don't know whether I'm accused of having been born or having been murdered. I sense only that, whoever my judges may be, if I'm acquitted I'll sleep in forgetfulness and be free of my memories.

PREPARE FOR YOUR TRIAL.

As soon as they appeared, those words on the window faded. They might have been fleeting, but I had no doubt I had seen them. How I would prepare for a trial, alone and not knowing the charges, struck me as grotesque and senseless. The absurdity of the situation filled me with an unexpected hilarity no less irrational than this supposed trial of mine. Twisted over an arm of my orchestra seat, I laughed wildly, like a madman, a mad dead man, my palms at my temples. I stopped laughing when I realized that if life and reason were exceptions lost in the firmament, this other universe too, the one of our spiral, could be just as pointless, just as alien to human consciousness. Therefore, once everything had been taken into account, I was still under the same constraints. I was being exhorted to prepare for a trial but not being told what crimes I was charged with. At the same time, by means of a design as obvious as it was inexplicable, I was infused with the certainty that acquittal would represent eternal forgetfulness, the limitless freedom of sleeping with no dreams and no memories.

Agitation suddenly brought me to my feet and took me up the corridor to the next theater. I was carried away by the presentiment, more than unjustified, that there I would find part of the answer to my uncertainty. As usual the theater was empty, on stage and in the

49

seating area. And yet, for the first time, I was stopped by a sensation unknown in that place. I always believed that whoever stayed there rarely evoked his past, because I never saw his memories on stage. I even thought we dead were blind after all, like the ghost of that Gypsy girl of mine, because we saw only one another's memories without being able to tell to whom they belonged. To add to my solitude, in that theater I didn't even confront the man's evocations. It was then, on one of my walks around the deserted theater, when I observed that each dead person was a Robinson Crusoe sitting on the head of a pin, taking on the entire guilty conscience of the universe.

For no reason, but with absolute certainty, at that instant I changed my mind and told myself that the auditorium, its proscenium and stage, all of it was empty. Whoever had been punished there had been acquitted at his trial. He slept now without dreams in hell, and for that reason, freed from consciousness and memory, he no longer was anyone. Never again would he turn his gaze to the shades of his past, and these would not appear again on stage. Immediately, and in an unconscious synthesis of terrifying realities, I thought that perhaps the spiral was not another universe the size of all humanity, where each dead person had a corresponding theater. It was conceivable that it had closed, while people still lived in the world with their foolishness and hope. Perhaps the seats and stages of those who had been acquitted and freed into nothingness, where not even memory exists, were waiting for other people and the staging of their memories.

Hypotheses entwined and knotted like threads. I was obliged to wonder whether some unknown but not inconsequential reason connected those who stayed in the same theater. It was possible that not having known one another on earth, secret analogies had governed their lives, and as a consequence they were assigned the same orchestra seats and identical stages. Perhaps, in the final analysis, an analysis as logical as it is ironic, that and only that was humanity's reason for being. In contrast, and maybe with identical verisimilitude, I could imagine the opposite was true. In other words, suppose that irony was sarcasm, and attribute to senseless chance the successive passage of different ghosts through the same theaters. I was shaken by the idea of randomness so great that if I were acquitted at my trial, Ruiz Alonso would one day be assigned my space in hell so he could eternally watch my arrest in Granada.

It was this anticipatory, irrational fear—my theater and stage inherited by Ruiz Alonso—that took me up the corridor and under the skylights to the next theater. Again and as always, I called to someone there who I supposed was allied to me in feelings or in interests. "Who are you? Where do you come from? What was your name among men?" And now, for the first time I wanted to ask: "Who judges us? Why do they try the dead?" Only silence replied, harboring the echo of my questions. Perhaps the one chosen to fill that theater by himself was still alive, and his memories and fantasies preceded him along the road to the proscenium. At least, this was always my belief in the next theater, where the gigantic cross of the Risco de la Nava appears. Here, for arbitrary and inexplicable reasons, I was not as certain of my presentiment. In any event, if the man had died, we would not be able to meet in our sleeplessness, for we were incapable of hearing or seeing one another in the theater or along this corridor that curves and moves up the endless spiral.

Regardless of whether his memories preceded him, they began suddenly to illuminate the stage. Where once there had been a parade of gentlemen in top hats, monarchs with ruffs around their necks, storks flying over Baltic cities, white-skinned ladies with their hands in muffs, sleepy elves, herds of reindeer gleaming with frost, hunters huddled over the pot of eucalyptus, fishermen with green eyes, Aretino's double, the thirteen twins around Blasco Ibáñez's table, the prostitute whose face was crossed by a whip, fields of fennel and thyme covered by bees, and the enlightened nude who was the *ragione chiara* acclaimed by the musketeers, there now appeared the glass front of the Lyon across from the Post Office, its window overlooking the sidewalk of Calle de Alcalá. The café had changed very little since the days when I would sit there with Buñuel or Alberti, after the theater. The same sofas leaning against the wall, which at first were made of plush and then of oilcloth. The same bar covered in zinc and marble, in front of the same shelves of illuminated bottles. Identical tables and chairs in the usual places. Two men were talking beside the window at the entrance, but their voices came through the glass very clearly. One was tall and must have measured a good two meters, as the peasants of my childhood used to say. He wore his pitch-black hair brushed back, flat against his skull. The scar from an accident or a knife blade divided his cheek, darkened by the sun and bluish because of his beard. From time to time he wrote in a notebook lying open on the table or toyed with an aluminum ashtray. He was a stranger to me and could have been any age, between mine when they shot me and plunged me into hell, and fifty.

The other man must have been close to eighty or perhaps older. He had reached that point in elderliness when people stop aging and turn into their own vanished likeness. I couldn't identify him until I heard his voice. With a disengaged coldness that did not fail to surprise me, I realized he would be someone I knew very well. His cottony kinky hair was thinning now, and his angular, large-jawed features had grown smaller around his dark eyes. His shoulders too, which once seemed to belong to a stevedore or a large, husky man, were collapsing, defeated by the years. His hands, stained by time with liver spots, rubbed the space between his eyebrows or stopped with the edge of his palm a yellow dribble that kept appearing at the corner of his mouth. It was Ramón Ruiz Alonso.

They were talking about me, even though they made a curious effort, as if by mutual agreement, not to ever mention me by name. The man with the scar on his cheek nodded occasionally at Ruiz Alonso's words with a vague gesture, almost for the sake of courtesy.

Most of the time he seemed to listen without believing most of what Ruiz Alonso was telling him. They never looked each other in the eye, but they were absorbed in their conversation. Two cups of coffee grew cold on the table.

"Here, in this very place, I spoke some years ago about that poor gentleman, God rest his soul, with an Englishman or an Irishman who picked up everything I said, in secret and without my knowing it, on one of those things, what do you call them?" Ruiz Alonso stammered.

"A tape recorder," the man with the cut on his face suggested.

"That's it, a tape recorder. Then he published it in a book about the death of that poor unfortunate, may he rest in peace. Can you imagine the lack of principles?"

The man with the scar did not venture a comment. He limited himself to tracing in his notebook two parallel, very short lines, which he then crossed with another vertical, drawing a kind of Cross of Lorraine.

"I don't have any tape recorder," he said as if he were talking to himself.

"I don't doubt it. I don't doubt it." His emphasis betrayed Ruiz Alonso's hidden uncertainty. By then he already must have regretted agreeing to the interview. "You're a gentleman."

"There isn't a single creature on earth capable of knowing who he is," the man with the cut face replied, quoting Léon Bloy.

"It's possible. It's possible, though I don't really understand these things. I'm only a poor retired typesetter." He hesitated a moment, as an actor would who gauged his audience before uttering an obscenity in the middle of a mystery play or a classical tragedy. "I'm a son of the people."

"Excuse me, what did you say?"

"I said I'm a son of the people."

"Son of the people or not, you will pass into history, Señor Ruiz Alonso. Or, to be honest, you've already entered it, because once a poet was murdered whom you had arrested," the man with the sliced face replied, with no irony.

"I didn't arrest him. I was ordered to arrest him, God keep him in His glory, poor thing! Yes, I was ordered to arrest him and I had to obey because we were at war, when all orders are sacred. I swear by the Blessed Virgin!"

"Is this the truth?"

"This is the beginning of the truth," he specified after thinking about his answer. "The governor of Granada was visiting the front that day. An officer whose name I forget because with age even the most terrible memories become confused and grow dim, gave me unavoidable orders. 'Look,' he told me, 'this gentleman has to appear in the offices of the Civilian Government because that's what the governor has ordered. He wants to find him here when he returns from the front, with no delays and no excuses. He's very interested in talking to him and wants him brought in duly protected: no one touches a hair on his head. For this service he has thought of a person with authority and prestige, like you, Ruiz Alonso.'"

He spoke in a very quiet voice, almost in whispers that the man with the scar sometimes made note of beneath the Cross of Lorraine. He said the most terrible memories became clouded but seemed eager to please as undoubtedly he hadn't been when he was sent to arrest me, assuming everything had happened in the way he said. The yellow dribble had dried at the corner of his mouth and his hand trembled when he persisted in wiping it away with his palm.

"I was familiar with that version of the orders you say are sacred in wartime." Again he spoke with absolutely no irony, looking at the cups of cold coffee as if they were a still life by a master, while Ruiz Alonso nodded his head. "As you must understand, it's impossible to believe."

"Yes, yes, I understand that too. But that's how things were back then. We were at war, an all-out war to the death, don't forget that. I can swear to you by all the saints in heaven that this is the truth of the matter." He stammered now and was ashen, as if he had reached the end of his strength. Suddenly he flared up, hitting the table with his fist. An unexpected rage brought him back to life. "Then all kinds of atrocities were told to slander me. They're so absurd that I laugh, yes, I laugh, when I think of them."

"What do you laugh at, Señor Ruiz Alonso?"

"Let's do one thing at a time and put things in some order! Yes, in some order, eh? All right, well look, to begin with, that gentleman, may he rest in peace, was a degenerate. When I say it like that, with my usual frankness, I don't intend to insult his honorable memory, because everybody knows and talks about it. Look, I'm a man from another time. A time that today seems very distant to me, in light of so much pornography and crime. Well, with my sense of morality and my religious piety, I say that his aberration doesn't matter to me at all because it's part of his private life. Yes, sir, his private life . . . "

"And with his death, even more private."

Ruiz Alonso stopped speaking to look at him indecisively. Suspicious and vulnerable, he seemed fearful of missing any sarcasm at his expense. Then, unexpectedly, blinking as if dazzled, he thought he understood. His eyelashes were growing in white, and a labyrinth of small veins flared on his pale cheeks.

"Yes, yes, I understand. Death is as private as life, because no one can live or die for another person. You can't for me, and I can't for you."

"Or you for that man."

"What man are you talking about?"

"The one you arrested or were ordered to arrest."

"Ah, yes, may God have pardoned him! I pray for him every Sunday at Mass, though they wanted to crucify me alive. I was getting to that, but I lost the thread and forgot what I was saying! I said I didn't care whether that gentleman was queer or not, if you'll excuse my plain speaking, because more than anything else I respect the privacy and dignity of a human life, follow? The disgraceful thing, the unspeakable thing, is what they did to me."

"What did they do to you, Señor Ruiz Alonso?"

"Defamed me. Yes, sir, defamed me in writing and in printed books. That Englishman or Irishman, the one who secretly picked up everything I said on a . . . What did you say it was called?"

"A tape recorder."

"Yes, that's it, on a tape recorder. Well, he told me a Frenchman had written a biography of that gentleman who was shot, may he be in glory! And it said, just as it sounds, that I arrested him because he caused jealousy and arguments among us homosexuals. I admit that when I heard an insult like that, I lost my temper, because each man has his honor and mine is double: being very Christian on one hand but also very much a man on the other. 'You tell this French gentleman,' I said in just these words, or others like them, 'that if he doubts my virility he can bring me his mother, his wife, or his daughters, and though I'm an old man I'll use them as they deserve, given their profession, which the police in their country have on file.' I wasn't boasting, I swear, because here where you see me, a decrepit old man, I still get a hard-on that's a joy to see."

The afternoon was dying over the Sierra on the stage in hell. The sky reddened like the mouth of a furnace. Then it moved to ocher and scarlet, like the onyx slipper snail in my last dream in Madrid. ("It's called *Crepidula onyx*, which is its exact technical name in Latin. In the tropical Pacific, it's known as the onyx slipper snail," Dalí had told me in his accent of a Catalan comic. Then, with no transition: "Have you read Proust? No? Never? You still need to be educated, but with a little luck I'm going to smooth and varnish you until you begin to look like an authentic poet. As a child, before he was taken to the theater for the first time, Proust thought all the spectators were watching the same drama but remained isolated from one another. In other words, the way we read history or a

voyeur shamefacedly spies through the keyhole.") The lights went
on in the Lyon and at that uncertain hour Ruiz Alonso's shrill voice
grew louder, proclaiming his attributes. Loving couples on sofas and
old men engrossed in open newspapers suddenly looked at him,
smiling.

"Everyone is looking at you, Señor Ruiz Alonso," said the man
with the scar in the same quiet, uninflected voice.

The old man pretended he hadn't heard, or perhaps he hadn't,
since he was lost in his farce, as unreal and outsized as that of a clown
in the earliest films. He didn't turn to confirm the presence of his
unexpected audience, but he lowered the tone of his complaints.

"And I forgive everything because at my age one knows that we're
nobody. I forgive everything, I do, but I don't understand what
pleasure these foreigners find in harming us. In another time I
would have said that this is the eternal anti-Spanish conspiracy.
Now the truth is I don't know what to say." He shook his head
wearily, but again, suddenly he seemed to recover. "Listen, where
were we?"

"According to you, the acting governor ordered you to arrest
him."

"Ah, yes! That's the truth. 'Take the protection you need and arrest
him immediately,' he repeated. I said I didn't need any, and my
prestige and courage were enough. 'Even so you should take along
an escort,' he said unwillingly and as if it pained him to tell me the
whole truth, 'because he's hiding in the house of a Falange officer. A
high-ranking officer.' The news surprised and even shocked me, because back then I was very young and inflexible. I called a spade a
spade, understand? Either them or us, period. Anyway, I stood firm
in my intention to arrest that gentleman, may he rest in peace, all by
myself, because my morality and reputation would open all the doors
in the city to me."

"There are very different versions of events. Even today people
swear that soldiers and armed men in civilian clothes, all following

your orders, occupied the street, and that you even stationed men on the roofs to prevent a poet from escaping."

"Lies! Nothing but vicious lies! The people who were hiding him, I'm ashamed to even say their names and not because I hid him, of course, but because of the vile things they said about me, they were the ones who circulated those rumors. They claim I assaulted their house protected by an army, as if it were a fortress. No, sir! I did it alone and unprotected because, as I told you, I'm very Christian but also very macho."

"On this point I can't believe you."

"What? What did you say?"

"I said that on this point I can't believe you. There are many witnesses who claim the exact opposite. The street was occupied."

"Lies! Nothing but vicious lies! If you knew the number of falsehoods that distort the truth of events, almost all of them intended to dishonor me! Look, let's take an example that refers more to that poor gentleman, may he rest in peace, than to myself. They've told the fairy tale of his pathological panic. Being a queer meant he also had to be a coward. That's how their minds work, these evil, primitive people who then pass themselves off as educated . . . "

"Who?"

"What? What did you say? . . . "

"I asked whom you were referring to."

"Well, all of them! Who else would I be referring to? The Englishman or Irishman, the Frenchman, and you too if you don't believe the truth when I testify to it on my word of honor. The fact is this: that gentleman, God rest his soul, always maintained a courage that deserves to be commended. I'll swear to that with my hand on the Bible. I told him to hurry, but I allowed him to say goodbye to the people who were sheltering him. He came back almost immediately and spoke to me very calmly. 'Well the family here says the best thing is for me to go with you. But why do they want me at the Civilian Government?' 'I have no idea,' I replied, not lying to him.

'They've only asked me to guarantee that you arrive safe and sound. I have no other mission. Will you come with me?' 'Well, then, yes, in that case I'll come with you.' 'Very good, very good,' I agreed. 'Then let's go.' When we entered the Civilian Government building, someone tried to hit him with the butt of a short musket, because there are cowards like that everywhere. I jumped in like a wild animal; I ordered him to attention and shouted: 'How dare you, you wretch? In my presence!' That poor gentleman, may God have mercy on him! felt so grateful he offered me a cigarette. 'No, thank you very much. I've never smoked. But if I can be of service in any way, you need only ask.' 'No, sir, I wanted only to give you my thanks and an embrace . . . ' Those were his exact words: ' . . . give you my thanks and an embrace for your kindness to me. I'll never forget how you've behaved.' We embraced and I was going out, leaving him under guard in the governor's waiting room, when it occurred to me to say: 'At least permit me to send an orderly for some chicken broth. A nice broth, even if it's a Maggi, never does any harm,' because that's how courteous and gentlemanly I am. 'All right, some broth then,' he agreed, and those were the last words I heard him say, because yours truly left then for his house. I never saw him again, and never imagined on that afternoon that they would kill him. That's the complete truth, and I'd repeat it if we were in the presence of Our Lord Jesus Christ, nailed on His cross. That's also how I'll testify before His divine tribunal, when my final hour comes and I appear for judgment . . . "

"There are other versions of events very different from yours. Testimonies from people who would also confirm them in the presence of God or any man, yourself included. You've been quoted as saying, at the moment you arrested him: 'I've come to arrest you and take you to the Civilian Government because you did more harm with your books than others have with their pistols.'"

"Death and damnation! May God strike me dead, right here at this table, if that isn't the biggest of the lies! By the Holy Sacrament! . . . Are you listening to me? By the Holy Sacrament, I swear to you again that this is the vilest of all the libels." Ruiz Alonso spoke very quietly, and the man with the marked face frowned as if making an effort to hear him or believe him. "How could I have said anything so absurd if I hadn't read any of his books back then?"

"And you've read them now?"

"Yes I have read them, after I bought the leather-bound edition of his *Complete Works* in a single volume. I've already told you that as the years go by, even the worst memories become muddied and cool down. Still, you must understand that I couldn't sit down alone with his poems if I felt responsible for his death. When he was arrested I had only heard about one of his poems, the one about the unfaithful wife, because at that time all of Spain was reciting it . . . All right, what do you want me to say? I'm going to be very sincere about this too. Back then I thought it was an obscenity, because I'm essentially a Christian gentleman and believe that sins like that, and I'd never throw the first stone, should not be available to innocent, impressionable young people."

"You said you still had erections that were a pleasure to see, Señor Ruiz Alonso. You added that it wasn't a boast."

"And it isn't, my dear sir, it isn't because even though I'm devout, I'm a man and a sinner. I'm also older and find in that poem artistic merits I couldn't see before. Even so, I still don't like it. The one I love is the one about the man who's told he's been summoned by death on June 25th and on August 25th he lies down to die, with the supreme dignity of heroes and saints. Look, it has so much grandeur in its simplicity that sometimes tears came to my eyes when I read it and remembered the poor gentleman accepting his final broth from me."

"Very well, go on."

"I don't want to hide anything from you. I, my dear sir, am an open book. If you ask my opinion regarding the death of that unfortunate . . ."

"I didn't ask you for it."

"I know, but supposing you had, as the man with the tape recorder did not refrain from doing, I'd answer as I answered him. I believe his shooting was reprehensible, because as a practicing, pious Christian, I condemn the death of man at the hands of man. I don't care if the victim's red, white, or polka-dotted. I'm an enemy of violence no matter where it comes from. On the other hand, if you ask what I think of his death in relation to his work . . . "

"I didn't ask you about that either."

"I'll tell you anyway, with my usual sincerity, that if the death of the man was a sin, the death of the writer was a benefit to him because at the end he was producing only nonsense and blasphemy; may God have forgiven him for that at the hour of judgment. Without changing the subject, but also without biting my tongue, I'll add that I don't understand the prestige he enjoys today, even greater abroad than in this country, I believe. Why so much interest in what he did and what he wrote? It must be because the poor man died the way he did, that's what I tell myself, because if he had survived nobody would remember him."

"Not the bulls, or the fig trees, or the horses, or the ants in his house," said the man with the cut face, looking into Ruiz Alonso's eyes for the first time.

"That's what he says, may he rest in peace, in his elegy to Sánchez Mejías; I understand very little of it though I remember almost the whole poem," replied Ruiz Alonso. "You see now that a poor typesetter also has a right to memory, though memories are sometimes his curse. Why don't we all forgive one another for the sin of being born? Why don't we let the dead bury the dead, as Our Lord Jesus Christ wanted? Why do you, Señor Vasigli, a Spaniard though your name sounds Italian, insist on writing a book about that unhappy man instead of dedicating a Mass for his soul?"

"Vasari, Sandro Vasari."

"Fine, Vasari. Why do you keep returning, Señor Vasari, to those times, when you must have been a boy, to tell us about the life or death of an unfortunate who had so many crosses to carry, from his homosexuality to his shooting and including his wasted talent? Better to let him rest in peace, wherever he may be rotting, waiting for the Final Judgment."

"I don't want to write a book, Señor Ruiz Alonso, but a dream."

"A dream?"

"The one I had on April 1st of this year. I dreamed about hell and saw it as an endless spiral, along which a carpeted corridor ascended." The man with the scar folded down the last written page in his notebook and drew a view of the spiral on the next one. Three equidistant lines crossed it, which he pointed at abstractedly with the tip of his pen. "Some theaters open onto the corridor, and a dead person corresponds to each of them. And in one of those theaters, the man you arrested and, according to what they say, also denounced, is waiting for judgment . . . "

"I didn't denounce anybody! I'm not an informer!"

"Be that as it may. In my dream, the man you arrested evoked fragments of his past in pieces and flashes. Those memories materialized immediately and were represented on the stage of his theater. From his orchestra seat, he seemed to watch and see them from a bird's-eye view, becoming aware of everything in my nightmare in the sight of God. I said to myself: 'This is impossible, you went crazy while you were dreaming.' And then: 'While you were dreaming you went to hell.' Parts of that nightmare, perhaps the most terrible ones, disappeared when I woke. As you said, Señor Ruiz Alonso, the most terrifying memories become muddied with time. Dreams too, as the hours pass. In this way, forgetting preserves our sanity. Still, I remember having seen him while he was still a boy, on a stage transformed into the Carriage Drive in the Retiro. Another boy his age was with him and two little girls, perhaps younger than the boys; they were clearly his siblings. Their parents, dressed in their Sunday best and very provincial, proudly encouraged them. They all commented frequently on this, the children's first trip to Madrid, capital of the kingdom. An open carriage passed where Machaquito and

Vicente Pastor were talking and laughing. They both wore Panama hats and high boots that buttoned with a hook. Vicente Pastor combined a white silk neckerchief with a three-looped watch chain across his chest and a carnation in his buttonhole. The carnation, very red and full, seemed to have just opened on that luminous morning."

I was deceived when I thought Ruiz Alonso would take him for a madman. On the contrary, the fatigue that at first had thickened his voice was completely gone now. Gradually his spine straightened beneath his weary shoulders as he listened attentively to Sandro Vasari and strained his eyes contemplating the spiral of his notebook. From time to time he shook his head with a gesture not of disbelief but of wondering astonishment. Finally, with an index finger stained by tobacco-colored shadows, he indicated two of the three lines that cut across the sketch, in the middle of one of its curves.

"In your dream, who appeared in these theaters?" he asked in a tone that was worried and urgent, though not lacking in firmness.

"The theater next to the poet's was vacant and dark, the stage empty," replied Sandro Vasari. "It would be impossible for me to describe the other one: the third of the four that ascended along the corridor."

"Why would that be? Tell me everything you remember. I beg of you."

"In its proportions it seemed identical to the poet's, as I've said, but on the stage his recollections didn't materialize but mine. Inalienable, untransferable memories, because they were imaginings of mine that had life only in my books." He shrugged almost disparagingly. "From this I deduce that I dreamed the theater I would occupy on the spiral if I had died. Or the future representation of my memories in the theater that will be mine when I die."

"You speak as if your dream were . . . I don't know how to say it, as if it were a real vision."

"I don't know whether my dream was or wasn't a real vision, as you call it. I know only that everything I saw seems truer than this café with its people and its tables, than this ashtray of what seems to be aluminum, than you yourself or my own image reflected in that mirror."

The old man almost didn't listen to him. Absorbed, deep in thought, he adopted the same posture and identical gestures as those of his unexpected appearance in the station when I ran into him there as I was leaving Madrid for the last time. If he was leaning his elbows on the bottom of the window then, he leaned them now on the edge of the table, looking at the floor as abstractedly as on that afternoon when he contemplated the platform. Even his jaws seemed to harden, the same as on that day in the distant past, while he strove to order memories, ideas, or fears in that gray head of his. More than aged by the passage of so many years, he seemed disguised as himself in the theater of hell. Dressed and made up by masters, though he was not sufficiently skilled to expand convincingly into the role of the old Ruiz Alonso. Without realizing it, he revealed the man he had been or, better yet, the man he still was and would continue being. ("This is merely a tamed worker! Nothing but a tamed worker! When Gil Robles grows tired of displaying him, he'll sell him to a provincial circus.")

"Did you ever see me on that stage of your dreams, where the poor gentleman"—he paused, as if my name burned his tongue even though he couldn't say it, or precisely because he couldn't manage to say it—"where the poor gentleman, may he rest in peace, watched the staging of his memories?"

Sandro Vasari, the man with the scar, shrugged and stood at the same time that he closed and picked up his notebook. He placed the pen in the breast pocket of his jacket and replied, not lowering his gaze to the old man's eyes:

"No, Señor Ruiz Alonso, I never saw you in my dreams when that man's memories were staged there. Not ever. If you lied to me, as I sincerely believe you did, because many testimonies contradict yours in almost every point, in dreams at least I couldn't prove it." He stopped suddenly as he was ready to walk away. "Excuse me, I did see you once and don't know how I forgot it. In my nightmare, he evoked his departure from Madrid and return to Granada in the summer of his death. His memories appeared accurately in hell. He arrived at the station accompanied by a friend, who carried his suitcase to the sleeper car and left it in the luggage net. They went out to the passageway to say goodbye, and there his manner changed. Filled with anxiety, he pleaded with his friend to leave right away so he could go into his compartment and close the curtains. In the corridor, his back half-turned and looking out the window at the platform, was a deputy for Granada with whom he didn't want to speak. That traveler, younger by almost half a century, was you. Secretly, so you wouldn't see or hear him, he told his friend your name: Ramón Ruiz Alonso."

Ramón Ruiz Alonso, expressionless and unblinking, contemplated the cups in their saucers. As it cooled the coffee turned gray and looked as if tiny spiders had climbed up from the dregs to weave their webs on the surface. He took a spoon and put it down again on the glass tabletop, making a clinking sound. Then he passed his gaze over his open palms, along the labyrinth of creases that seemed marked with the tip of a knife.

"It's very true, but also very strange," he said at last, shaking his head. "I don't know how you could know all that if your dreams didn't illuminate the past. Yes, that friend of his recounted the story afterward, and today his biographies say we met on the Andalucía express. This is the reality, and I never affirmed or denied it. I couldn't prove or disprove it, because I assumed I never saw him that afternoon. Even so . . . "

"Even so . . . "

In the café, which suddenly had begun to empty out, Sandro Vasari and Ramón Ruiz Alonso formed an unusual picture. The hunched old man, his hands still open, forehead, brows, and eyes reflected in the glass of the table; beside him stood the man with the scar, his energy and circumspection reborn, though not without an obvious note of astonishment when he was already preparing to leave. Together they resembled models for one of those biscuit-shaped pantheons from the period when our parents took us to Madrid for the first time and the French impressionists were on view at the Retiro. Pantheons signed by Mariano Benlliure or one of his outstanding students, in which a patrician old man, carved in alabaster statuary beside a marble table, like Blasco Ibáñez's, showed his empty hands to the exterminating angel.

"I did see him and see him again now just as I did then. As you say you witnessed the apparition in your memories, in your dream. A man was with him, almost as young as he was, who resembled a sheep. He must have had his head shaved a little while before and a curly fuzz was beginning to darken his skull." Ruiz Alonso continued, not looking up from his open hands, his words growing quieter and more spaced apart. "I noticed how he avoided me, obliging me to keep leaning out the window in the passageway, pretending to look at some rustics right out of a zarzuela like *The Festival of La Paloma*. I don't know if you understand me because people like that are rare now in Madrid. Women in long polka-dotted skirts, shawls with long fringe around their shoulders, and kerchiefs on their heads, escorted by men in caps pulled to one side, tight trousers, and starched handkerchiefs around their necks, armed with willow branches like foils. I don't know how much time I spent looking out the window, watching them run along the platform, sometimes to catch a train that wasn't ready to leave yet, other times buying pink candied almonds, or simply showing themselves off as if the station were a theater, while I knew I was obliged to listen to their laughter, their remarks, their shrieks. That kind of sentence, imposed by the gentleman, may he rest in peace, seemed as endless to me as eternity itself."

"What else happened?"

"Nothing else. The man who resembled a sheep left, and the poet, God rest his soul, said goodbye to him from the car steps. I watched, pretending not to see anything, so they in turn wouldn't see me. After so many years, the whole scene must seem completely crazy to you. But I know very well what I felt . . . "

"What did you feel, Señor Ruiz Alonso?"

"That gentleman went back to his compartment and closed the doors and curtains, as if I were carrying the plague," said Ruiz Alonso, not listening to him. "Yes, exactly as if I were carrying the plague, or was a leper or monster. Look, he had no right to treat me that way. He didn't, I assure you. I'm a poor typesetter, a workman, retired now, and proud of it. But back then I was also a deputy and author of a book about corporatism, with a prologue by Señor Gil Robles. Above all and more than anything else, I was an honest man, a Christian gentleman even though I was a worker, which doesn't discredit my honor but increases it. Yes, sir, increases it! I had a name that now they want to stain with all kinds of lies, because these days and in this country there's no honor and no shame. I moved through the world with my head high because my conscience was clear, and I knew that Almighty God, at whose feet I will soon lie prostrate, looked upon my face as He looks upon it today."

"Did you also hold your head high when the governor asked you to arrest that man, Señor Ruiz Alonso?"

"The acting governor."

"Fine, the acting governor."

"Lieutenant Colonel Velasco. That was his name. I don't know why I remember it now."

"Did you hold your head high when Lieutenant Colonel Velasco asked you to arrest the poet?"

"Yes sir, I did, because an inevitable justice, divine justice, seemed to settle our debts! If he hadn't avoided me on that train, I still would have taken him prisoner, but then there would have been no pride or satisfaction on my part, limiting myself strictly to fulfilling my duty. If I had known they were going to kill him in a few days, I would have been horrified, but I still would have arrested him because, as I told you before, in wartime orders are sacred. Command is hard and obedience can be even harder. If I insisted on carrying out my duty alone, it was to show him that I didn't hide behind the curtains at the moment of truth. I, a humble typesetter, could take him to the Civilian Government building with my face as our only escort, because my presence was enough to keep anyone from assaulting him." He paused, shaking his grieving head, only to raise it immediately and face Sandro Vasari. "Am I as reprehensible as they say—the Irishman, the Frenchman, and someone from Barcelona who's from a very pious family so I don't know how he turns up—when heaven decreed I could arrest him, knowing its will coincided with my satisfaction for the insult in the Andalucía train? Answer me from the bottom of your soul: Am I or am I not an honest man?"

PREPARE FOR YOUR TRIAL.

If man is the guilty conscience of the universe, the only consciousness that can detect its almost absolute dehumanization, then man, alive or dead, on earth or in hell, is perhaps the most complex of its constructions. Sandro Vasari ("Why do you insist, a Spaniard though your name sounds Italian, Señor Vasigli, on writing a book about that poor unfortunate instead of dedicating a Mass to his soul?"), I repeat, Sandro Vasari, born perhaps after other men killed me or a child when they did, dreamed about me in hell, awaiting trial. He saw both the seats and the stage, which one day will be assigned to him on the spiral, and this seems an even greater portent to me. Here and now, in the interminable wakefulness of my own death, and returned to my assigned theater, I perceive with dismay the close correspondence between dreams and eternity in the warp where life and death are interwoven and become identified. I would also affirm, though I can confess this certainty only to myself, that literature is the closest key to this labyrinth where the living and the dead are commingled.

PREPARE FOR YOUR TRIAL.

To die is to sleep or perhaps to dream, says Hamlet. Immediately, and having a presentiment of his destiny on this spiral, which at one time or another we all inhabit, he asks himself with surprising clairvoyance what dreams await him in death. That consideration leads him to reject suicide, fearful of the worst nightmare: this long insomnia that only acquittal at trial can bring to an end. Three centuries after Hamlet, Proust believed as a boy that each spectator watched performances at the theater in isolation (" . . . In other words, as we read history or a voyeur shamefacedly spies through the keyhole"). When he was finally taken to see Berma in *Phèdre*, he discovered the stage shared by the entire audience. He then deduced that artifice, an inheritance of Greek democrats, transformed each person into the center of the theater. In hell, I now deduce that in this way we would have a Ptolemaic world, the boxes, orchestra seats, mezzanine, and top balcony, in the middle of a Copernican firmament. Two concentric universes, their signs forever opposed.

PREPARE FOR YOUR TRIAL.

Perhaps a way of preparing myself before I am judged is to evoke Hamlet and Proust in order to infer their oblique presentiments of hell and their sojourns there. The theater Proust imagined, to the admiring praise of Dalí, where each spectator would observe the staged work isolated and separated from the rest of the audience, is nothing but his own conception of *À la recherche du temps perdu*: a dead time of people and places destroyed and devastated by war, which the novelist patiently resuscitates in a bedroom lined with cork in order to better remove himself from the other world around him. At the same time, and perhaps this is the most original of his portents, it is an oblique analogy to hell, where every deceased person awaiting trial or condemned at trial contemplates the return to the life of his past, blind to the others and exiled among them. In another, no less notable, coincidence, the *Recherche* begins under the sign of sleeplessness and sleeplessness is hell, where the dreams in death feared by Hamlet become staged memories. Or where at times the staging of memories also precedes the arrival of those predestined to watch them in their corresponding theaters.

PREPARE FOR YOUR TRIAL.

On earth they never tried me. They killed me without imposing a sentence. Until the day Ruiz Alonso and his underlings came to arrest me in the house on Calle de Angulo, 1, which perhaps no longer exists in Granada though it rises again on my stage, I thought I was as safe from death as if I hadn't been born. I didn't know then either how to prepare for my trial, which, ironically, would never come. The house, which belonged to the Rosales family, is all white on the stage beneath that August's sun. It has two stories and a terrace, with a well-lit door on the narrow, shady street. It has a courtyard, a fountain, a marble staircase, a grilled window facing the sidewalk, and another side door. This opens onto narrow steps that lead to the second floor, almost isolated from the rest of the property. The window illuminates the library of my friend the poet Luis Rosales, who is almost never here now except at night. Luis has hidden me on the upper floor with the complicity of his family, even though all his brothers are Falangistas and the Civilian Government has decreed the death penalty for anyone who shelters a fugitive. The Rosales family hid others as well or arranged for their escape from Granada. On several occasions I was wakened from an uneasy sleep by strange voices and footsteps on the ground floor. I never asked anyone anything. Surviving in this city of terror these days is as private and shameful as an act of love between two men.

PREPARE FOR YOUR TRIAL.

If the systematic memory of my dying were part of my defense before the hidden judges, they would condemn me again with no trial at all. Recollections of the Civil War, when the fields of Spain filled with the dead as I predicted to Martínez Nadal, are not in order. They are jumbled together in streaks of images, glittering, almost flashing behind the stage. Luis Rosales, back from the firing lines, comes one night to my hiding place. The front must be very odd, because the unmarried Rosales brothers often return from there at nightfall to sleep in their parents' house. Luis has come from the Motril sector, where, as he assures me, he can get me to the Republican lines without any danger, as he has done already with many others. And to be fair, he says he also helped several fugitives from the government to escape to this side. "In those fields you get lost without hearing a shot or finding a soul," he reiterates in a low voice so as not to wake his aunt Luisa, who shares the upper floor with me and takes care of my cavalry almost like a mother. "Taking you to the other side would be the easiest thing in the world." I shake my head and say I don't want to be hunted down like a rabbit coming out of a wood or beside an irrigation ditch. On several occasions we've had the same useless debate, and now Luis withdraws and unexpectedly concedes, perhaps so as not to make me think that he and his family are moved by the desire to be free of my presence. "Whatever you want," he agrees, shrugging. "In the final analysis, they can't arrest you here either."

PREPARE FOR YOUR TRIAL.

"In the final analysis, they can't arrest you here either." After the panic of the first few days, I almost began to believe it. But in some buried part of my soul throbs the clouded presentiment that I am not master of my fate. There, in that chamber excavated, perhaps, in the center of my being, I knew I had lived my final day in Madrid before, step by step and instant by instant, it was enough to abandon myself to that obscure memory, lost in an existence earlier than the irrevocable time of clocks, to almost predict forgetting the coffee cup on the balcony or the presence of Ruiz Alonso on the express. I also know now that if I had yielded to Luis's advice, I would have passed over to the government's side through Motril. In a war where officers of the Falange, like the Rosales brothers, sleep at home at night, the front is undoubtedly deserted in many places. And yet I even exaggerate my fear of escaping when Luis suggests it to me, resorting to the memory of my extreme panic when I came to hide in this house. In reality, and given the reign of terror that the rebels imposed on Granada, the risks of those of us who hide in the city are greater than the dangers of a flight across the countryside. I fell into similar contradictions even before I hid on Calle de Angulo, when Luis himself urged me to seek refuge in the house of Don Manuel de Falla. In his opinion, I would be safer there than with his parents because no one would dare burst into the home of a universally celebrated composer so well known for his piety. I guessed immediately he was right, and sensed that Don Manuel, who had been so fond of me in my early, more ambitious youth, would have helped me gladly even if only not to miss the chance to perform a charitable act. Even so, I rejected his urging and cited the fact that Falla had silently become angry when I decided to dedicate the "Ode to the Blessed Sacrament of the Altar" to him. A Catholic as traditional and sensitive as he would never forgive me for having compared the Lord of his devotions and mine, though I was a nonpracticing believer, to the heart of a frog pierced by a needle. The truth is I chose the Rosales family's house as a refuge and want to remain here until they come to arrest me, because in this way I fulfill my inevitable destiny. One might say that the book of my life and death, including my sleeplessness and banishment on the spiral of hell, precedes me and determines my fate and my actions.

PREPARE FOR YOUR TRIAL.

In the house on Calle de Angulo, 1, life glides by as if on tiptoe in the midst of the crimes of war. Partially hidden behind the latticed window of my bedroom, I see the Rosales father leave punctually every morning and afternoon for his stores called La Esperanza. Downstairs, on the floor with the courtyard with the fountain and white columns, he leaves behind the mother, their daughter Esperancita, an ancient cook who looks as old as the world, and a twisted little maid who stutters. Upstairs, on the second floor, which is almost a separate dwelling, Aunt Luisa says goodbye to me to go to early Mass. "God be with you, child, and don't do anything foolish. I'll pray for you." "Pray for everyone, Doña Luisa, the living and the dead, the victims and especially their killers, who will find it so difficult to enter heaven." At midmorning, Esperancita brings me a coffee with two cubes of sugar and a copy of *El Ideal*. Every day, as reprisals for the bombings, it announces executions by summary judgment and doesn't conceal the shootings with no trial at all. In moments of distress, and always insisting on getting me over to the other side, Luis has confessed to me that they also kill hundreds by the cemetery walls and ravines in Víznar. My brother-in-law Manolo is one of the prisoners, if he's still alive after having been the socialist mayor of Granada for ten whole days. My poor sister, with her young children, must be suffering unimaginable torment, though it's shared by thousands of women in Granada. In spite of this vast tragedy, which perhaps lies in wait for me, coming closer each night, it imperceptibly moves away from my spirit, as if it were someone else's dream. Esperancita has a Falangista fiancé in Madrid, and at this point she doesn't know whether he's alive or dead. She tells me about her love, her anguish, even her nightmares of a girl in love, as if I were her older sister or we both loved the same man. I do what I can to calm her: "Don't worry, dear, everything will work out. Before you know it this absurd war will end and you'll go arm and arm with your fiancé to the opening of my next play." She smiles through her tears and asks what I'm writing now. "The destruction of Sodom and Gomorrah by the wrath of God Almighty and the invention of incest by Lot and his daughters." "Jesus, how awful! It must be more barbaric than *Yerma*. When will we see a play of yours with people who love each other, marry, and have children as beautiful as angels?" she asks, still smiling, while she dries her eyes with an embroidered handkerchief. "Never, Esperancita, because people have forgotten how to love, marry, and conceive children like angels. They give birth only to monsters and buffoons in their image and likeness." "You may be right," she agrees, very serious now. Then she picks up the coffee service, says goodbye, kissing me on the cheek, and leaves quickly. We see each other again in the afternoon, when they bomb Granada. Doña Esperanza Rosales calls up to her sister and me to take refuge on the ground floor. We all squeeze together into a tiny room filled with carved credenzas and embroidered scenes. The women pray or sob to the boom of explosions and the interminable howl of sirens. I'm frightened by my serenity when I recall my earlier cowardice. Two days later *El Ideal* says another fifteen prisoners chosen at random have been executed in very just revenge for the attack. Another page in the same issue carries the note of protest from several prisoners over the most recent bombardment, which even damaged the Alhambra. It is addressed to His Excellency the Military Commander of the Garrison ("We sincerely hope that all Spaniards will echo our sentiments and cease spilling so much innocent blood, for the good of Spain. Long live Your Excellency!"), and one of the signers is my brother-in-law Manolo. In this way I learn he is still alive.

PREPARE FOR YOUR TRIAL.

At my request, Esperancita has brought up *À la recherche du temps perdu*, in the translation by Quiroga Plá and Pedro Salinas. If I remember correctly, which in this case would be an unavoidable irony, Proust publishes the first volume of his vast novel, *Du côté de chez Swann*, on the eve of the Great War. Perhaps there's no other in the entire saga in which the visual evocation of what he has experienced, from the bell towers and shop windows of Combray to the flowering hawthorn and ruined medieval spires in the domain of the Guermantes, is so transparent. Perhaps the invocation of the past, by the grace of Proust in this part of the *Recherche*, has no rival in the history of any literature. I even wondered sometimes, after I was dead, whether Proust had managed to see in life and from his asthmatic's bed the anticipated staging of his memories in his theater in hell, only to translate that afterward into precise words. Up to that point, the work is also the retable of a paradise lost and re-covered by memory. Then, with the passage of time and in the transition from Combray to Paris, Marcel moves from Eden to Sodom and Gomorrah. From the idyllic little room in his parents' country house, where the child narrator reads, dreams, and inadver-tently perceives his memories, we come by way of jealousy and the perversion of all love to Jupien's brothels for queers. The world of the novel and its context in the history of those times matured, were corrupted, and became ready for the wrath of God.

PREPARE FOR YOUR TRIAL.

The reasoning for my defense and my examination of conscience return me to my own *Sodom and Gomorrah* (" . . . When will we see a play of yours with people who fall in love, marry, and have children as beautiful as angels?"). This persecution and enclosure were neces-sary in order for me to think about Proust and guess the real signifi-cance of the play I proposed to write. It all fits together now like the implacable cogs of a watch that shows the hours not of time but of destiny. I supposed I conceived this work of mine, which I already foresee will be unfinished forever, as a Voltairean reply to Don Man-uel de Falla for his anger at the appearance of my "Ode to the Blessed Sacrament of the Altar." Yet, and it's always worth repeating, I'd swear with identical certainty that my poem was written by a believer, and that in spite of himself Falla would have taken me in and hidden me in his house. I also think it's undeniable that my purpose in writing *Sodom and Gomorrah* was very different from and of course much more complex than that small vengeance. As I once said to Gerardo Diego, and I think he cited it in that poetic anthology of his that so resembled a hodgepodge, every creative act is a man or a woman going astray in a dark wood, which perhaps ought to coincide on never-drawn maps with the dark night of the soul, where poets lose their way because they don't know themselves. In fact, and even setting aside my pederast's remorse and pride, *Sodom and Gomorrah*, or I should say, the idea of *Sodom and Gomorrah*, was nothing but the allegory before-the-fact of this Civil War, in which the wrath of heaven is the rage that leads us to persecute and torment one another. After this catastrophe, perhaps we won't even conceive of incest. But the world of our youth, the one where Ignacio Sánchez Mejías, Rafael Alberti, José Antonio Primo de Rivera, Luis Rosales, and I reached the age of reason and attained our manhood in the same grouping that shrank or expanded in very few years, will have disappeared forever. Nothing will remain but shattered vestiges scattered by the winds of time, like the pilasters, caryatids, and broken statues of a dead Middle Ages, which Proust found in the meadows along Guermantes way. Perhaps one of these broken ruins is my own work. In another time I might have wanted to believe this was so. Now, the possibility of my writing surviving or not leaves me indifferent. In any case, my *Sodom and Gomorrah*, unfinished forever and never really started beyond some sketches, would have been not only the foretelling of this slaughter but also the last will and testament of our generation.

PREPARE FOR YOUR TRIAL.

It is Sunday and August whitewashes the sky of the theater on the stage in hell. The swallows fly very high over Calle de Angulo, chasing one another. Church bells are announcing Mass when my father telephones from Huerta de San Vicente. He speaks in a very low voice, which is difficult for me to recognize and understand.

"Son, they've killed Manolo. A priest who had already talked to his mother came to tell us. Conchita doesn't know yet."

"   . . ."

"Your mother went to tell her. I didn't have the courage, I admit it. Those poor children! My poor grandchildren!"

"   . . ."

"Son, promise me you'll be careful! Swear it, yes, you have to swear to me!"

"   . . ."

"Son, we've had arguments and differences in this life. But none of that means anything. I swear to you too that even now it was worth the grief of having been born to bring you into the world. You are my greatest treasure, and there's no father on earth prouder and more boastful than I am."

" . . . "

"Son, I'd give everything for your sake, including your mother and your brother and sisters! May God forgive me! Be very careful! You can't fail me, never, never, never!"

" . . . "

Abruptly he hangs up the phone without saying goodbye. " . . . We've had arguments and differences in this life. But none of that means anything." He speaks to me as if the two of us had died and together on this spiral were taking into account the smallness of the world. Sprawling on a chair, my head down on my chest and my arms wide, I would like to think about Manolo and my sister's grief. And yet I can recall only my last nightmare in Madrid. Or rather, I don't recall it, but it comes back to me intact, like one of those unexpected dreams, enveloped in an amphibian, resplendent light, which submerge us in their brightness when we fall asleep suddenly after a very long period of fatigue. Again I see the alabaster shell and the other shell resembling a split log that at the same time was the eye of a Cyclops. The white Bally shoe, in a sea of crimson clouds, at the foot of the cut-down torso of the Grace with the apple in her hand. The goddess embracing the red scallop shell and Paris sleeping, perhaps dreaming everything just as Manolo may be dreaming us now. "A priest who had already talked to his mother came to tell us. Conchita doesn't know yet." "We hope all Spaniards echo our feelings and stop spilling so much innocent blood for the good of Spain! Long live Your Excellency for many years!"

PREPARE FOR YOUR TRIAL.

The cacophony of many cars abruptly braking in the gutter and on the sidewalks brings me to the window, constantly covered by curtains embroidered, I had been told, by Aunt Luisa. A swarm of

Assault Guards, all armed with rifles, occupies the street corners and doorways. Others appear immediately, leaning over the railings on the flat roofs beneath the indifferent flight of the swallows. Out of a convertible Oakland come Ruiz Alonso, dressed in a blue coverall, and five other civilians, among whom I recognize Juan Luis Trescastro, a member, like Ruiz Alonso, of Popular Action. Quickly and without looking at one another they invade the home of the Rosales family, escorted by several police officers. Now I know with no room for doubt or hope that it is all over, or that I'm very close to the irreparable end. Again the old fears and terrifying panic that brought me to this house seem as distant and alien as if another man had suffered them. Not me, precisely, in a far off time, but someone who in an equally remote tomorrow describes me, aware of and surprised by my serenity during these moments. Mine is an indescribable calm, but not very different from the patient fortitude, bordering on indifference, that paralyzed me when the curtain went up at any of my openings, after all the torments of the spirit and anguish of the flesh. Whatever it may be, the will of God shall be done, if it hasn't already been done under these same circumstances.

PREPARE FOR YOUR TRIAL.

Aunt Luisa has appeared next to me, as white as a dead woman or one resuscitated. She makes an effort to smile at me sadly, with those bright, large teeth of hers that resemble a sheep's. She takes me by the hand, just as if I were the son she never had, born a man and almost lost at the same moment.

"Child, now let's pray."

She has me kneel beside her before a Sacred Heart she keeps beneath a lantern and on the chest of drawers where she stores the sheets, scented with quinces from the plain. With my eyes closed I hear fragments of her Ave Marias, but I cannot give myself over to any of the prayers of my childhood without committing the worst blasphemy for a believer and a writer: taking the name of God or man in vain. I would like to see my parents in the camera obscura where my reason for being is centered. But also a part of myself, the part that silent, nameless, always opposes my most fervent desire and has erased their faces from my memory. Instead I see Ignacio Sánchez Mejías, as I described him in my elegy, having bled to death and transformed into an apparition that climbs the stands in the deserted bullring under the full moon. I'm alone in the arena and know I'm alive, for I'm afraid again even though I may not know the cause of my terror. I call him by name and he turns around, smiling. "You refused to visit me in the hospital and we'll never meet again on earth or in hell," he shouts at me. Again I scream his name because I don't know how to answer him. He laughs openly and responds: "At least I had the death I chose. The one I didn't want for my son. ('Son, I'd give everything for you, including your mother and your brother and sisters! May God forgive me! Be very careful! You can never fail me, never, never, never!') You'll die the death others impose on you because in this country of iniquity and misfortune, those who do not choose their death are doomed to be killed by imbeciles. Stupidity is our innocence."

PREPARE FOR YOUR TRIAL.

Ignacio falls silent in my imaginings and Doña Luisa's prayers fade away. Standing now, she calls to me from the window. Ruiz Alonso and Trescastro leave the house, gesticulating and apparently annoyed. They get into the Oakland and the driver speeds away even though the street, houses, and flat roofs are still occupied by the Assault Guard. On the first floor it has grown silent and only now do I realize how much my senses had already found out. On the ground floor, the raised voices of an angry dispute between Doña Esperanza and Ruiz Alonso have stopped, at least for the moment. From that moment on, time begins a pause, as unforesee-able as delays in an entr'acte of a drama where death is real. In any case, the dice have been thrown and at the edge of the table one must wait for their inevitable fall.

PREPARE FOR YOUR TRIAL.

The car returns and this time it carries Miguel Rosales along with Ruiz Alonso, Trescastro, and the driver. Miguel has his arms crossed over his chest and is frowning, like a communicant who unexpectedly had begun to doubt his faith. Beside him, sitting sideways, Ruiz Alonso speaks to him with great insistence and a good deal of hand waving. Miguel doesn't look at him or answer him. Instead he contemplates the two ways out of Calle de Angulo, the one that leads to the Plaza de los Lobos and the one to Calle de las Tablas, both occupied by Assault Guards. At the instant the Oakland stops in front of the house, Ruiz Alonso rests his palm on Miguel's shoulder, in a gesture in which a supposed affection is mixed with persistence in support of a repeated statement. Miguel moves his hand away, gets out of the car first, and crosses the threshold without letting them precede him. Trescastro and Ruiz Alonso hesitate and bump into each other when they attempt to follow him at the same time. Finally, almost simultaneously, they enter the half-closed door that a police officer opens for them. Another, on duty at one of the corners of Calle de las Tablas, obliges a girl to go back who came out of a doorway, unaware of everything or compelled to because of an emergency. When she turns around, he extends a long neck with a very prominent Adam's apple and pays her a compliment. Suddenly, with the same unexpected abruptness that ended the raised voices on the ground floor, the circling of the swallows stops. One might even say they all disappeared into the sky or vanished in thin air. As if the light were Lewis Carroll's looking glass, the one that can be gone through at will, with the world on one side and hell on the other. However, sounds of discord rise again from the first floor, more contained or more fatigued than the earlier ones. They cease and are followed by footsteps on the stairs, at first very hurried and then hesitant and slow. The door to the landing opens and Miguel appears. Up close, one would call him a soul in torment who comes through the walls. In the past few hours he has aged twenty years and little is left of the boy resembling a character in a satirical sonnet of Machado's: a versifier, lustful, a drinker, yet an anticlerical Falangista, and above all a devotee of the Virgin of the Alhambra. Little red veins set his eyes aflame with blood, though his lips, very white and numb, meet in an expression of anxiety and bitterness. He avoids looking at Doña Luisa, faces me, and even seems to stand at attention as if saluting a dead man being carried down the street. Then he murmurs:

"Get dressed, please, and while you're dressing I'll tell you everything."

At this moment, precipitated by the tone and timbre of Miguel's voice, I understand several truths just as the lightning flash illuminates a crossroads, a bell tower, a fountain with seven spouts, or a flowering apple tree where there were only dark shadows. Above all I realize that I'm still in pajamas and slippers. The house shoes with no back or sides Miguel lent to me, and the white pajamas, heavily starched by the one-eyed maid with a stutter, I brought from Huerta de San Vicente. I'm also aware that Miguel Rosales's proud, disdainful air in the Oakland, when with folded arms he ignored Ruiz Alonso's words, does not contradict the evidence that the latter's will has been imposed on his. Finally, I deduce that Señora Rosales refused to turn me over in the absence of her sons. The others must have been at the front, on those tours of vigilance and propaganda from which they return at night, and Miguel was the only one available in the Convent of San Jerónimo, where, according to what Luis has told me, the Falange has its barracks. In fact, Miguel himself will immediately confirm the accuracy of my assumptions. On the other hand, he is silent, though I guess it in his evasive glance, about the fact that if he had resisted Ruiz Alonso until the arrival of his brother Pepe, who has a great deal of prestige and is more powerful, they wouldn't have arrested me. In fact, and even though Miguel Rosales doesn't know it, he is no freer to save me than I was to escape through Motril or to ask Don Manuel de Falla for asylum. Everything is arranged and must be repeated as it has already occurred in this place and in another universe.

"This clown Ruiz Alonso wants you to go to the Civilian Government offices and make a statement, and he has a signed order to that effect," he says hurriedly, now when the two of us are alone in the bedroom where I'm dressing. "It will be a simple procedure, and I'll go there with you. I assure you that tomorrow morning you'll be back in this house."

"But what are they accusing me of?"

"Nothing concrete. This bastard, and may all the demons in hell shove it up his ass, told me you did more harm with your pen than others did with a pistol. What bullshit! You see, I'm talking to you with absolute sincerity because it's so absurd it's funny. Well, you'll be back tomorrow if not this evening. None of it makes any sense."

"It's a mistake . . . a hateful mistake."

I repeat this several times, while Miguel averts his eyes. My voice, belonging to another man lost in the depths of my being, is made larger by an echo that is determined to fill my soul. He, this stranger inside me, is still unaware of the destiny that awaits us. I pity him for his anguish and at the same time despise him, fearing that his abject panic, ironically born of a final, mad hope, will affect the serenity that regulates my gestures and dictates my composure.

"Yes, of course it's a mistake," Miguel Rosales agrees. "It will be corrected immediately and we won't stop until we've made Ruiz Alonso and his henchmen pay dearly for this."

"Find your brother Pepe. He's very influential and could set me free in no time. You will, won't you?"

"Yes, yes, don't worry about it, and I'll find Antonio and Luis too."

"But especially Pepe."

"You, stop worrying. I'll take care of everything."

"Miguel . . ."

"What."

"They killed my brother-in-law Manolo. My father called this morning to tell me about it."

It takes him a moment to recover while he shakes his head with lowered eyes, his hands clasped behind his back. I finish dressing and we go out together. Aunt Luisa doesn't come to say goodbye. She has shut herself in her bedroom and I'm certain she's praying for me. At the half-closed door to the staircase, Miguel has me go first as if we were going to a masquerade ball and I weren't heading toward my unavoidable death. For a moment he takes my arm and murmurs very quietly:

"I'm sorry. I assure you I'm really very sorry."

I believe I responded with a gesture, perhaps a look, as we began the descent to hell. The sun through the window silvers the tiles and glints on the rifles of the police posted on the terraces. The other man inside me, the one who suffers and fears so much, is silent now, shrinking into the depths of my being. Like an echo of the echo of his voice, I keep repeating that it's only a mistake, a monstrous mistake. In the courtyard we're surprised by the most unexpected of scenes. Beside the fountain, sitting at a small table covered by a cloth, Ruiz Alonso is having a snack of pastries and café con leche. He has a napkin tied around his neck with a bowknot to protect his blue coverall, and each time he leans forward to dip a piece of pastry, the curly locks of hair on his forehead fall to the rim of the cup. Across from Ruiz Alonso sit Trescastro and one of the unknown police who came with them in the Oakland. They seem somewhat discomfited by the snack, which the deputy himself no doubt demanded. On either side, mute and erect, Doña Esperanza and Esperancita look at him contemptuously.

PREPARE FOR YOUR TRIAL.

Ruiz Alonso stands and drains his café con leche in a sonorous gulp. He has great difficulty removing the napkin because the knot tightens in his fingers when he attempts to undo it. Finally free, thanks to the solicitous assistance of Trescastro, he wipes his mouth and sweaty forehead with a single swipe though the corners of his thick lips remain spotted with white. Only then does he turn toward me and greet me, lowering his forehead as if about to charge. ("The truth is that the gentleman, God rest his soul, always maintained a fortitude worthy of praise. That I swear to with my hand on the Scriptures. I told him he was detained but allowed him to say good-bye to the people who were sheltering him.")

"I have orders to take you to the Civilian Government," he says brusquely. "I'd be grateful if we make it fast because a good amount of time has already been wasted here."

"Miguel Rosales also advises me to go with you, though all of this is a mistake, a dreadful mistake. What does the Civilian Government want with me?"

"I have no idea. I've only been asked to guarantee that you arrive safe and sound. For the moment I have no other mission. Will you follow me?"

"I suppose I can't refuse."

"Very well. Then let's go right now."

Doña Esperanza embraces me and Esperancita kisses me on both cheeks. Secretly she hands me her embroidered handkerchief and in a whisper asks me to bring it back very soon. She would like to give it to me but can't because it's a gift from her sister the nun in Rome, she murmurs in a hurried, broken voice. Trescastro has the wheel and Ruiz Alonso sits beside him. Miguel and I ride behind. As the car begins to move away toward Calle de las Tablas, the Assault Guards disperse along the Plaza de los Lobos.

"Miguel, don't forget to find your brother Pepe right away. Pepe above all."

"Yes, yes, I promise. This has to be cleared up immediately."

"It's all a mistake, a monstrous mistake."

That man who lives inside me and at times cohabits openly with me to deny or contradict me, the one who desires men I'll never love or loves women I can't desire, the same one I hate for his fear and despise for his obstinate rancors, suddenly subjugates me as we cross the Plaza de la Trinidad on our way to the Civilian Government offices. Defeated, I begin to tremble like a jack-in-the-box and my teeth chatter between my jaws. ("At least I had the death I chose. The one I didn't want for my son. You'll die the death others impose on you because in this country of depravity and misfortune, those who don't choose their death are doomed to be killed by imbeciles. Stupidity is our innocence.") There is a flash of contempt in Miguel's reddened eyes. No doubt, and in spite of himself, he believes that at the critical moment I'd go to my death singing verses to the Virgin of the Alhambra and insulting the mothers of Ruiz Alonso and Trescastro. He pulls himself together right away and takes one of my hands between his, as if he were going to read the lines on my palm.

"Whoever expedited this denunciation will answer for it," he states in a loud voice so the members of Popular Action can hear him. "You'll be home as soon as I find Pepe. In the meantime, try to be calm."

"Send a blanket, please, and tobacco. I beg you. It's August and I'm shivering with cold."

"Yes, yes, of course."

"And find a lawyer too. Pérez Serrabona is my father's attorney, and he can put you in touch with him."

"I will, I will, though it isn't necessary. It's less than nothing, Pepe will resolve this mess and get you out. Be calm and don't despair."

Trescastro stops the car in front of the Civilian Government building. On the stage in this theater of mine, August gilds the streets. Two Falangistas, their shirts undone, stand guard at each side of the entrance. In a few moments, if I continue with the evocation of the afternoon under the last skies I'll see alive, one of the sentinels will try to hit me with the butt of his rifle. He'll do this without anger or ill will, as he undoubtedly attacks all the prisoners as they cross the threshold. He's almost an adolescent and has not yet tried to veil the liquid of illuminated surprise that lights the eyes of childhood. He is content to attack us with the irrational indifference of children who stone stray dogs or pursue lizards with a stick, precisely because in his eyes we cease being men and are transformed into a stupid, malignant species very inferior to lizards and dogs on the scale of the moral values of animals. It is also true that an angry Ruiz Alonso intervenes, though this is the only truth among his lies and is more a defense of his own pride than of my helplessness. "How do you dare, wretch? In my presence!" he shouts now on the stage as he had roared then on the street.

In reality, pun intended, everything is repeated punctually and precisely even though a part of my dead man's consciousness remains waiting for a variant, an inevitable discrepancy. (PREPARE FOR YOUR TRIAL.) Trescastro takes his leave of Ruiz Alonso and says he is going home. Miguel, on the other hand, goes with us into the Civilian Government building and shouts at Ruiz Alonso, in a voice loud enough for everyone to hear, that he wants to speak with the governor in his presence. Ruiz Alonso shrugs his laborer's shoulders in a way that is both disdainful and indifferent. Surprised, I understand that Miguel will use the name of his brother Pepe to attempt to avoid torture in my interrogations. I think of Manolo, for whom I never felt more affinity in my life ("They killed my brother-in-law Manolo. My father called this morning to tell me"), and I wonder how much he suffered until death became his desperate liberation. In the Civilian Government offices an unexpected silence reigns, interrupted only occasionally by the tread of boots or the clatter of a typewriter. And yet the building, like certain of Poe's houses ("Tel qu'en Lui-même enfin l'éternité le change." "You haven't read anything by Mallarmé either? *Fillet*, intellectually you're a virgin and martyr. A monster of the South, innocent and brilliant like a camellia in flames or a burning giraffe. I'll have to go to bed with you to sow my culture in your soul"), has an invisible life of its own that is ominous and sinister. One might call it a labyrinth of facing walls that terrified hands have scratched from the floor to the edge of eternity, or a collection of surgical instruments, the treasure of a surgeon turned torturer, fallen to the ground and transformed in this mansion by virtue of a miracle in reverse, a portent of the Black Mass. I look at Miguel and understand how much he fears and suffers for me at this moment. Suddenly I also realize that the entire Rosales family must descend from a remote line of converted Jews, though I never noticed it before and they had forgotten it in another century. It's enough to see Miguel's face now, when anguish deepens all his features with a chisel, and it's enough to think about the religious devotion of the entire family as well as their self-sacrificing solidarity with those who are persecuted, an apparent contradiction to their proven fascism.

PREPARE FOR YOUR TRIAL.

With no surprise, almost with the fatigued, sad indifference of someone waiting for the last inscrutable line that will close his poem, or the encounter with the man who will change the entire meaning of his existence, the inevitable difference between the past and its representation on the stage through my memories appears on a whitewashed wall in the Civilian Government building. Next to the office of the Pontius Pilate who presides over this place, at the height of the forehead of a smooth-faced soldier guarding the room, there was nothing but the stain of a good amount of damp on the day they took me there under arrest. A kind of unexpected plagiarism of a shadow puppet, improvised with the thumb, index finger, and middle finger of one hand, crossed over the wrist by the middle finger, index finger, and thumb of the other, to represent together a kind of seated rabbit. Now, on the stage, eternity copies everything in hell, including the silhouette of the young rabbit. In a manner where arrogance leaves no trace of caution, even at the moment of his victory over the Rosales family, Ruiz Alonso tells Miguel that the governor has gone to the front and today Lieutenant Colonel Velasco is his replacement. Miguel nods, not looking at him or responding, as a gruff prince would treat a gentleman-in-waiting suspected of stealing. ("This bastard, may all the demons of hell shove it up his ass, told me you did more harm with your pen than others with a pistol.") Nonetheless, and precisely on a stage of this spiral, which Miguel could not have devised with his imagination of a Falangista singer to the Virgin, above the shadow of the rabbit rampant, and just beside the wall, some letters erupt as golden and bright as the ones that appeared on the window of the Andalucía express. They end with a great question mark that seems to be of blinding gold, as if all a summer's wheat had melted on the scythe. In front of it, very large and well spaced, nine words ask me: WHY DON'T YOU PRETEND YOU'RE CRAZY AND BE ACQUITTED?

DESTINY

On stage the question in gold letters imprinted on the wall of the Civilian Government Building of Granada faded away. All that remained was the stain that outlined the shadow of a rabbit. Then the wall and door to the governor's office merged, as if sinking gradually into deeper and deeper waters. Finally the set appeared, empty of memories and filled with shadows. It was then, when he turned in his seat, that he saw the stranger sitting beside him, almost elbow to elbow, shoulder to shoulder. He had emerged unexpectedly in the alabaster light from the passageway.

He gave a start because he never had seen anyone in the corridor or the theaters of the spiral. With no particular feeling and naturally with no distress at all, he had concluded that the dead were blind and deaf only among themselves. "I'm dreaming," he said to himself and immediately recalled that death was eternal wakefulness if innocence was not proved at trial. (WHY DON'T YOU PRETEND YOU'RE CRAZY AND BE ACQUITTED?) Then he thought he had lost his mind: a phantom driven mad by the solitude of hell but still rational enough to be aware of his own insanity. Almost immediately he resolved that the presence of the other man, in the next seat, was not a dream or a hallucination. In silence, the stranger observed him carefully as if making an effort to recognize him.

He thought that if recollections of what had been lived and the memory of what had been imagined appeared on the stage, perhaps on the eve of the trial other phantoms would do the same in the orchestra seats. In any case, if that man was a shade of his reason or his delirium, he could not recognize him or leave his side even though no physical force kept him in the grasp of his seat.

With greater calm, almost with the cold curiosity an agnostic scientist would bring to the examination of a frog's heart, which he had compared to God Himself in his homage to Falla or, to be more precise, at a crossroads of his irrevocable destiny, he held the gaze of the stranger and in spite of himself began to observe him.

He was an old man of indefinite age, impossible to determine, with the ambiguous air of those who stopped aging one day in their senescence. Perhaps on the anniversary of their coming into the world, or maybe at the funeral of one of their grandchildren, or possibly one morning when they woke, as they contemplated the still bluish sun of dawn and wondered whether that light and that silence might not be the only reality before which our lives passed like the images of a film moving across the back curtain of the stage. The man was also shorter than he, though at one time he may have been taller before age bent him and made him shrink. His head was completely bald from temple to temple, as rosy as a child's above his forehead and mottled with dark spots at the temples. His eyebrows above the edge of rimless glasses with very long earpieces of thin gold were hairy, thick, and white. He dressed in black, with no affectation or untidiness, as if he simply wore mourning for himself.

For a lost instant, one of those moments that even in hell seem fleetingly suspended over the edge of a knife, he felt the temptation to touch the old man's hand or forearm. Immediately another impulse, more complicated and difficult to explain, held him back. Almost at the same time he told himself the intruder would disappear when touched, just as his represented memories vanished when he persisted in going up on stage to put his hands on them. He also thought that knowing the stranger was alive on the spiral, old but still animate and fragile, would be the greatest of horrors when at the back of his mind he still hoped he was nothing but an apparition of his own aberration. (WHY DON'T YOU PRETEND YOU'RE CRAZY AND BE ACQUITTED?) Then, almost without realizing it and as if he had lost control of his voice, he asked:

"What are you doing here?"

"Where am I?" he replied as if he hadn't heard him.

It was all too absurd, as Bebé and Carlillo Morla would say, shaking their southern, Chilean heads when he read them one of his surrealist pieces. He was afraid to experience when dead a passage added to his play, *The Public*, which he had entrusted to Rafael Martínez Nadal. ("If something should happen to me in this war that's at our door, swear to me you'll destroy the original of *The Public* right away.") In a brief rush of author's passion, over which the doors of hell or death did not prevail, he asked himself whether Rafael had carried out that request and replied he'd never have the courage to do it, just as he had expected when he handed him the manuscript. ("Precisely for that reason, because only I could suspect the importance of what I've written. If I die, *The Public* has no reason to be for other people.") His words back then seemed grandiloquent and pretentious. But he couldn't help identifying with one of his own mad characters in that farce, The Figure of Bell, The Centurion, The Prompter, or The Lady, when he insisted, facing the stranger:

"Do you really not know where you are?"

"No, I don't know. But I've come from hell."

He shook his bare head, too big for the shoulders reduced by age. When he moved it, it seemed ready to separate from his hunched body, and the vertebrae in his neck creaked with the sound of little bones being stepped on.

"This is hell," he replied in a tone of anger transformed into studied indifference. Without knowing why he began to hate the intruder. He was overcome by a dark rancor toward his voice and his astonished gaze beneath ashen eyebrows.

"This is hell?"

"Yes, yes it is, and it has the form of a spiral. Each dead person is assigned a theater, and this is mine. What are you doing here?"

"Your theater?" the old man asked in a tone of amazement. "What do you mean?"

Consternation opened the stranger's eyes wide behind the round lenses of his glasses. He told himself that in the past, in another world lost in a very remote time, his eyes had been large and dark. He didn't know then whether he remembered the other man's eyes or supposed he ought to remember him without being able to specify who he was. The old man's accent eventually disconcerted him, because free of intonation and inflections, in the end it disappeared. It made him think of a Trappist who, returned to the world after eternities in silence, spoke as if he had learned the language of his fellow men in the midst of a species other than human. In turn, and to his own annoyance, he caught himself speaking to the man in mourning in the tranquil, slow tone of someone who insists on proving the veracity of his words before the most cynical of deaf men or the most skeptical of judges.

"On stage my memories are revived when I evoke them. Only mine, though other dead people invisible to me must see them as well, as I sometime look at theirs in other theaters. If one of us is acquitted at trial, he obtains the grace of sleep freed from consciousness and memories. At other times, I believe that men's evocations precede their death and their presence in hell . . . "

He was cut off by the old man's laughter. It seemed uncontrollable, though he soon took delight in his own outburst. He laughed as if he were clucking, out of breath and trembling. Behind his toothless gums was the dark palate of a sheep dog.

"Where did you get this absurd idea of hell turned into a tower of theaters?"

"It's not a tower. It's a spiral. All you have to do is go out to the corridor to understand. The passageway climbs in very wide, open curves to all the theaters."

"A spiral!" Hilarity doubled the old man over as if he were a hook. It made him slap his knees with bony hands spotted by the years. "It's the most grotesque thing anyone could imagine! Hell a spiral of theaters. One for each man, I suppose."

"One for each man," he agreed, more and more humiliated and surprised, incapable of escaping from the phantom and even of ignoring his unexpected presence. "One for each dead person."

The apparition shook his head and for the first time looked away. His guffaws turned into panting with the coughs and snorts of an old rutting stag, though he soon gained control of himself. He spoke now with a kind of ironic commiseration, as an experienced and to a certain extent sadistic shepherd would with a very young apprentice goatherd.

"Boy, this isn't hell and we aren't dead. I'm very well acquainted with hell, to my sorrow, and I can assure you it's on earth." He turned to face him, as if trying to convince him with his sincerity after abusing him with his sarcasm. "Do you know where we really are?"

"Where do you want me to say?"

"I haven't wanted anything, my boy, not even to go on living, for a very long time. But facts are facts, even though they may be dreams. This supposed spiral of hell, these theaters where, as you so absurdly say, their memories at times precede the dead, the other stage set of your ridiculous vocations, the eternal sentence to wakefulness and memories, the possible liberation in forgetting, all of it, absolutely all of it, is nothing more or less than my nightmare. You're not anyone, only a crazed phantom in one of my dreams, from which I'll wake whenever I please."

(WHY DON'T YOU PRETEND YOU'RE CRAZY AND BE ACQUITTED?) The crazy one was that man, whoever he was, placed in his path by an inexplicable but perhaps not completely irrational destiny as he prepared, or should have prepared, for his trial. If that withered creature was truly mad and not simulating derangement, perhaps the purpose of an oblique providence was to offer him as a model for his own feigned madness. On the other hand, the man believed both he and hell were his dream, the nightmare of a possible mega-lomaniac who perhaps feared being immortal. ("I haven't wanted anything, my boy, not even to go on living, for a very long time"), but Sandro Vasari had also dreamed the endless spiral, him in his assigned theater, and even some of the memories that preceded Vasari himself into eternity. One by one, the words of the man with the plastered-down hair and the scar on his cheek came back to him: "I said to myself: *This can't be, dreaming you went crazy.* And then: *Dreaming you went to hell.* Parts of that nightmare, perhaps the most terrible ones, disappeared upon waking."

"If I'm your dream, who are you?"

"I don't want to tell you my name because it's my curse. At one time, when I was as young as you, I was vain about having the name I have. Now I wish I had never been born."

"I became proud of mine too. I was dazzled to know it was repeated and proclaimed. Now I agree with you, it would be better never to have been born."

"Be quiet and don't interrupt! Even in my dream you're too young to understand prestige like mine, the prestige I had at your age. People recognized me on the street and came over to shake my hand, as if I had worked miracles. At first I told myself: 'It's fair because I am who I am.' Then I started to ask myself: 'Can they be talking about me? Can they be talking to me?' You'd never understand . . . "

"I understand you perfectly because the transformation in my own legend, I've experienced that too."

"I told you to be quiet! At your age what do you know about me and the times I'm referring to? If you interrupt again, I'll stop talking. But then you won't find out what hell really is."

It was the most ironic of threats, but he made it unaware of the sarcasm. Perhaps he was sincerely convinced he was nothing but part of a dream, though that dyspeptic old man with no accent seemed accustomed to deceiving himself. With an effort he controlled the anger provoked by the old man's presence, though he could control himself only to the point of replying:

"I'm not a phantom in your nightmare. You're an apparition in my derangement, and since I can't explain how I ever imagined you, I must conclude that you're right and I've lost my mind."

"What? What did you say? Repeat everything more slowly."

Suddenly he was pretending to be deaf, or at an unexpected moment age had deafened him. He cupped his right hand behind his ear, and he could see his palm crossed by lines and wrinkles. His hand trembled, as if his words had pierced it.

"I think I've lost my mind. But you aren't dreaming me in your nightmare. In fact you exist only to the extent of my hallucination."

"How do you dare to say I don't exist?" He flew into a rage, threatening him with his desiccated index finger. "For precisely this reason, for existing and having the name I had, they wanted to kill me like a dog. Ah! What can you know, you fool, about a tragedy like mine! How to make you understand at your age the manhunt and horror I had to live through!"

"Yes, I understand because I've suffered them too. Be quiet and go away because you tire me. You didn't come to hell to tell me anything new, and I have to prepare for my trial."

From being his hallucination, as he almost came to believe, he must have taken on a life of his own and delighted in displaying it. He passed from anger to a kind of sardonic contempt, stretching out on his seat and smiling at him as he would at a shadow he could brush away or illuminate on a whim. Perhaps that stain on the wall at the Civilian Government building next to Commander Valdés's door, though it was also Lieutenant Colonel Velasco's in Valdés's absence, that plagiarized the shadow puppet of a rabbit and above

whose memory the most disconcerting advice had lit up: WHY DON'T
YOU PRETEND YOU'RE CRAZY AND BE ACQUITTED? Yes, why not, in
fact, he wondered again, insistent on convincing himself: on trans-
forming the question that was beginning to gnaw at and devour him
into an academic one. Because simply put, dementia was much
more difficult to represent than reason, in the savage comedy of life
or the incomprehensible wakefulness of hell. To the exact dimensions of a civilization that for centuries had been calling itself rational and enlightened, men simulated a sanity that would disappear at the first opportunity they had to exterminate one another in
the name of their beliefs, without the victims, who probably became
executioners when they stopped being victims, able to defend themselves in any way other than to cry out in vain about the mistake, the
monstrous mistake, of their sacrifice.

. . . And the intruder continued to delight in his living presence,
stretched out in his seat like a challenge or an insult. He wanted to
change his desperate desire to have him disappear without a trace
into muffled shouts at some wailing wall of the soul. With useless
nostalgia he thought about the characters in his plays or poems
whom he would bring down at will at the most unexpected and at
the same time the best moment. The man finally dying in peace at
the end of a ballad. The Gypsy repeatedly stabbed by envy. The
woman possessed and abandoned by her scornful lover when he
learns he's been deceived. The child lost in the sky holding the
moon in his hand. They all disappeared immediately, obeying creative demands. "A painter never knows when he's finished or should
finish his painting," Salvador Dalí had told him, repeating another
phrase of Picasso's he wouldn't discover until much later. "A poet,
on the other hand, never fails to know," he replied then, truthfully.
Now he ought to retract it, because this phantom of his wakefulness
in hell, if it really was an image from his hallucinations, remained at
his side, imperturbable and tenacious, pointing at him several times
with his finger and at other times placing his lined palm behind his

ear in order not to miss any of his words or to feign a deafness that might be derisive.

"What did you say you're preparing for now?" the old man asked, like a burlesque echo of his own thoughts.

"For my trial. You came only to get in my way and interfere with me."

"You're not preparing for anything because you don't know what you're talking about," he clucked again, with that exasperating, almost womanish laugh. "I spent all these years in hell, but not in limbo. I have very precise reports about you and yours."

" . . . About me and mine?"

"Yes, sir, that's what I said. Have you become deaf? You're a swine, a real swine. When I think about all the sacrifices and suffering of my own youth, of its capacity for devotion and its idealism, the depravity of this gang of yours still seems worse, much worse, than our crimes."

He thought of Ruiz Alonso telling Sandro Vasari that in view of so much pornography and delinquency, his own times seemed very far away. He thought of his own father, not the father whose words on the day of his brother-in-law's murder and his own arrest were to tell him he would give anything for him, including his mother and his siblings, because he could never fail him, never, never, never, but the other one: the one of that morning in the Retiro and of his adolescence, standing before Monet's *La Gare Saint Lazare* and railing against the impostures of some delinquents who didn't know how to attract the attention of the ignorant. He thought of himself that day in Madrid, wondering for a moment, which he would then forget until this other instant in eternity, whether he would ever feel and express himself as his father was doing then. Thinking about all this, and in an unconscious transposition that he would immediately understand all too well, he asked:

"Who gave you those reports, the ones you alluded to?"

"Who else would it be? Luis, naturally."

"Luis . . . "

"Luis Rosales." He said the name impatiently, as if it were taken for granted. "I'll never leave his house again; it's where I hid in the summer of 1936. I slept there last night and I'm dreaming you now. How many years have I been hidden in these two rooms on the second floor? Forty, forty-five, fifty? I lost count, but I didn't forget my decision not to leave there alive. In one winter or another all the Rosales family died except Luis and Esperancita. Now they visit me very rarely, though she knocks on the door three times a day with the flat of her hand and leaves my meals on the floor. They know I prefer not to see them or speak to them because I chose hell and not the world. I can't free myself from Luis as easily as I avoid Esperanza. He has a key, and from time to time he bursts in, at the most unexpected moments, to talk to me for hours. In the end we almost always argue and I still don't know whether he wants me to go or expects me to die in his house, God knows when . . . Just yesterday I told him . . . "

"Be quiet! Be quiet! Damn you! I don't want to endure this martyrdom!"

(WHY DON'T YOU PRETEND YOU'RE CRAZY AND BE ACQUITTED?) No, I can't pretend to, when I really did lose my mind, and after I was dead. I created this awful hallucination, the image and likeness of my caricature, and now it not only has a life of its own but has come to usurp mine, in another hell that's a sinister parody of this spiral. What does this implacable old man want of me, the man I would have turned into if I had lived? Is he trying to tell me that my derangement is my only truth and he has become the avatar of my madness? Or perhaps the truth is just the opposite, as he proclaims, and I'm part of the dementia of an old man driven crazy by loneliness? If Ruiz Alonso, Trescastro, and the thugs in the Assault Guard hadn't arrested me that Sunday morning, perhaps everything he's telling me is true now and I stayed hidden in that attic of a sort on Calle de Angulo. ("I have orders to take you to the Civilian Government. I'd be grateful if we could make it fast because a lot of time has been lost here.") Or perhaps, in the most absurd of possibilities, the thugs from the Assault Guard, Trescastro, and Ruiz Alonso never went to Calle de Angulo, 1, and his entire Calvary, with his arrest, interrogations, being shot in the back, and wakefulness in hell were nothing more than the recurrent nightmare of the old man, who he must be as well.

"Be quiet! Be quiet! Damn you! I don't want to endure this martyrdom!"

He raised his hands to his ears because a rough sea, one of those metallic oceans by Dalí or Patinir, suddenly agitated and disturbed by a storm of blazing volcanoes, seemed stirred up inside him and threatened to blow apart the bones of his skull.

"Be quiet! Be quiet!"

He heard the old man's words through his hands. But he could distinguish only the dark echo of his own shrieks. An echo that began to irritate and embarrass him, because it wasn't the broken bellow of the pederast he always knew he was but the screaming of the fairy he never wanted to be. At the same time and in the light of a bright flash of memory, it brought to mind the first time his father guessed at his homosexuality, one infinitely distant summer between his first trip to Madrid and his first stay in Cadaqués, when he dedicated the ode to Salvador Dalí where he said he wasn't praising his imperfect adolescent brush but his longings of an eternal visionary. It was another Sunday afternoon, because his destiny always seemed to be decided on Sundays, and he was playing from memory something by Chopin on the piano at Huerta de San Vicente. He stopped suddenly when the final ray of late afternoon slipped through the half open window, divided in a prism of the chandelier, and stained his right hand with all the colors in the spectrum. Only then, as he looked at the rainbow on his fingers and perhaps began inadvertently to write a line published years later, where he spoke of a hyacinth light illuminating his hand, did he become aware of his father's presence, sitting in the semidarkness of a corner in the living room. A mirror reflected his eyes and in his glance he saw the infinite sadness of the first man on earth, different from the monsters that had preceded him, when he discovered loneliness after the death of a child.

"Yes, yesterday afternoon Luis showed up unexpectedly on his return from Madrid," continued the vampire who was dreaming him or the apparition of his own madness. "He came with the excuse of picking up some recent books he'd lent me. Collections of poems by people your age, or perhaps even younger. Scattered over the floor where I had thrown them, he tripped over the books. 'If this is the garbage that's current, that they're writing today, tell me why a generation of poets like ours ever lived?' I asked him at the outset. He shook his head, not daring to look me in the eye, and tried to respond with some fallacy about the previous regime, which in its fumbling had castrated the people intellectually. 'Don't try to convince me with that kind of specious reasoning. I'm the victim of that regime, locked away in your house for almost half a century, not these kids whose mental capacity doesn't go beyond impudence and commonplaces. Ours was a generation of exceptional poets and masterpieces. When I say this, I'm not indulging in vanity but summarizing the true history of literature. We were also a group of free men, at least in the best and happiest years. Don't tell me now about the new pieties, with the people as an object of worship, when we've survived so many idiotic catastrophes that we've turned into two old wrecks. We're all people, the two of us, the mason who's whitewashing that house on Plaza de los Lobos, and even the ones who murdered half of Granada in the name of God. In the universe there's no effect without a corresponding cause and . . . ' He interrupted himself suddenly while he was quoting himself almost in shouts, as if he had forgotten ideas and words. ' . . . And besides, besides.' Listen, where was I?"

"You said that in the universe there's no effect without a corresponding cause," he replied, not unaware of the irony.

"Exactly, yes, sir, that's what I said and he couldn't answer me. 'The only origin of all our misfortunes, the slaughter of hyenas that our war was, the dictatorship that followed it, and even the foolishness that passes today for poetry, is reduced to this people of yours who have never measured up as an intelligent, civilized community in the eyes of history.' He found himself obliged to agree, though unwillingly. Then he spoke to me about men your age and others even younger, all of you who could be my sons, though you're only a splinter of my dream . . . "

"I'm not your son and I'm not your dream. I'm a dead man who reasons and has delusions. You're an apparition in my hallucination."

He affirmed it now without conviction, as perhaps his father had tried to tell himself that Sunday in Huerta de San Vicente that a pervert could not be a son of his, that he was a ghost who would vanish with the last sun of the afternoon. Besides, the old man, absorbed in the memory of his shouting and diatribes, wasn't listening to him either.

"He described a generation of supposed poets, dressed in rags in the American style, like hoboes in the films of King Vidor who cross the United States from coast to coast, hiding in a freight car on the Union Pacific. All of them poisoned by the drugs they consume like candied almonds because they're incapable of thinking and feeling for themselves. 'Luis,' I said to him, 'you talk nonsense and want me to return to this world I have absolutely nothing in common with, though according to you my works are read and performed among those tribes. In the midst of those people I'd live enclosed in an invisible bubble, like an alien. Like those lovers in Bosch, in *The Garden of Earthly Delights*, imprisoned in a soap bubble or a bladder mislaid at a witches' Sabbath. If you remembered who we were, you wouldn't even dare suggest it . . . And furthermore, furthermore . . . ' Listen, what else did I say to him?"

"That he shouldn't advise you to return to *The Garden of Earthly Delights*."

"I already know that, imbecile, and I don't intend to repeat it!" He was becoming enraged as he caressed his pink baldness. "Ah, yes! Then I thought it was my duty to add: 'If in addition to remembering who we were you maintained the dignity that should be ours, you'd also turn your back on that jungle and hide away here with me.'"

"And he replied he wasn't free to do that because his destiny was as irrevocable as yours."

"That's true, he said that! How did you know?" he asked without too much interest, shrugging. "Perhaps you're not as foolish as I thought because, after all, you're my dream. He replied . . . "

"He replied that each person has a role in the great theater of the world and the parts in the play were indivisible and nontransferable."

"Yes, yes, that's what he said, as if I'd never read Calderón. I was assigned captivity, for this was the destiny imposed by my name. For having the name I had and being the man I was, I had to hide in his house when they wanted to kill me. Now, so many years later, my pride in being who I am keeps me from returning to a country that doesn't deserve my presence. He was assigned a role different from and subordinate to mine in the farce. By means of inexplicable chance events, he became my guardian or, if you prefer, my jailer and confidant. He was no freer now to reveal my existence so I would be honored as a man come back to life than he was before I was denounced and condemned to be murdered."

"But one way or another that situation had to end. Nothing is saved from the passage of time, not the stone in the air or the man on the ground. If such an absurdity still exists, it's because it's one of my hallucinations, just like you."

The old man was only half listening, not granting any credit to his words, as he blinked uneasily beneath ashen eyebrows. He himself didn't dare entirely believe what he had just said. ("Nothing is saved from the passage of time, not the stone in the air or the man on the ground. If such an absurdity still exists, it's because it's one of my hallucinations, just like you.") Then he thought of that female patient of Charcot or the elder Huxley, the uncle or father of the novelist, whose case Luis Buñuel told him about before he happened to learn he had actually read it in Proust and in *Sodome et Gomorrhe*. (*La femme aura Gomorrhe et l'homme aura Sodome.*) A woman of the highest British society, who renounced all the receptions of her class, for as soon as her host would offer her a seat, she saw an ancient gentleman sitting there, refined and smiling, with a green frock coat and a lorgnette. Incapable of determining where the illusion lay, in the gesture that offered her the armchair or the formally dressed individual who occupied it, she turned to Huxley or Charcot to resolve her doubts. Supposedly cured, she went to a private concert to test herself. As soon as she was offered a seat in the first row, facing a very well-known soprano, the stranger with the lorgnette appeared to her again. Nonetheless, this time she controlled herself. She drew strength from her weakness and accepted the chair of carved Victorian mahogany, driving away forever the very urbane and distinguished phantom.

Unlike that lady of another time, he couldn't decide whether he should or should not touch the hand or arm of his presumed parody, just as he hadn't been able to decide that earlier. It was fitting that the usurper of his identity and even of his life snatched away by bullets would disappear at his touch, in precisely the way Charcot's or Huxley's patient finally had dispensed with her own ghost. It was also fitting that he himself would be the one to disappear then, if *it was the truth* (what sense would truth make in hell?) that he was the man's dream. Surprisingly, that possibility of melting into interminable nothingness and sleeping with no memories or nightmares, beyond time and space, frightened him for the first time. It was still his absolute, most fervent desire finally to forget himself, but he didn't want to achieve it by those means or through fear.

"That's what Luis Rosales came to tell me," the other man agreed, this time almost exulting. "In any case, he insisted, we ought to settle what was left unfinished. I think I've indicated to you my suspicion that after so many years he might want to be rid of me, at any price and by any means. Perhaps it would please him if that were possible, but naturally he wasn't free to do it. 'Luis,' I said to him, 'think back and remember the days when I taught you what an hendecasyllable was. Now it's my duty to show you who and where we are. This is the second floor of your house, the house that belonged to your parents, but it's also hell. The two of us are condemned to immortality, for reasons I don't know and besides do not concern me. I'll remain in these two rooms forever, and you'll come to visit me occasionally across entire eternities, to repeat this conversation in identical terms or in others very similar.'"

"One of the rooms is the bedroom," he interrupted on an impulse. "It has a single bed with legs and headboard of curved, very thin iron. The walls are white, though perhaps the years have darkened them, and the fringed bedspread is lemon yellow. The bedroom opens on to a kind of small sitting room that has a window with embroidered curtains that faces Calle de Angulo. It has a Pleyel piano, shelves that hold books from the Library of Spanish Authors and some wretched translations of Proust that Pablo Salinas was in charge of. I also recall a chest of drawers where Luis Rosales's aunt perfumed the sheets with lowland quince. Above the chest and inside a lantern stands a Sacred Heart of Jesus with open arms."

The old man listened with no great surprise, nodding at times and other times smiling. He seemed to congratulate himself for the detailed description, as if it were his. He wiped his glasses with a large handkerchief, in one of whose corners he saw the initials of his first and family names. Then he pretended to applaud.

"Well done, young man! Everything correct and as it should be! The kingdom of heaven must be made up of men like you. It doesn't surprise me that you know my hell so well, since you're one of my dreams. In a sense I could even say you'll turn out to be me."

"In a way," he corroborated, fully conscious this time of his irony.

"Only in a way," the old man tried to be specific. "If you were my age you'd be much wiser. I have to explain your destiny to you as I did to Luis Rosales, since yours is very similar to his. You're chained to my dream, as he is to my wakefulness, and you'll continue to appear on nights like this so I can talk to someone other than Luis and loneliness doesn't drive me crazy. As you can see, youngster, the laws of hell are very judicious even though the legislators are invisible. Even assuming I wasn't immortal, in which case Luis Rosales wouldn't be either, you and I would turn out to be inseparable because when I'm dead I'd go on dreaming you for all of eternity."

"You'll disappear as soon as I touch your shoulder with the palm of my hand, because you're not anyone. They killed me a long time ago and you're only my false shade: the man I wouldn't have wanted to be if surviving meant turning into someone so different from myself."

"Are you sure they killed you, my boy?"

"I'm as certain of that as I am of our being in the true hell, the only one that exists."

The apparition laughed again, but his laugh was different. Perhaps harder and less shrill. Without having grown any younger, and without ceasing to be himself, he was changing his appearance, like someone trying on various disguises on the cold eve of a carnival. His shoulders broadened and his spine straightened, until he had the bearing of man very advanced in years but more accustomed to moving through the world and clearing the way with his hands than in spending almost half a century in two rooms with a Sacred Heart of Jesus, a Pleyel, a single bed, the Library of Spanish Authors, and the translations of Don Pedro Salinas.

"You're not sure of anything because life, death, even eternity itself are the fruits of infuriating chance. No destiny determines them because there's no providence other than the one made and unmade by every one of us at each instant and in each step we take."

"Who are you now?" he interrupted, not listening to him, and in a tone that surprised him again because it indicated a horror and perplexity much greater than what he felt.

"I know who I am," he replied, quoting Cervantes and still smiling, as if he had pronounced a sacrilege. "In other words, the man you could have been."

"I know who I am too! Why do you persecute me this way?"

"I'm not persecuting you. You said that I'm at your mercy and it would be enough for you to touch my shoulder with your hand for me to disappear immediately. Why don't you try it?"

The old man's skull was growing a white pelt like that of a Moorish shepherd very advanced in years, while his rimless eyeglasses disappeared. And the tone of his complexion, so pale on his cheeks beneath that pink baldness, darkened and blurred the spots on his temples, as if he had spent a long time exposed to many suns. Only the hobgoblin's clothes and shoes, the attire of someone in mourning for himself, remained unchanged.

"I'd like to know what you want of me . . . "

He abandoned the lament in his plea, though he noticed he had put himself at the mercy of the ghost, clearly similar to the man he would be now if his killers had been pleased to let him live. ("I'd like to know what you want of me.") He thought of the days of *La Barraca*, when he traveled all over Spain in trucks with a troupe of young men and women who idolized him as if he were a god dressed as a mechanic. In Burgo de Osma they had been joined by an adolescent, still in school and now on vacation, whose parents allowed him to go away with the actors because even in Burgo he was a public figure. ("You're still young but very justly celebrated. You have a natural talent no one can deny without offending you"), a kind of grown prodigious boy in the eyes of the entire country. "What do you know how to do?" he asked the boy, constrained by his slim bearing and those deep black eyes where two points of gold (WHY DON'T YOU PRETEND YOU'RE CRAZY AND BE ACQUITTED?) flashed in two embers: like the fawn devoured in Aleixandre's *Destruction or Love*, quivering in the eyes of a Bengal tiger, transformed into a tiny fleece. In a voice with very good timbre for his age, the boy recited for him lines from the Archpriest of Hita's *The Book of Good Love*. "Oh, Lord, and how lovely is Doña Endrina in the square! / What a figure, what charm, what a long neck like a heron's! / What hair, and what a sweet mouth, what color, and what good luck! / With arrows of love she wounds all that her eyes look upon." Then he welcomed him to *La Barraca*, though in reality he wouldn't have wanted to ask him. Afterward, while he lived with the company, he tried in vain to forget him. One night he was surprised to find himself strolling with the adolescent along very old streets in Soria, with greyhounds and fishes in the carvings of the houses silvered by the moon. They stopped at a fountain to drink, and while the boy smiled at him and dried his mouth with the back of his hand, he embraced him and impulsively kissed him on the lips. "What do you want of me?" he had asked in the identical tone of voice, astonished and terrified, that he had directed to the aged shadow of himself. "Nothing, nothing, forgive me. I only wanted to forget who I am and why I was born the way I was born, but it was useless."

"I don't want anything from you," the ghost said, returning him to the reality of hell. "How could I if I'm only your sham reflection? Why don't you forget about us and look at the stage in this theater?"

He obeyed almost knowing what he would see, even if it weren't the staging of his recollections but the dramatization of his double's memories or fantasies, this phantom of his in a new metamorphosis. The stage opened again onto the station platform and the Andalucía express. He and Rafael Martínez Nadal were returning to the compartment with seats upholstered in large dahlias and Rafael was lifting the suitcase onto the rack, above the yellowing photographs of the Rhine in Basel and the Loire in Amboise. Then he put a hand on his friend's back, and with a look that seemed more helpless than affectionate, accompanied him to the platform to say goodbye from the step.

"What do you think will happen now?" his double asked in a voice low enough not to annoy other spectators, without names or visible shapes, who perhaps were sitting around them throughout the theater.

"Nothing that hasn't happened and I haven't seen before, on this very stage," he replied, irritated and impatient.

"Are you sure? In your place I wouldn't insist on it. I've already said we're nothing but the whim of chance or many intertwined chances."

On the train platform and as he talked to Martínez Nadal, he unwittingly turned toward the open door to the passageway. There, in the corridor, absorbed in contemplating the platform, he saw Ruiz Alonso, the tamed worker. Yet at the precise moment he should have been surprised at the similarity his jaws established between that man and his own father, the scene froze on stage and the three of them, he, Ruiz Alonso, and Martínez Nadal were immobilized in a station as still and quiet as Aunt Luisa's Sacred Heart in its high lantern above the Rosales family's chest of drawers.

"What's going on?" he asked the apparition that was at once his parody and the double of the man he might have been. "Why did everything in the scene stop?"

"Shhhh!" The old man brought his index finger to his lips. "Don't raise your voice. If this is hell you might wake the innocent dead. Those you claim sleep free of memory." Then, almost shouting, he threw the question back at him. "What do you think will happen now?"

"The same thing that happened then. The past isn't foretold because it's irrevocable. I'm going to ask Rafael to leave, and I'll hide in my compartment so that man doesn't see me."

He was going to observe that Ruiz Alonso had seen him in any event, though he didn't find that out until after he was dead and living in hell. ("If I insisted on carrying out my duty alone, it was to show him that I didn't hide behind the curtains at the moment of truth.") He felt tempted to add that as soon as he returned to the compartment, life again frozen in a *tableau vivant*, and prepared to close the curtains on the window after closing the ones to the passageway, letters of cast gold would blaze on the glass. PREPARE FOR YOUR TRIAL. He immediately restrained himself because the old man's mordant smile, resembling that of his first incarnation, gave him a sense of foreboding about the uselessness of such details.

"I think you're wrong again and everything happened very differently. Or else the past is revocable after all, though you say otherwise."

"Rafael," he said to Martínez Nadal when the petrified memory was reanimated, "I changed my mind and I'm staying in Madrid. Please go to the compartment and get the suitcase. Don't ask me anything else now." "But you're deranged!" "I beg you, Rafael. I can't, I don't want to go to Granada with that man: the heavyset one leaning out the window in the passageway." "You've lost your mind! Before you know it you'll bay at the moon like a rabid dog!" "Whatever you say, but do as I ask. Or leave the damn suitcase on the train. I'm getting out of here and I'll wait for you in the station café." "All right, all right. Whatever you say," Martínez Nadal agreed in this unexpected variation on his destiny. Afterward, as if what happened in the theater melted into sudden darkness only to dawn again in a different scene after a transition too fleeting even for the eyes of the dead, he and Martínez Nadal appeared together in the restaurant. A waiter in a stained swallow-tailed jacket was serving them another two cognacs, while the man with the head of a sheep, still worried about and exasperated with him, seemed to be taking care of the suitcase. Again he paid for their drinks and the tip, as he had done in Puerta de Hierro. He drank and continued to face his friend, who silently seemed to be demanding a full exegesis of his lunacies.

"What does all this mean?" he asked, more impatient now than disconcerted.

"This means absolutely nothing, because life has no meaning. It's only what happened a long time ago. The result of one of my hastiest and smartest decisions. Listen for a moment and you'll hear my reasons."

"Rafael," he said to Martínez Nadal on the stage, "a premonition made me see my destiny if I went to Granada. In a few days there would be or will be a military insurgency. They'll believe they're carrying out a coup to avoid an attempt at revolution. But they'll precipitate the revolution and war that will fill the fields and streets of this country with corpses. In Granada the insurgents would win and hunt me down like a wild boar, not for what I did, since I haven't done anything, but for being who I am. To escape their fury I would have to hide in the house of some Falangista friends. But this man we saw on the train, the one with the jaws of a mule, would come there to arrest me. Then, without a trial, they'd shoot me in the back, calling me a queer." Then the voice, broken, on the verge of a lament and perhaps not very far from weeping, seemed to become calm. "Yes, this would be my fate if I'd gone to Granada now," it resumed dispassionately, as if stating universal laws known to everyone.

Once again Martínez Nadal seemed to have forgotten his irritation in order to observe him with an absorbed expression. "I'm the one who advised you to stay in Madrid if your panic is so great." Deep inside, and in a certain sense in spite of himself, Martínez Nadal felt convinced that everything he'd just said would have occurred inevitably if he'd left on the Andalucía express. "Here at least you'll be out of danger," he mumbled to escape his own thoughts. "We won't be out of danger anywhere. But at least here I don't know my fate. In Granada I know it too well to forget it." "In short, God's will be done, as you've said so many times. All right, let's go. We'll take a taxi and I'll ride with you to your house." "No, not to my house, no! I beg you. Even now I'm very, very afraid. Rafael, couldn't I hide in your mother's house, with my suitcase and my play *The Public*, a work so absurd that only God knows whether we're all characters in it?"

"This never happened!" he exclaimed in agitation, pounding the arm of his seat, for all of it seemed a mockery of his tragedy, as personal and untransferable as his own existence or voice, which no one could live or speak for him.

"How could it not have happened if I'm here now! If I'm dreaming you whoever you may be! Look at the stage and don't be insolent."

Another of those transitions, still invisible to the eyes of the dead, occurred and changed the scene. The sky was a concerted howl of sirens and a latticed brilliance of searchlights. In the distance, an increasingly remote Madrid blazed and trembled beneath the bombs. He was in a bus that seemed to be traveling on the Valencia highway. The almost full moon lit the road like a parody of those medieval tales where the Milky Way led pilgrims toward the west. He woke after a brief sleep to which he had surrendered out of anxiety more than fatigue. The vehicle advanced hesitantly, its headlights turned off, past endless fields. ("Rafael, these streets and the fields around Madrid will fill with the dead, covered in their own blood. This city will be shelled and bombed until many of its neighborhoods crumble into ruins.") By the light of the moon he recognized Don Antonio Machado, sitting next to him with bowed head, his hands on his knees. With his mind still befuddled and half awake, he thought and said to himself that this sick and aged man, for whom he never felt greater admiration and who, in turn, despised everything he had written, was the greatest Spanish-language poet of the last century, as he himself was of the present. He was certain the old man's poems and his own would survive the ideas and aberrations of the men bombing the city, the men defending it, and perhaps Madrid itself in another time. He repeated in the deepest part of his being that history did not exist, because it almost always was reduced to its own suicide, and only art and literature biologically justified the presence of a people on earth. Then he found himself obliged to admit that as a reader of his own work, and of Machado's verses, it all left him indifferent, and he hoped only to survive the unspeakable madness of a murderous war.

Looking around the bus flooded with moonlight, he recognized the poet's entire family. His mother, a tiny, wrinkled old woman who seemed a centenarian or halted at some imprecise point between a century of life and a useless immortality. Two of his brothers, his sisters-in-law, and his nieces. Ten or twelve souls, frightened and numb, like a tribe at the dawn of the world, fleeing the last monsters they would soon fight for the earth, or perhaps pursued by the ghosts of forebears who lived and died without ever having been completely human. On other seats, with their wives and household goods, he saw Ramón Menéndez Pidal, director of the Academy of the Language, with his squared beard; José María Sacristán, another director, but this time of the asylum at Ciempozuelos; Dr. Arturo Duperier, president of the Spanish Society for Physics and Chemistry, for whom each year the press predicted a Nobel Prize; Isidro Sánchez Covisa, of the Academy of Medicine; the poet and painter José Moreno Villa, who drank pitchers of beer in a single, indifferent swallow, and many others half hidden in the silent semidarkness. When his mind cleared he remembered that all of them were part of an expedition of intellectuals, privileged brains, as old Valle Inclán might have said ironically if he hadn't had the good taste to die shortly before so great and preposterous a tragedy, whom the Alliance of Antifascist Intellectuals evacuated from Madrid to Valencia to keep them out of danger in the ambiguous name of a doubtful posterity. At that precise moment he felt Machado's hand, a palm too hard and firm for so sick a man, resting on one of his knees as if looking for a place to lean on. "Do you remember the first time we saw each other?" he asked in a quiet voice. He pretended to have forgotten in order to please the old man and not tangle the threads of those memories he was weaving laboriously at the back of his narrow, half-closed eyes behind his glasses. "I'm not really sure, Don Antonio. I think I was still a boy . . . " "Exactly, you were a boy and were going to school in your village. I happened to visit it with an inspector for elementary education whose name I never found out. I was surprised by your eyes, too sad for a boy your age. I asked what you wanted to be in this life and you replied in a way that was oblique but very clear: 'I like poetry and music.'"

"It's absolutely true!" he exclaimed, unable to contain himself, but he did refrain from grasping the clothing or arm of the apparition, the virtual image of the man they kept him from being if he had lived.

"Of course it's true! It all is except for you, you're my dream. Don't raise your voice or wake the dead who've been acquitted! How many times will I have to reprimand you for that? And don't wake me up either, though I'm alive and haven't been tried. Look at the stage again."

The landscape was different and the bus had changed into an ambulance. Now they were crowded together: Don Antonio Machado, his mother, smiling and mummified in a no-man's land between the world and eternity, his brother José, his sister-in-law Matea, and himself. Machado was thinner and older, almost as ancient and fleshless as his own mother. From a green thermos that a little while before he had held against his chest, he was pouring them coffee into Catalan bowls. Another city lay behind them, this time Barcelona, also being gutted by bombs. They were traveling on a highway that was covered with an exodus of cars, carriages, trucks, horses, wheelbarrows, other ambulances, soldiers, deserters, men, women, the wounded, children, beneath a quartz winter dawn. "I don't know how long it's been since I've had coffee so early," Machado said to him. "In any event, this coffee must be made of peanuts or who knows what it's made of. Whatever it is, how courteous the Catalans are, as Cervantes already testified at moments of bitter humor, though his critics still haven't noticed that aspect of his parody. The coffee we drank at night in Madrid probably wasn't pure either. Do you remember when we left Madrid? The city seemed about to fall at any moment, but ironically, it's still resisting and now we're about to lose Barcelona, the aforementioned Cervantean fountain of good breeding, which I suppose will welcome the Fascists with open arms. What was I saying? Recently, in no time at all, my mind wanders." "You were speaking about the night we left Madrid," he replied, warming his hands on the sides of the bowl. "That's right! They evacuated us in that bus for privileged brains, as you repeated, quoting poor Valle Inclán. Save the intellectuals and afterward, in due course, pregnant women, the old, and the mentally retarded. Do you remember those nights in the Madrid cafes? Don't you think we did harm to Valle Inclán by telling so many stories about him and enlarging his legend beyond the conceivable?" He didn't reply because he seemed to sense that the dying man wouldn't have listened to him. "At least now everything will be clear for the historians, the strategists, and the foreign diplomats. Before you know it Barcelona will fall and from the point of view of history, which is what we learned to call destiny from the Greeks, we'll have lost the war. Humanly speaking, I'm not so sure. Perhaps we've won it, though the time hasn't come to be aware of that."

"What happened to Don Antonio Machado?" he was surprised to find himself asking the apparition, as if admitting his reality without noticing it.

"A better question is what happened to me and how did I come to dream you in the image and likeness of my youth. It's curious; perhaps, even if it's paradoxical, I ought to speak now of my old youth. We think of age as the accumulation of years at the present moment. But we also refer to it when we evoke times lost in the past: our adolescence and even our childhood," his ghost continued, between reflective and pretentious.

"For example that Sunday in another era, when my parents, my brother and sisters and I saw Machaquito and Vicente Pastor cross the Buen Retiro in an open calash in front of *The Fallen Angel*," he interrupted almost in spite of himself, as if wanting to put to the test this shade that, being the ghost of a man who never was, also tried to be the phantom of himself.

"Precisely!" the old man agreed. "That same morning I saw Monet's *La Gare Saint Lazare*. My father ridiculed the painting, which he even called a blotch. Our mother told us that Monet, like Velázquez himself in another century, tried to capture the lights, air, and chiaroscuro of a fleeting instant: the moment the locomotive enters the station. Notice that it all fits together. Individual life and collective history are merely the sum of impressionistic moments subject to the law of chance, which is the negation of all laws."

He stopped before he could reply. With a gesture in which there was a touch of the effeminate and another touch of the authoritarian, he pointed at the theater, where the scene was quickly changing again. Once more he was seen on the stage, though now and at the front of the proscenium one would call him considerably older. His age oscillated between how old he was when they killed him (" . . . shot in the back, calling me queer"), how old he thought he looked in hell, though there were no mirrors on the spiral, and the age of either of the ghosts transformed into two versions of his supposed advanced years. The setting represented a semicircle, very similar to certain classrooms at Columbia University when he was there as a hypothetical student, recovering from the sorrows of dark love following a failed suicide attempt during the ruinous days of the Depression in America. ("Dazzling streams at the feet of the line of unemployed workers waiting for Al Capone's charity soup at the refectory of Saint Patrick's.") At the front of the classroom, facing the desks of boys and girls arranged in tiers, he was speaking in English about Don Antonio Machado. Now he had white hair and was visibly thinner. With the weight he had lost, and bent over by half a century, beneath a head widened by white temples, he looked almost as broad-shouldered as his father had been. His English was that of a calash driver from Gibraltar, and he was convinced that his American students, who seemed to be scribbling notes, did not understand a word of anything he said. Only a girl with green eyes, like the Melibea, perhaps Jewish, of Rojas, or Proust's Albertine, who may have been an adolescent boy in Sodom though she was also a lesbian in Gomorrah, watched him, smiling, with no pretensions of writing down absolutely anything. "In the Spanish Civil War" (perhaps without knowing why he made an effort to say it with capital letters), "I had to lose two cities, Madrid and Barcelona, with Don Antonio Machado . . . We were evacuated from Madrid in the fall of 1936, and from Barcelona to France in January 1939. I've never felt closer to him, a sick, dying man at the time, than in those circumstances of a mass exodus. I couldn't say the same about his work, which I always admired, though at a distance, never identifying with his poetry. In 'A Young Spain,' Machado attempts to summon in extremely solemn terms a future redemptive youth. He calls it divine, clear, pure, transparent, and even clear-sighted. He compares it to fire and to a diamond. Forgetting the relationship between cause and effect, though strangely conscious of the depraved decadence of his own time, he delegates to the youth of the near future a regenerative task, as they liked to call it at the time, born of spontaneous generation and parthenogenesis. As he says in 'Portrait,' an autobiographical poem, in his veins there are drops of Jacobin blood, though his verses do not necessarily correspond to his political convictions. However, in another poetic portrait, this time a sonnet dedicated to *Azorín*, the old anarchist who shifted to the right, he calls him an admirable reactionary precisely *for his disgust with Jacobin squabbling*. The Spain that dawns in 'Ephemeral Tomorrow,' after a polar night filled with yawns, will be the Spain of rage, of ideas demanding vengeance with torch in hand, according to Machado's rhetorical prophecy. To this kind of retributive utopia, forged, he says, *in the solid past of the race*, forgetting that from the same quarry comes the other Spain, which he always denounced, the Spain of bullfighters, flamenco dancers, and church bells, the Spain of philosophers nourished by monastery soup, the devout Spain of Frascuelo and Carancha . . . " Strident bells rang and he ended the class. The students picked up their notebooks and went out in groups. Only the girl with green eyes, like the possibly Jewish Melibea of Rojas, or Proust's Albertine, who perhaps was an adolescent boy in Sodom though she was also a lesbian in Gomorrah, slowly approached the dais to speak to him.

They were conversing quietly when the scene froze anew in the light projected by the windows upon the semicircle. With their heads very close together, the two of them remained on stage, the young woman paralyzed like Lot's wife on the road to Segor ("I shall give you my daughters! I shall give you my daughters for you to know them and conceive in them! All of you use them and heal your sickness before the One, The One Whose Name Must Not Be Spoken, destroys this city as punishment for your sins!"); he was stopped at the very moment he was closing his briefcase, still listening to her.

"What does that mean? What place is this, where in the United States?"

"How many times must I repeat that nothing is anything and probably we're not anyone? As for the place, I know it very well because I live there now. But its name doesn't matter, because every point on earth is the same point. We're on the edge of a different period in my life," the apparition continued. "Though you, in your innocence, or rather your ignorance, couldn't predict it. Everything happened as you're going to see it, though it could've happened some other way."

"Everything? What's everything?"

"Nothing, just like us, as I just told you so you could immediately forget it. You're incorrigible," replied his grotesque, aged double. "But I won't lose the hope of educating you, if you remain in my nightmare. Prepare to witness the most didactic of spectacles."

(WHY DON'T YOU PRETEND YOU'RE CRAZY AND BE ACQUITTED?) The madman, or madmen, who controlled the magic lantern of a sort, changed slides but not protagonists. A window covered by Venetian blinds, like the ones he had seen during a distant summer in Vermont, opened onto a copper late afternoon, similar to the ones that had dazzled him so often when he left the Columbia library or on the bridges over the East River. At the height of the windowsill, and in a room that the half-light infused with a vague aquarium atmosphere, stood a bed with a yellow bedspread, identical perhaps to the one on his single bed in the Rosales house. Yet in this new retrospective incarnation, he had never taken refuge on Calle de Angulo or been pursued like a mad dog, because he had stayed in Madrid, obeying an accurate presentiment. In a whirlpool of memories and contradictory feelings, where for a few moments he thought he might drown, his recollection of the single bed where he had spent so many nights awake, trembling and afraid he'd be arrested before dawn, became confused with the other bed on stage, at the bottom of the Venetian blinds, in the scarlet of dusk. A shriek of horror, scandalized though not free of a certain complacency, very similar to the one Falla perhaps gave vent to when he read for the first and last time the "Ode to the Blessed Sacrament of the Altar" and the dedication that began it, broke off at the back of his throat. In the bed next to the window, slim and with white hair, the way he had looked in the classroom but completely naked now, he was embracing the girl with very green eyes, like Fernando de Rojas's Melibea or Marcel Proust's Albertine, who was completely naked too. They were going to make love but were still talking in whispers that spread throughout the theater in hell. They were going to make love, with the inevitable fatality that very soon the sun would set, perhaps in obedience to identical laws, but their intimate murmurs sounded all over the theater. "I never was with a woman before," he confessed, "with men, yes, and perhaps with too many because I desired very few and loved even fewer. I did love others and never dreamed of going to bed with them. ('I looked into his eyes. He lowered them and his shoulders seemed to collapse under the overcoat tailored in London. My attendants, the flamenco boys, began to smile at one another and exchange depraved whispers.') My ode to Whitman is my proof of identity and my confession." "I was with only one man, my father, who raped me a year before he killed himself," replied the girl with green eyes who perhaps was a youth in Sodom though she was also a lesbian in Gomorrah. (*La femme aura Gomorrhe et l'homme aura Sodome.*) "Since then I've made love with several women, whom I never desired though I couldn't repudiate them either. I thought I gave myself to them out of hatred for my father and all men. Now I see that in their embraces and caresses I was looking for you without realizing it." "You also must have looked for your dead father in me, since at my age I could've been him," he replied, holding her to his body. "You would've looked for him to bestow your forgiveness, because the same wind will sweep away all flesh and perhaps he raped you to justify his suicide. If we don't have the courage to pardon one another, we won't deserve having been born." The sun set and night came through the window. From the orchestra seats, and perhaps because he had never loved anyone, man or woman, the way he loved his poems, or to put it more precisely, his own vertigo, standing at the boundaries of the universe when he created them, he thought of his verse where the evening left with the night over its shoulder. On the stage, darkened now, there were sounds of moans, groans, murmurs, sobs, panting, and howls. Afterward, nothing, only silence. An interminable silence.

"Was this absolutely necessary?"

"Necessary or not, that's how it happened," the apparition replied.

"And afterward?"

"Afterward? Did you believe perhaps that life is a serialized novel? There is no afterward or before. Only an eternally perishable present whose fiction yellows in photographs."

"Or in the theaters of hell."

"Or on the stage of this nightmare of mine, which you insist on calling your hell. So be it, if it makes you happy, but don't miss this scene, which will be the last."

The scene changed again and in a sense revolved around itself.

Now he saw the garden that the bedroom window, protected by Venetian blinds, overlooked. Completely transformed into that ghost, with the same head and identical tanned age, he was pruning laurels at the foot of some pines. A flock of blackbirds, like those at the rear of *The Garden of Earthly Delights*, flew beneath a slate-colored sky. ("In the midst of these people I'd live enclosed in an invisible bubble, like an alien. Like those lovers in Bosch, in *The Garden of Earthly Delights*, imprisoned in a soap bubble or a bladder mislaid at a witches' Sabbath.") That woman, the one with green eyes like Melibea or Albertine, came to the window and called him by name. From the orchestra, it took him a few moments to recognize her, and he could identify her only by her voice when she began to speak to him in English. She too seemed older or prematurely aged, with short white hair around a face where only her eyes, perhaps of a Jewish girl of the Renaissance or a youth who had been a girl, like the Mercuries of Giovanni da Bologna in the precise words of the poet Rubén Darío, on the eve of the Great War, and at the time that two bullfighters rode in a calash past *The Fallen Angel* to the astonished admiration of some Granadian provincials, and as a gay, confident world lazed indifferently at the wrath of God ready to destroy it, only her eyes were the same. "The cultural attaché of the Swedish embassy called and is on the phone. He is desperate to speak to you and says they've given you the Nobel Prize in Literature for . . . let's see if I remember exactly, ah, yes! *una contribución sin precedentes, unprecedented contribution to the poetry of Spain and to Western Civilization, a la poesía de España y a la civilización occidental.* No, no, excuse me! *To the Cultural Heritage, la herencia cultural de la civilización de Occident.* You can't tell me it doesn't sound harmonious and beautiful even though it seems somewhat rhetorical." From the bottom of the firmament the blackbirds returned, tracing a figure eight in the sky. He left the pruning shears on the ground and waited, looking at them, open and motionless, like a parody of a stork, while he rubbed his chin with the back of his hand. "Listen, what shall I tell this man?" She pretended to be impatient. "You could tell him that so notable a distinction doesn't belong to me because my life is a loan. I'm convinced they would have murdered me in Granada, just as they killed my brother-in-law Manolo, if I had boarded the Andalucía express on the afternoon Martínez Nadal took me to the station. ('Rafael, I changed my mind and I'm staying in Madrid. Please, go to the compartment and bring my suitcase. Don't ask me anything now.') If I survived it was at a very high price, since from that time on my poetry has seemed the work of a stranger: a man very different from me who is embarrassed that all of you wrote so many theses on his dead work. Standing shades make up the literary kingdom of Mr. Nobel, that right-wing dynamite maker. But in the final analysis, I must answer to my conscience for what I write. Tell this Swedish gentleman that I renounce his prize in order not to repudiate myself." "It would be better if you told him personally." "I will in due course. As soon as I finish cutting the laurels," he replied, shrugging his shoulders. The two burst into laughter and the scene shattered like a stained-glass window broken by a stone. Then the stage sank into the darkness of a dreamless sleep.

"Lies, all lies!" he yelled in exasperation in the orchestra.

"Why is that?" his apparition asked, his expression between astonished and confused.

"Because everything, absolutely everything I saw is a cruel mockery of what happened!"

"Are you sure about what you're saying? Why are you shouting like that? Really, boy, you'll end up waking me if you haven't already roused the innocent dead."

"Sarcasm and a carnival trick! . . ."

"I thought it was a very faithful interpretation. I don't know why you're protesting so much."

"I'm not your dream, wretch!" Almost without realizing it he began to use familiar address with the latest intruder. "I took the Andalucía express that afternoon, because in a sense I was obliged to."

"Who would oblige you to?"

"The same destiny you denied. I mean, the sensation of fulfilling a fate lived through twice, once that day and the other in a very distant time, perhaps before watches and calendars."

"You're completely mad! Why would I dream about a lunatic like you, so similar to who I was in my youth? This is the only mockery, and now I wish I had wakened. Go on, shout louder and wake me!"

("I believe I've lost my mind. But you aren't dreaming me in your nightmare. In fact you exist only in my hallucination.") Thinking about his words to the other ghost, the one with the pink bald head, dark temples, and eyeglasses, he lowered his voice until it was almost transformed into a murmur that the apparition made an effort to follow, coming close to his face.

"I reached Granada and then Huerta de San Vicente just in time for them to kill me. With the uprising triumphant and the reprisals started, I hid in the Rosales family's house. But they came for me even there. ('. . . he told me you did more harm with your pen than others with a pistol.') An individual named Ruiz Alonso seemed in command of the men who arrested me. He took me to the Civilian Government building, offered me some broth, shook my hand, and left me alone in a room with scratched walls that smelled of dried blood. I could describe for you in detail each instant of what happened but I prefer to cut it short because any victim is ashamed of his suffering. Those who are proud of their martyrdom are the ones who think they deserve it. I wasn't tortured physically, thanks, I believe, to the good offices of the Rosales family. At least, that's what Pepe Rosales told me when he visited a short while before my death to promise I would be released. I remember that, overcoming the contempt I must have inspired in a hot-blooded drinker like him, more for my chastity than my pederasty, he pinched my cheek when he said goodbye and said: 'Sleep well tonight, my boy, and tomorrow we'll all hug you at home and I'll kiss you on this cheek if you promise not to pinch my ass.' I smiled and lied, saying I would pray for the victory of the military. He looked around, even though we were alone in that drab room, and said in my ear: 'Don't pray for anybody, my boy, because we all deserve hell. This war has divided Spain in two, like a river, and on both sides the only ones doing their duty are the killers.' The acting civilian governor interrogated me in person and in terms that don't concern you. Aside from Pepe Rosales, Don Manuel de Falla visited me the night before the crime. He came to beg my forgiveness for having hated me. But I won't say more about this either because what we spoke about is none of your business. I forgave him everything and didn't want to forget anything, since rancor is a completely useless passion in eternity. My hating those who killed me would be as absurd as my parents' despising having given birth to me. I'll keep the end to myself, because it's inalienable and mine though you might want to misrepresent it. It's impossible to imagine but simple to describe. Some shots in the back at the edge of a ravine and another, the coup de grâce, to shatter the heads of the dead."

"Exactly right!" the intruder corroborated. "The coincidence cannot be clearer!"

"The coincidence? What are you talking about now?"

"Everything you told me is the same thing I often imagined in my house in America. In other words, my fate in Granada if instinct hadn't taken me off the Andalucía express that afternoon. It began as a game and turned into a kind of obsession. I even understand your reticence in refusing to comment on certain passages of the farce. I didn't want to confess any of that to my own wife. Still, one day I'm going to write it, just for myself. When one has refused the Prize of the Dynamiter, flatly and unhesitatingly, one can allow oneself moderate pleasures."

"Enough! Enough! I'm not going to tolerate this parody of my tragedy from you!"

"How would you stop it, wretch? When did dreams ever govern the dreamer?" He paused and smiled, shrugging his shoulders. "You wouldn't try to destroy me after absolving your imaginary killers?"

"I'm not trying anything. I want only to be left alone. Alone with my memories, if I can't free myself or they don't want to free me from my sleeplessness."

"I'll go, I'll go," the apparition yawned. "Dreams, like the flesh, end in tedium. It's time to wake and perhaps write about our dispute. Didn't you ever think about an interminable autobiography, infinite, really, where you told not only all we were but also all we could have been in all their variations? It would be the only appropriate kind for any life. Even in ours the two of us would fit, and who knows what extended multitude of men in our image and likeness" —he was shaking off his drowsiness and rubbing his eyes with sharp knuckles. "All together, like dice thrown from the same cup. You know, son, *un coup de dé jamais n'abolira l'hasard.* The combinations of the fortuitous are infinite, in all the avatars of identity and their Ortegan consequences. Here, for example, are you and I like a pair of facing mirrors, in the middle of the same desert, though each comes from a different time. You, arrested in my youth and on the day I didn't take the train going to Granada. I, shackled in my present old age."

"And the desert?"

"I call my dream the desert and you say it's hell. Perhaps we're both right."

The old man was becoming blurred, as if someone were erasing him with a fingertip, taking away volume, outlines, and profile. Eventually he disappeared without leaving a trace or vestige in the theater or his seat. Alone again, he looked around him. The stage became a dark emptiness, the proscenium open to infinity, like the mouth of a tunnel excavated in the middle of the firmament. He heard or thought he had imagined the sound of footsteps in the vicinity of the corridor and the alabaster lights. Immediately he became aware that he was isolated and abandoned or abandoned and isolated on that spiral, where the dead were blind or invisible to one another. His doubles, the phantoms, having disappeared, the notion of his insignificance oppressed him. Eternity was the greatest of sarcasms, an illogicality more absurd than perishable life. In this untransferable theater before his trial, he was nothing but a spectator of his past in an endless succession of shades condemned to the same wakefulness. Perhaps the first of them, his most distant ancestor, saw on the stage memories of a recent time he had experienced when still a gorilla or an amphibious fish, with the eyes of a man, in the dark jungles of the beginning of the world.

The last of his aged replicas, the one living in the United States with the woman in whose eyes and behind the gates of Gomorrah Melibea and Albertine had met, told him his martyrdom in Granada was only a dream of his, as were Ruiz Alonso, the Rosales family's house, the yellow bedspread, the piano, the Sacred Heart, the translations by Salinas, the window facing Calle de Angulo, the Rosales family themselves, and Valdés's interrogation. Of the two nonsensical grotesques in their hypothetical old ages, the one with white hair and dark traces seemed more hateful. He imagined him in an America very different from the one he had known. The one of the unemployed, the beggars, the supplicants in lines for watered soup, the one of despair, of prostitutes, of suicides. The America that he predicted would be devoured one day by hissing cobras climbing like lianas to the highest terraces. (*Brother, can you spare a dime?* The one of the multitude that urinates, of the multitude that vomits, of the blacks disguised as janitors, the one of the king of Harlem tearing out the eyes of crocodiles and banging the hindquarters of monkeys with a spoon, of narrow defiles of masonry and brick under an empty sky, of the moon buried in the Jewish cemetery.) All of that America at the edge of the apocalypse, waiting for a resurrected Bosch to paint it before the fall. (" . . . and Dalí still very young, not dressed as a janitor like the king of Harlem, whom he would take many years to meet, but as a soldier, the newest replacement, when his brush was still imperfect and he struggled to imitate everybody, from Picasso, naturally, to Chagall, passing through Matisse, telling me in his deep voice and Ampurdanese accent: *Each painter responds to his environment, just as each child is nourished by the juices and salts and potash and will-o'-the-wisps and lotteries and cellos that constitute the maternal womb. Here in Cadaqués, I can't paint like Bosch in Flanders.* And I, giving him almost inadvertently the advice that would transform the little soldier and amateurish dauber into one of the most original painters of this insane, suicidal century: *That's precisely why you should keep painting like Bosch. You could spend your whole life in the undertaking, but you'll end up discovering the great artist you have hidden under your blood, in your unconscious.*) That America, yes, indelible and magnificent in its vast tragedy, stretching from coast to coast and from ocean to ocean with its pus and its ringworm, its lice and its scabs, transformed into the other America of gardens with laurels, bedrooms with pale ironed curtains, and the Swedish cultural attaché announcing the granting of the Dynamiter's Prize in Literature.

He began to pity the simpleton who attempted to represent him in an old age snatched away by bullets. He imagined living in another unspeakable hell where he would be incapable of writing because he had lost his identity. A hell that ironically, paradoxically, was not the real one, the spiral of wakefulness, but the one he had feared so much in life: the renunciation of all he had been on earth. As on so many other occasions, he thought again about the conversation with Alberti and María Teresa León, at the foot of the Maqueda Castle, while the three of them in their incredible, vulnerable youth, appeared on stage where they again experienced the teasel and the merlons. Alberti confessed his uncertainty when it was time to choose between two horrors, ignorance of his own fate in death or its unending eternity. He immediately replied that his panic had another name: the loss of his self, the being who had never been, in no-man's land. If the destiny of the second apparition had been realized, a very conceivable fate beginning with a fact that only seemed insignificant, his giving up the trip to Granada in time, he would still be living in an America different from the one in his *Poet in New York*, but at the same time he would be totally distinct from the one who had written that book or, in fact, any other of his more typical works. Stripped of his identity, as you divest yourself of an old, shoddily made suit, he would dream occasionally and always in vain of death at the hands of other men, which in Granada had fulfilled the doom anticipated in some of his plays and poems: in one of the two songs of the horseman, in "Ballad of the One Summoned," in "Sleepwalking Ballad," in "Surprise," in *The Public*, and in *Blood Wedding*. An execution that confirmed not only the fate written and described in his own hand but also the universal dimension of his renown as poet, prophet, and martyr.

Old, incapable of writing, and exiled to the American hell of gardens with pruned laurels (*Les Lauriers sont Coupés*), he could still go on dreaming his destiny, his arrest, and the endless spiral itself. He could dream himself murdered in the fullness of his creative talent. Lost afterward in his orchestra seat or in the curving corridor, until he became aware that the strange construction, a Tower of Babel where shades witnessed their memories without seeing one another, was nothing more or less than eternity. Always in dreams with a woman whose eyes combine Melibea and Albertine, he would feel nostalgia for any lived moment no matter how often memory obliged its representation on the stage, and a desperate desire for nothingness to put an end to insomnia. From the darkened theater and in those nightmares, he would deduce the trial and acquittal of certain of the dead, while Sandro Vasari's orchestra seats and stage made him infer the anticipatory staging of the memories of the living. Finally, dreaming beneath the window with Venetian blinds, he would see himself in the third theater along the corridor: the addition to the theater that would be Vasari's one day and where now, without his guessing it on earth, his future dead man's memories were holding a general rehearsal. Occasionally he walked the distance that would take him to the damn theater, knowing the terror it held. In that theater, identical to the others but frosted with cemetery cold, he would witness the appearance of a gigantic cross above the Risco de la Nava, between Portera del Cura and Cerro de San Juan, crowning the basilica that housed the tapestries of the Apocalypse. "And the four beasts had each of them six wings about him; and they were full of eyes within: and they rest not day and night, saying, Holy, holy, holy . . . "

The recollection of one apparition restored to him the memory of the other: the irascible, myopic one with the bald head, pink and polished like rare porphyry. The one who stated with certainty that after almost half a century he still lived hidden on Calle de Angulo, first because of fear of losing his life and now because of disgust with the present world and its vanities. ("If in addition to remembering who we were you maintained the dignity that belongs to us, you too would turn your back on that jungle and shut yourself in with me here in hell.") According to that ill-tempered phantom, hell was the upper floor of the Rosales family's house, where they hid him in a long-ago summer to protect him from the fury of crime unleashed. The world considered him dead and disappeared, to his moderate satisfaction, since his extreme passions were reduced to rage and rancor. His protector and jailer who, believing he was saving him, shut him away in a refuge that resembled him, was no freer now to resuscitate him than he was before to betray him. Furthermore, the old man thought himself eternal and also said he dreamed of him on the spiral to the precise extent he needed him in order not to lose his reason. ("You're chained to my sleep, as he is to my waking, and you'll continue to appear on nights like this so I can speak with someone other than Luis and solitude does not eventually drive me mad.") Seized with the fear of having really lost his mind, as he must have felt at other times in his dialogues with phantoms (WHY DON'T YOU PRETEND YOU'RE CRAZY AND BE ACQUITTED?), he began to ask himself whether that old man, half demented and driven wild by loneliness, wasn't correct when he called him one of his dreams and for good measure would not dream of the second ghost, the one who thought he lived on the other side of the world with an ambiguous woman and a garden of laurels.

Nightmares and apparitions brought him to the memory of a living man, the one he had seen talking with Ruiz Alonso in the Lyon. ("I dreamed about hell and saw it as an endless spiral along which a carpeted corridor ascended. Some theaters open onto the corridor, and a dead person corresponds to each one. And in precisely one of those theaters, the man you arrested and, according to what they say, also denounced, is awaiting trial . . . ") Ruiz Alonso became impassioned then, replying that he wasn't an informer and did no more than follow other people's orders in arresting him. Evoking his protests in a parenthesis, he had a presentiment that the truth would never be clarified. He himself, victim of the obscure intrigue, was indifferent to it, not because he had forgotten the arrest and the shooting, even less because he had forgiven them, but because everything on earth, including personal tragedies, was material as distant in eternity as horses, ants, and men on the beach from the far-off perspective of the ocean.

Another distancing of a moral order was imposed by Sandro Vasari with regard to Ruiz Alonso. Though they both sat at the same table, one would say he separated himself from him with an invisible rod, as if his presence were as irritating as it was inevitable. From the beginning of the interview, marked with crosses of Lorraine, Vasari had been his absolute master. He made Ruiz Alonso confess to truths perhaps hidden until then and turned a deaf ear when he assumed he was lying. And yet, toward the end, he didn't seem as sure of himself. Almost without taking a breath between

sentences, he told Ruiz Alonso he had never seen him on the stages
of hell when he dreamed them, then immediately said the contrary
and admitted that in a nightmare he witnessed the poet's arrival at
the Andalucía express in the company of Rafael Martínez Nadal
while Ruiz Alonso, looking out a window in the passageway, pretended to be unaware of his presence. Returning to Sandro Vasari
and Ruiz Alonso, he thought he detected a correlation of analogous
situations, like those of a single text in various languages on one
palimpsest, between the meeting of those two men in a Lyon filled
with amorous couples and readers of rustling newspapers, and his
own dialogues with his extremely aged doubles in hell. In all three
cases an old man apparently at peace with his conscience con-
fronted a young man who turned out to be his hidden, buried truth.
Except for all the distances and variants, the coincidence could not
help but amaze him. He even asked himself whether that conversation between Ruiz Alonso and Sandro Vasari (" . . . *What did they do
to you, Señor Ruiz Alonso? / Defamed me. Yes, sir, defamed me in
writing and in published books*") had ever happened. In other words,
the words of a very obvious academic question, wasn't everything his
own dramatic imagination, performed on the stage of the theater
that one day would belong to Vasari after his death? He even supposed an unconscious reason for the three phantasmagorias, the
one in the Lyon, and the appearances of his ghosts. The three cases
were no more and no less than embarrassing versions of the perpetually insoluble dispute between him and his father. Between his
pederasty and the old man's patriarchal virility.

Almost immediately, and with no effort other than letting himself
be carried along by the evidence, he found himself obliged to change
his mind. The quarrel with his father had been settled since the day
of his arrest on Calle de Angulo. In reality, it had never existed ("Son,
I'd give everything for you, including your mother and sisters and
brother! May God forgive me! Be very careful! You can never fail
me, never, never, never!"), even though his brother-in-law had to be

shot and I had to fear losing him to find the courage to make that confession. In this way, and emphasizing the evidence, he saw how his entire reasoning or, to be more accurate, his attempt at reasoning, was invalidated by that call to the Rosales family's house. A few days later, and after suffering as cruel as it was absurd, they killed him like an animal. There was never the slightest doubt, he told himself ironically, about that fact. Everything else, however, seemed debatable and uncertain. From that point on, the questions stopped being academic and were restated in a different context. Was it even possible that death was merely nothingness, plain and simple nothingness, as Luis Buñuel predicted and proclaimed so often in his obsessive atheism? ("Death, my dear, is nothing more or less than deafness and blindness forever and ever, amen. Without sight or hearing, the other senses encyst and petrify.") Influenced perhaps by those words, he described death as a heap of extinguished dogs in his requiem for Sánchez Mejías. No, though it might be in the briefest of parentheses or a hurried note in the margin, that line in his elegy came from a more complex source. Almost unwillingly, he confessed it to himself. A few summers before the fatal goring, he had been with Alberti and María Teresa at Fernando Villalón's farm. It made him uneasy when the other three began to talk about spiritualism, and Fernando, as if subdued by sleepiness, boasted of being able to conjure the souls of dead dogs. It was a motionless, silent night, studded with stars like spurs and fragrant with jasmine and mint. Suddenly, and panting heavily, Villalón slipped into sleep and the horizon filled with the barking of a furious pack of hounds. It stopped as suddenly as it had begun when that cattle-raising medium and surrealist poet awoke. He remembered nothing and was very surprised to see everyone overcome by fright.

What happened afterward should have been reduced to a collective hallucination. He tried to believe this even knowing he was translating it into the terms of a rationalist club. Dogs and men really ended in a silence of muffled voices and yelps. This was how he had ended forever, yes, forever, when they shattered his back with bullets and he fell into the ravine on the night of the crime. There was no sleepless consciousness, no hell in a spiral, no orchestra seats, no corridor ascending in alabaster light, no prosceniums, no scenery, no memories revived on stage, no apparitions, no gold letters on windows of trains, no trial, no possible redemption. Only death, which was nothingness. And yet, yes, yes, and yet he could not deny the incontrovertible evidence, because the existence of redemption and judgment was obvious to him (WHY DON'T YOU PRETEND YOU'RE CRAZY AND BE ACQUITTED?), as well as train windows where the process and hearing were announced to him in letters of fused, burning gold, as clear as the ghosts of his two doubles, or the prosceniums and stages where memories were represented for a population of shades invisible to one another in the alabaster light of passageways and orchestra seats. Paradoxically, all that was as undeniable as absolute annihilation in the rectangular, interminable peace of death. After all, Fernando Villalón himself, a man who said he lived among the living and the dead at the same time, once declared that the important thing wasn't existing or not existing but knowing who one is.

From I he passed to he, or rather, to be clear, from himself to Sandro Vasari, the man with hair flat against his skull and a cut on his cheek. He thought he was slowly unveiling his own truth, just as Dalí tore successive layers of rice paper from his collages until he revealed the intended composition, or the one that appeared by virtue of the Calderonian magic of art, where all dream was life. His absolute death was possible, the death of body and soul, of desire and memory, beside the ravine of so many crimes. In that case, all that remained of who he was, the little boy dressed as a girl and a knight on a pony of papier-mâché at the age of one in a photograph hidden in his parents' bedroom, the boy wearing a knitted tie in the Retiro, the lover of Dalí, the comrade of Sánchez Mejías, the pederast who paid for the kisses of Gypsies and then hated himself for hating them, the author of his verses and plays, the bard who scandalized Bebé and Carlillo Morla reading them *The Public*, the poet who also offended the piety of Don Manuel de Falla when he dedicated the "Ode to the Blessed Sacrament of the Altar" to him, believing it would please him, the man who saw the aurora borealis over the lake at Edem Mills and the long streaks of the rainbow on the Manhattan asphalt, all, all of it, all, all of him would be nothing but a handful of mute bones rotting in the ground.

Sandro Vasari told Ruiz Alonso that he wasn't trying to write a book but a dream. "The one I had on the first of April of this year. I dreamed about hell and saw it as an endless spiral along which a carpeted passage ascended. Some theaters open on to the corridor and each of these corresponds to a dead person. And in one of the orchestra seats, the man you arrested and some say also denounced awaits judgment." When they had reached that point, Ruiz Alonso protested fiercely, shouting that he hadn't denounced anyone. Sandro Vasari let him have the last word, perhaps without believing him, and continued the account of his nightmare. Perhaps what had happened after his death could be reduced precisely to the dream of the man with the cut cheek and the hair smoothed flat against his head. Or rather, to put it better, to the dream he wanted to write, as he confessed to Ruiz Alonso, and perhaps was writing. In such circumstances, which to a spiritualist cattle rancher and poet like Villalón would seem as evident as the appearances of the dead, he would have no other voice, no other being than the ones lent to him by his author. The man who drew crosses of Lorraine in a notebook as he listened in the Lyon to the confidences of Ruiz Alonso without looking at him, would have begun to sketch a spiral in the same notebook when he was barely awake on the morning of April 1st in some year. Then, he would have drawn lines resembling the arms of the crosses along the spiral at four distinct points not very far from one another. One would be his theater in eternity, the next the one of the stranger acquitted and freed from wakefulness, the third the orchestra seats prepared when the day arrived for Vasari himself, the last the parterre of that being whose name he did not know or whose name he did not care to recall, before the setting of the Apocalypse. From then on, and as Luis Buñuel said to him one day, quoting René Clair, the dream of the man with the cut face would be transformed into a book and needed only to be written.

He himself knew how fragile, though not invisible, were the boundaries between dream and literature. As he said to Gerardo Diego, the poet was a creature lost in the dark night of the soul where he went hunting, blind and ignorant of the prey he pursued. How and why verses arose, with their essence and form, from so much disorder no one knew, or at least he would never know. He had only the certainty, he added then in a way whose rhetorical pedantry he could not escape now, that he could destroy the Parthenon every night and erect it again from the beginning every daybreak. He had other certainties as well as doubts in that hell constructed to the measure of his destiny by Sandro Vasari. Above all he wondered what the extent of his liberation would be, if in some way he became free, in the book that undoubtedly bore his name. Were his acts, his feelings, his reflections his own or were they all foreseen, as he foresaw the fate of El Amargo in his "Ballad of the Summoned One"? The messages interpolated in the staging of his memories, PREPARE FOR YOUR TRIAL, WHY DON'T YOU PRETEND YOU'RE CRAZY AND BE ACQUITTED? Were they real advice from his creator or merely false short cuts to lead him into dungeons of paper and words in a monstrous board game? If he could have spoken to Sandro Vasari, supposing the partially conceived creature were capable of arguing with his biographer in hell, he would ask him only to be as fair with him as he was with his own characters. In the days when he published volumes of poems and staged dramas, when his unexpected fame preceded him wherever he went, he never considered himself better than the helpless humanity in his verses and plays. His was the brittle abandonment of the roll call of Gypsies, statues, dead men no one knew, women denied maternity, girls seized by black grief, blind dead women, knifed smugglers, blacks covered in mushrooms, crushed squirrels, minotaurs, bullfighters gored open from top to bottom, goblins, masks, girls drowned in wells, chimeras, and marvelous shoemakers' wives. Perhaps the reason for his success with the public and even among people who despised his pederasty was the vulnerability intimately shared with his characters. So that flattery would have been one side of the coin of his fate. The other was being shot to death in the back, which perhaps had been carried out to determine whether he was a creature of flesh and blood or a creature from his books.

Suddenly he felt terribly tired. With almost amused curiosity, he wondered whether the fatigue was his or had been imposed by the implacable Sandro Vasari. In any case, if he had been able to sleep without contradicting himself and without having been acquitted at trial, he would have sunk into an endless sleep, like the sleep of someone who sinks into a lake and encounters a blind mirror as the center of the world. From those hypothetical ciphers of a futile language, the lake and the world, he moved to the spiral that Vasari would believe as certain as himself, if he was a truthful, authentic writer. He told himself, or believed he sensed it, that then it wouldn't be enough for their creator to point out the four theaters where his novel took place. He also would have to write down the action and divide it into another four acts whose names were revealed to him, as obvious as his life or his death: THE SPIRAL, THE ARREST, DESTINY, and THE TRIAL.

THE TRIAL

The bolt slides and the same soldier who tried to hit me with his musket ("How do you dare, wretch? In my presence!") opens the door. Startled at first, then immediately terrified, I recognize him by the childish dewiness that still fills his eyes.

"Move, you son of a bitch, the governor wants to question you!"

"The governor? . . . "

"You're lucky, you damn queer. The governor is as good as a saint. If I didn't have orders from him to bring you to his office in one piece, I'd squash you like a scorpion, you fucking red, and we'd save the bullets we'll shoot you with."

"I want to see Pepe Rosales! Pepe told me yesterday I'd be released today! I want to see Pepe Rosales!"

"We shot Pepe Rosales at dawn for hiding you. You'll see him soon in hell!"

I guess that he's lying, not even stopping to think about it. I read it in his twisted smile and dewy eyes, while he takes me by the arm and pushes me toward the open door.

"No! Pepe's alive! He was here yesterday and swore that today he'd take me to his house!"

I'm frightened by my own voice, the resonant tone of my reply. ("Sleep well tonight, my boy, and tomorrow we'll all embrace you at home, and I'll kiss your cheek if you promise not to pinch my ass.") I believed him and last night I could sleep for the first time since my arrest. Dreamless sleep, as if I had been born blind or had just lost all my memories. Sleep indifferent to the screams of the tortured that previously had driven me to bang my head against the walls, like an enraged minotaur. Sleep, though it was on the floor with my arm for a pillow, since there wasn't even a cot in the room they gave me for a cell.

"Yeah, right, whatever you say." My shouts seem to have moderated his obtuse cruelty. Through my panic, and in a kind of revelation, I imagine a mountain village where this boy, now armed, endured taunts, stones, and gobs of spit. "We'll play the call to arms, we'll surrender our weapons to you, and you'll leave here under a canopy, like the Virgin."

"Pepe's alive! Pepe can't abandon me! He'll be back right away to release me. You'll all have to answer to him!"

"Yeah, fine, we'll answer. Get moving, you fairy, or I'll break your back with the butt of my gun. Look at those hips, like a little whore from the Albaicín."

Again the corridor and the door to the governor's private office. Again a beardless soldier standing guard beside it. Again the unexpected copy of shadow play that dampness drew on the wall. The man with the toothless smile speaks for a moment with the sentinel and rings a bell beneath the stain. Without waiting for a reply, he pushes me and lifts the latch.

"At your orders, Excellency. I have the detainee you asked for."

Behind a carved desk covered by thick glass and an embossed leather desk set, stands a dark-haired, very thin man dressed in a military uniform, his eyes reddened and vague with lack of sleep. One of his long hands, very white and bony, indicates a wicker chair on the other side of the desk.

"Sit down, please, I'm Commander José Valdés."

At a signal from him the boy withdraws and closes the door behind him. The civilian governor drops into an armchair upholstered in garnet-colored velvet. Beside a golden inkwell where two gold roosters attack each other with outstretched wings, he has a newspaper diminished by several folds, with a short article circled in red pencil.

"Read this, if you'd be so kind, and then tell me what you think of it."

I read in silence though my lips tremble at each word, as if in that paper and precisely that article I was struggling to learn the letters. The paper is from Huelva and the report has my name, followed by a comment that closes the headline: "Now they're killing one another." It says that among the many corpses found every dawn on the streets of Madrid, mine has been discovered. "The disorder among the reds is so great they don't even respect their own. For the author of *Gypsy Ballads* it was no help being Azaña's coreligionist in politics, literature, and unresolved sexuality."

"Well, what do you think of our press?" the governor insists.

As on the day of my arrest, in the Rosales family's house, I divide into two beings. One thinks coldly about a poem of mine where an anonymous lament tells a story that has no names either. The one about a stranger who turns up dead, with a dagger in his chest, under a streetlamp shaken by the wind. ("Oh mother, how the lamp trembled!") No one dares look into his eyes opened by death and the dawn. People are more shocked by his being abandoned, a stranger lost forever among them, than by the crime itself and the terrible certainty that someone in the village had become a murderer for dark, unknown reasons. Paradoxically, I had to come to the office of Commander José Valdés to realize that the germ of a tragedy I would never write lay in a thirteen-line poem. The impossibility of bringing to the theater a situation like that one, barely outlined but so rich in dramatic power, overflows with despair at my fate and leads the other man in me, the one I would call the man of flesh, to give a despicable reply:

"It could be true if the war had found me in Madrid. My heart was always with the military! I want to give everything to the Insurgency!"

"I expected another answer from you." Valdés shrugs. "Or perhaps I no longer expect anything from anybody. Just to sleep and wake in a hundred years."

"In a century?"

"Perhaps by then the Final Judgment will have come and we'll all answer to God for ourselves." More than indicating it, his gestures affirm it. "Do you think that people will remember our war in a century, with or without a Final Judgment?"

He is my judge and my executioner. I know with identical certainty that each moment confirms the impossibility that Pepe Rosales can save me. And yet something in his helplessness, in the insomnia that makes his eyes blaze and the sickly softness of his hands, prevents the man of flesh from telling him that from the ruins of war the foundations of a new Spain will be born, or some other cowardly stupidity. I hear the other man in me respond on his own:

"Probably not, because the dead bury the dead in the Gospels and besides, you're the Christians in this battle."

"We almost agree." He picks up the newspaper and throws it in a wastebasket after crumpling it. "The dead will bury the dead, but their lies should survive them. Tomorrow, when they think about this war, which should have been only a coup, they won't be surprised by our sacrifices or our crimes. Only our lies, your side's lies and this Spain's, will astonish them."

"This is the fate we deserve," I murmur unexpectedly.

"No doubt about it." He agrees again with complete conviction. Then he shakes his head, half engulfed by sleep, as if these considerations consumed his last strength. "Did I tell you that this isn't the first time we've seen each other?"

"I don't think I remember ever having seen you . . . "

"It's true. You didn't notice me, and you had no reason to. I not only saw you but observed you for hours."

"Where, for God's sake? What monstrous crime do you want to accuse me of now?" The panic of the creature of flesh who inhabits half of me becomes an equally burning curiosity. He moves from one passion to another as if crossing rooms without walls.

"No crime at all. As for the rest, it was logical you wouldn't see me because I was nobody. Only a modest commander in the Corps of Military Inspectors, buried in Granada as a commissary general by the Republic because I was suspected of patriotism. Even these signs of identity were reduced to my uniform, without which it was as if I were naked or had never been born. And so, naked or without a body, that is, dressed in civilian clothes, I requested a leave and went to Madrid for a week to have an ulcer treated. In a café on the Gran Vía I came across you and recognized you immediately from newspaper photographs. I thought it strange to run into you there and never to have seen you in Granada, where I had lived since the year the Republic was established, as I've said. I understood immediately that only coincidence could bring us together, because in Granada we lived in very distant worlds in a very small city. Yours, which I suspected in part from gossip, was revealed to me by the two flashily dressed Gypsy boys escorting you that morning in the café on the Gran Vía. Should I add more? . . . "

"It was a few months, I don't remember how many, before Sánchez Mejías was gored in Manzanares."

"Very good, that's exactly what I was getting to. Sánchez Mejías himself came into the café and approached all of you, as if he were following you in an inevitable, embarrassing way. I recognized him right away too, from the papers and because I had seen him fight several times. From my table I heard everything you both said and I wasn't ashamed of listening. At first my dignity as a soldier disapproved, even though I was dressed as nobody, a civilian. Immediately I told myself that if you, being who you are, appeared with those Gypsies, then I could lower myself too, to the point of eavesdropping on a conversation you held in loud voices even though it was private. I hope you can forgive me . . . "

"I can't forgive you for anything, Commander Valdés, because I'm a dead man. I don't even understand why I'm still alive. And I understand even less what the point of all this is."

"Excuse me if I seem long-winded. I've had too many sleepless nights and it's hard for me to state ideas precisely." He raised his palms to his temples and then folded them over the pit of his stomach, rubbing his tunic. (" . . . I requested a leave and went to Madrid for a week to have an ulcer treated.") His hands were paler than ever, their whiteness resembling that of a boiled or frozen monkfish. "Sánchez Mejías, that rock of a man, all fiery courage, pleaded for the privilege of your company and you persisted in denying it, reproaching him for his affair with a foreign woman when he was Argentinita's lover. He requested permission to go with you to lunch and you replied drily: 'Nobody's invited you.'"

"He said a restaurant was a public place and he could have coffee there if he wanted to. He left to wait for us in the street and then follow us. He sat at another table, in the rear, and ordered a manzanilla sherry."

"Precisely! It seems incredible that you remember everything and have forgotten me because I also followed you to the restaurant, as if I were the shadow of the two of you. Your shadow or your dog. You threw out the Gypsies and called to Sánchez Mejías. 'Come on, man, tell me what you're having and how the bulls will turn out this summer.' Hesitating, but more overwhelmed by fatigue than by doubts, he went to your table and let himself be invited."

"I still don't understand . . . "

"You don't know how much I admired you then. And I couldn't decide what astonished me more, your authority or your compassion. Perhaps my respect for your pity was greater than what I felt for your dry power over that giant, because I've always had the gift of command and more than enough opportunity to demonstrate it here in Granada, since the beginning of the war. I never felt pity. Not for my neighbor and not for myself."

"Not for yourself and not for me."

"Exactly, not for you and not for myself. No sir, neither one, though I recognize that it's more to my advantage to be compassionate even if I were a coward. On the other hand, you must admit that pity makes no sense in this country and in this war. The duty of all of us, your side and ours, is to exterminate one another without caution or hesitation, until one or the other is incapable of killing. It doesn't pain me and I don't reproach you for it because we all obey orders and follow moral principles. If we must devour one another like wolves, I'd hope only that we don't lie to ourselves as men."

I wouldn't know how to lie to myself now either, when my other self, the desperate and fearful one, is lost in some desert in the solitudes of my soul. I'm as much a master of myself as I was that morning in Madrid with Ignacio, even though it's Valdés who leads me to control myself. In this serenity of a man who at the end of his life discovers a scalpel in the exact center of his being, I realize that the stabbed stranger in my poem is myself. I'm dead in the middle of the main street of any village, which at the same time is the world. People approach my open eyes and wonder who I really was and why I was murdered. Never, until this moment, was I so clearly aware of the oblique autobiographical meaning of poetry. A man writes an eleven-line poem with no purpose other than giving lyrics to a guitar rhythm ("the guitar that weeps for hidden sorrows and distant dawns"), and in reality leaves proof of his destiny, denounces his death, and signs his will.

"Are you sure you're telling me the whole truth, Commander Valdés?"

"No, no, this isn't all the truth."

"What are you hiding from me then?"

"My envy."

"Your envy?"

"The envy I felt that day for you and Sánchez Mejías. I asked myself then, as I again ask myself now, why it was my duty to recognize the two of you while you were bound to ignore me. Why did fate choose to give the two of you, being so different, fame among men and deny it to me? Do you have an answer for that?"

"No, no I don't, just as you don't have the right to ask me that."

"Of course you don't. How was I to explain such an injustice to myself? I'm going to surprise you with a confession that perhaps you won't understand either. Even in these circumstances, and you being who you are, I'd trade my fate for yours. Did you understand me? My fate for yours!"

The man of flesh in me is silent now, as I myself am silent. If he weren't so removed from my spirit at these moments, if he were to break brutally into my voice with his panic, I'd respond to the absurdity with another piece of foolishness. I'd tell Valdés that he, that is to say, I, would also trade my destiny for his. Provided he would go on living, the man of flesh in me would change with pleasure into a murderer, master of the gallows and the knife in this city, whose deepest and sole precept in the war was to hate his neighbor as himself. And yet I reply:

"Not I, Commander. We belong to very different species."

"I know that very well! That's exactly what I'm talking about! Your species is the one of people whose names are called to survive them. Mine is the one of people who will die as if we hadn't lived. Or would be better off never to have existed. Imagine someone writing a book about you in half a century. Someone trying to imagine this interrogation, to give it a name, which people suppose I subjected you to. 'Valdés'—he would say eventually or say explicitly—'was nothing but a vulgar killer.' I was born for that, my dear sir, so that in half a century somebody, whoever he may be, can call me a vulgar killer.

"And yet it shouldn't have been like this. No, sir, it shouldn't have been like this. The real injustice, the most monstrous injustice, isn't the crimes we commit in Granada or your side perpetrates in Madrid. If the dice had fallen another way and this were a civilized country, those who kill here or there would go to work, to the office, to the brothel and be decent people incapable of killing anybody, not even in dreams. The real injustice is the destiny of men like me, born to be someone and doomed to be no one.

"Here where you see me, and again supposing this were a civilized nation, I'd be a hero honored by everyone, not the killer they now call me behind my back and later will call me openly. Sixteen years ago, when I was a lieutenant, I thought I'd entered history through the main door and by my own right. Look, I was on leave then in Zaragoza, the year had just begun, and during the coldest, windiest January, the troops at the Barracks del Carmen rebelled one dawn. With a couple of Civil Guards, I was the first to arrive and lay siege to them. I ask you to believe me, even though you think it's pure humbug. Only the three of us, those two guards and yours truly, were enough to hold them for almost an hour from the roofs of nearby houses. We were good shots and knew how to stay calm. The soldier who looked out a window or doorway to answer our fire was a soldier we finished off with a bullet. When my father arrived, he said: 'Son, keep up the fire and I hope you conduct yourself to the measure of my expectations.' 'Colonel,' I replied, 'I hope I have already conducted myself to the measure of Your Excellency's expectations. Now I want to be worthy of mine.' And he, in a quiet voice: 'Damn, but that's true too! What a wild boar you turned out to be, boy!' I'll cut it short because the day that should have been the day of my glory would later turn into a source of resentments and regrets. My father left me his command for all practical purposes, like another father, an ordinary painter, secretly cedes his palette to the son who turned out to be a prodigious artist. With a good shot I mortally wounded one of the soldiers who led the movement. The door of the barracks opened and I quickly climbed to the rebellious unit and at gunpoint obliged them to line up in the courtyard. No one said a word because that morning, all modesty aside, and as my father told me afterward, I seemed to be the god of war.

"I believe that during the Great War Ludendorff took the fort at Liege in a very similar way. And you see, they gave him the German equivalent of our Laureate Cross of San Fernando and made him a marshal. Well, just as we were saying, this will never be a civilized country and we're a thousand years behind the rational, cultivated world. Do you know my reward for taking the Barracks del Carmen? No, of course you don't know, since nobody knows! A miserable simple red cross. Yes, sir, though you may not believe it! A simple red cross, as if I had rescued the general's Persian cat or taught the multiplication tables to his favorite grandson. A simple red cross, with the hypocritical excuse that there was no other reward at that time!"

He's insane. A raving madman, though his derangement had remained hidden until now. Lost in the depths of a rancor that obedience and discipline made him forget about without realizing it. This war was needed so he could obtain power and prestige, and though he looked for them as a hero, he would attain them as an executioner. Absolute master of a city and consumed by sleeplessness, he shoots rashly and takes revenge on the vanquished for the contempt of a world that did not make him a Ludendorff when he had taken the Barracks del Carmen. Spurred on by his insanity, the creature of flesh returns to me. He returns but is shaken now not by horror but by fury. His enraged, effeminate voice raises mine until it's almost a shout.

"Are you trying to tell me that I was arrested because sixteen years ago you obtained only a simple red cross instead of the Laureate Cross of San Fernando? Or will they kill me because on another day, in Madrid, you envied Sánchez Mejías and me without my even realizing it? How am I to blame for being born or for our being conceived so differently?"

"My dear sir," he responds, suddenly very calm, though with a certain irritation in his voice. "I'm not responsible either for your finding yourself here with me now. Ruiz Alonso arrested you when I was at the front, with or without the consent of Lieutenant Colonel Velasco, since that's something I still haven't been able to determine. I can only assure you I did not order your arrest and learned about your return to Granada only in a newspaper from before the war . . . "

"All of this is a mistake, a monstrous mistake," the creature of flesh wails again. "Why don't they release me?"

"In due course. You accused me of having taken you prisoner and I have the duty and the right to defend myself. Look, I was so unaware of your arrest that when Pepe Rosales came to reproach me for it, without my knowing anything about anything, I said to him: 'Pepe, old friend, if this Ruiz Alonso arrested your friend and searched your parents' home, take him to an empty field and shoot him a few times.'"

"Then why don't you order my release?"

"In due course. In due course. Granada is filled with violent men who make war on their own and prefer killing behind the lines to fighting at the front. If I released you in daylight, they'd arrest you again and shoot you against the cemetery wall, and I wouldn't be able to stop it."

"You're the civilian governor. Where's your authority?"

"I have very little. I hope God isn't blind and can see that."

"You hope only that God isn't blind?"

He sighs and closes his eyes, but opens them again immediately, as if he were afraid of falling asleep unexpectedly. Suddenly he looks into mine and murmurs:

"When I told you I would trade my fate for yours, it wasn't a lie. I have cancer and I'm dying. For the first time since the war began, I was able to see the doctor yesterday for a few moments. He spoke to me openly and I thanked him for his frankness. 'Commander,' he said, looking at me as I'm looking at your now, 'you don't need a surgeon, you need a confessor. The end will come in a few weeks or a couple of months. From now on, I can prescribe for you only the morphine I don't have.'"

I'll never know whether his claim that Ruiz Alonso arrested me behind his back and without his knowledge is true. Yet I know with certainty that he isn't lying when he speaks to me of his imminent death. Fatigue, which I supposed was devouring him whole, consumes him only in part. His earthen color, his features drawn with a knife and a bevel, his slow and at times petrified gestures give him the air of a dead Castilian who has turned the color of earth beneath the frost.

"I'm not your confessor!" my other self manages to reply. "I don't know whether or not you're resigned to your death. I'll always rebel against mine, because it's an inconceivable mistake."

"I don't want to confess either!" he shouts. "I mean, I don't want to confess yet. I'll do that in due course."

"What do you want from me then?"

"To talk. Just to talk."

"Why with me? Since I entered the Civilian Government building, I'm not anybody anymore."

"Because one day I envied and respected you, even more than Sánchez Mejías himself, and because I sense you won't stop listening to me."

"You could talk to your soldiers and your family."

"I have no family. I'm alone in the world." He states this without pitying his solitude or taking pride in his independence. In the same straightforward way, bordering on indifference, that he might use to confess his ignorance of a foreign language. In the identical tone he continues: "My officers and my soldiers, I don't talk to them. I give them orders, and they obey, just as I obey when Queipo or Franco give me their orders from Sevilla."

"As you could give instructions for my death at this moment."

"I suppose so. It would cost me nothing to do that." He shrugs, and a rapid shadow of tedium crosses his fatigue. "Yet I didn't bring you here for that," he explains without a hint of irony. "And I don't want to talk about you, or Franco, or Queipo, and in a sense not even about myself. No, sir, all of us and this war really aren't anything but clouds, ants, nothing."

"You wanted to talk to me about God, Commander Valdés."

He looks at me with eyes that astonishment widens around his bloodshot whites and inflamed irises. For the first time I dared to say his name ("Commander Valdés"), as if I or the man of flesh—I'm not exactly sure which one—had found the strength to exorcise him. Also for the first time, I realize he doesn't want to shoot me, that this executioner consumed by cancer and delirious from lack of sleep, absolute master of the city with the authority of Queipo and Franco, a murderer who during this time has arranged and sanctioned hundreds of deaths, as Luis Rosales, almost in tears, finally confessed to me, has decided to free me from his squads and underlings for reasons that neither he nor I will ever understand. Awareness of my salvation, perhaps dimly sensed from the moment they burst into the house on Calle de Angulo to arrest me ("This son of a bitch, and may all the devils in hell give it to him up the ass, told me you did more harm with your pen that others do with a pistol"), sends me to a kind of no-man's land where, sometimes calmly, and sometimes with irresolute apprehension, I confront the certainty of freedom.

Inside me as well, and to my irritated astonishment, the creature of flesh turns around and reacts very differently. He grows and shouts recklessly. He is seized with a coward's delight when he believes himself safe at any price. His horror and panic, which had moved him earlier to say that he prayed for the victory of the military, now would lead him to impetuous extremes that courage cannot even conceive of. My only fear is of his audacity, for I'm aware that so much daring is nothing but an inadvertent desire for self-destruction.

"How did you guess? How did you know I was referring to God without my even naming Him?"

"That doesn't matter now, Commander. Please continue."

It is he who obeys, nodding, and it is the man of flesh who gives the orders and raises his voice, affected and possessed of an Andalusian accent that so many years of living in Madrid served only to confirm and emphasize, across from the impersonal speech of this man in agony.

"Are you religious?" he asks me, a not entirely unexpected question.

"I am, though I've never been observant since I've had the use of my reason."

"I've always been observant but was never really religious. I went to church on Sundays because a garrison officer has certain duties in a right-thinking society. I took communion on Easter Sunday because I'd been doing that since I was a boy, in Logroño. I took the name of God, perhaps in vain, in my war speeches in Africa and took it again in Zaragoza when I wanted to persuade the two Civil Guards that the three of us alone had to subdue the Barracks del Carmen. Yet I realize now that when we put down the uprising, I forgot to thank God for our victory. Nothing more, but also nothing less. It's not much, is it?"

"It isn't everything. You also fought with God on your own when they gave you the simple red cross and after you saw Sánchez Mejías and me in Madrid."

"Yes, sir, that's true too! How did you know? You read me as if I were an open newspaper. I fought with God, that's the precise expression. When I asked for His reasons, knowing He would never answer, I always called Him Your Excellency, as if I were addressing a case to Him, petitioning for late payments. Does it seem strange to you, does it seem comical?"

"It doesn't seem anything. Go on."

"'Your Excellency,' I said to Him in Zaragoza, 'You know very well that few officers would have exposed themselves to this kind of courageous action without guarantees and almost without possibilities of surviving it. I recognize that if they didn't kill me then, I owe it to Your Excellency, because getting out of that alive and escaping without a scratch when I subdued the rebels alone, with a revolver, is nothing but a miracle . . .'"

"Did you stop to think that if you'd been killed, then perhaps the king would've awarded you the Laureate posthumously?"

"Of course I stopped to think that! I'm not a man lacking in imagination!"

"Though you can't manage to understand your destiny on earth. I don't understand mine either."

"'Your Excellency,'"—he continued speaking to the shadows—"'You granted me life as an ironic act. To oblige me to accept that humiliating bit of charity: the simple red cross. So that once imposed, everyone could forget about me again. At this price, death followed by the eternal remembering of my name would be preferable.'"

"You didn't have to wait that long because the war made you master of Granada. You've entered history through the main door, Commander Valdés."

"I entered through a door I never wanted." He takes a square handkerchief from his cuff and wipes the sweat from his forehead ("I have cancer and I'm dying.") "I've killed a good number of men in Africa. Many more than I could count. I never attributed much importance to those deaths because they were all Moors and Moors are inferior to Gypsies in my personal code. Do I shock you?"

"I'm listening."

"If you had seen the heads of our soldiers in Barranco del Lobo and Annual, cut off with an ax and piled in the sun for the flies, you'd understand me perfectly."

"That's possible, though I doubt it. Luis Rosales told me the same Moors are fighting at your side. Do they continue to cut off heads with an ax, following their customs?"

"I wouldn't be surprised, if they're permitted to. I was actually getting to that and I'm glad you reminded me. Sooner or later, all our reason for being can be explained in the light of this war. I never, ever believed it would take place, and therefore never imagined myself as governor of Granada. When we were preparing the uprising, we all felt certain the coup would be almost bloodless and the government would fall at a single breath, like a house of cards. Your friend Pepe Rosales was the most optimistic, perhaps because he was the most unthinking. 'Look, Valdés,' he said to me during the days of the conspiracy, 'in no time we'll be in power and then we'll establish the National Syndicalist Revolution.' It bothered me that a rich spoiled civilian, and especially a rich spoiled kid like him, his eyes fried by so much manzanilla sherry, would address me informally as if we were related. I tolerated it only because it was a foolish custom in the Falange. 'Look Pepe,' I replied, 'this matter of National Syndicalism feels like a kick in the stomach to me. I don't know anything about politics and I don't understand how we're going to prevent one revolution only to impose another. I'm in this so Spain can have peace, order, and work. In other words, so the country can move forward the right way, which is with the discipline of a barracks. Forgive my frankness, but all the rest seems like very dangerous chatter to me. If we, the members of the Falange, are going to turn into the Communists of this Spain of ours, I'll turn in my membership card and that's the end of it.' "

"But here there's no peace and no order. And the only work is killing your neighbor."

"The coup did not succeed either, in spite of Pepe Rosales's optimism." He shrugs. "We only have a war to the death that will last longer than I do because it will take years and I'm living on borrowed time."

"A war that brought you the renown you pursued so intently, and with renown, immortality, though by unexpected paths. Allow me to say it again," my other self indicates cynically. "You could say that God was ironic with you, but don't accuse him of being unjust."

He looks into my eyes again and persists in pressing his palms onto the desk. He seems to murmur something, his very thin lips half open and trembling. One would say that the cancer gnawing at him now follows cardiac arrest: what the old folks from the Andalusian lowlands called a soul attack when I was a boy.

"I don't accuse Him of being unjust, because I know very well He's lost his mind," he mumbles in a very quiet voice.

"I'm sorry, what did you say?"

"I said that God has lost His mind and since the start of the war

I've never hidden from Him my certainty of His madness. 'Your Excellency gave me Granada, which I never asked for, and with Granada the duty to defend it against the reds,' I've often prayed to Him. 'I don't think I did a bad job, because we took it and they haven't taken it back. Thanks to Your Excellency, the day also arrived that I had always hoped for: the one when everyone recognized me and said my name with the same devotion as if it belonged to a rich, all-powerful relative . . .'"

"Don't look at me when you speak to God, Commander Valdés. Don't look at me when you say these things, or I won't be able to believe you."

He doesn't hear me or pretends not to have heard me. His face doesn't change its impassive expression as his terrifying prayer continues. But he bows his head and contemplates his hands near the edge of the desk.

"'But at this price, and if I had been consulted first, I'd never have accepted my glory,'" he continues, his tone of voice immutable. "'No, at this price, I'd prefer death and oblivion.'"

"What price did you have to pay, Commander?" the man of flesh asks him, as if he actually had become his confessor.

"A price too high in blood and too easy to satisfy," he says to his hands. "The guarantee of our survival was the death of hundreds of men in three weeks. I've blindly given orders, and orders to shoot, and I've blinded myself intentionally when I was denounced for crimes committed behind my back by the Black Squads, to settle an old dispute, to carry out personal vengeance, or simply not to lose the habit of killing. Pepe Rosales burst into my office one afternoon . . ." His voice breaks quietly and he shakes his head.

"What did Pepe Rosales want?"

"He moved the guard aside with a backhand slap when he tried to block his way. He kicked the door open, rushed to this desk, and began to pound it with his fist. 'May I ask how you'll put a stop to the murderers' crimes? How long will you permit this rabble to dirty us all with their crimes?' 'Pepe, sit down, be quiet, and listen to me,' I replied very coldly. 'No matter how many people are killed by this rabble, as you call it, it's less of a sacrifice than if I have to shoot someone against my will. Here there's no time to try anyone. When I hesitate over the name of a prisoner, I consult Sevilla by phone, and Sevilla always orders me to shoot him. On very rare occasions I've come across acquaintances, because I never had friends and you're not one of them. I also called Sevilla then, to tell them that on my own responsibility I was releasing the man, and no one argued with my decision. This is a war without mercy or quarter in which I would have requested any duty except executing Spaniards as if they were rats or Moors. This obligation and no other fell to me because that's how God wanted it. I probably differ from the men in the Black Squads only in that they enjoy killing, while I can't sleep when I think about the shootings. Yet some of us continue to meet an unavoidable responsibility, which is safeguarding the civilian population.' Frowning, his head lowered, his rage subsided, he asked me what position suited him in Granada, realizing he hadn't been born to be an executioner or a murderer. 'Pepe,' I replied, 'the first thing you should do for the greater glory of the new Spain is to go and sleep off all you've had to drink today.'"

"You wouldn't talk to God the way you talked to Pepe Rosales."

"No, I told God that same day: 'Your Excellency must have lost Your mind over the years.' Just like that, just what you've heard: 'Your Excellency must have lost Your mind over the years.' I didn't know then that I was going to die. I knew I was sick because I always had been but couldn't have imagined the end would come so soon. When the doctor decided to tell me the truth, I came back to this office. I gave orders not to be disturbed until they heard from me again, took all the phones off the hook, and prayed again. 'With my days numbered, I ought to reaffirm my conviction. Your Excellency has lost Your mind in Your old age and don't know it yet. I, on the other hand, know I'm going to die and for this reason ought to tell You about it.'"

"Commander Valdés, I'm not God, only an innocent man who's been persecuted and taken prisoner. I beg you again to tell me only the reason for my presence here and the motive for your confession."

"I supposed you would have guessed them," he mumbles without looking up from his hands.

"I can't because I never imagined anyone like you."

"Then leave. Tonight I'll call Sevilla and tell them that tomorrow I'm going to release you. Your fate doesn't concern me once you've left the offices of the Civilian Government, but I hope you know how to survive me."

He's telling the truth and his truth means my life. But suddenly the man of flesh understands his double inability to write from now on, and to live without being able to write. A good part of his indifference infects me on this night that resembles a stranger's delirium, though in a certain sense it seems as distant as my earlier panic. As remote as my brother-in-law's death as recounted by my father. ("Son, promise me you'll be careful! Swear it to me, yes, you have to swear!")

"You won't release me and won't dare to kill me either without telling me why you interrogated me personally. Or why you pretended to interrogate me, because in reality you didn't do that either."

"I promised Pepe Rosales."

"That's not enough and you know it very well."

"Before you know it I'll be in the presence of my Maker and I'll respond to all his charges. The last must be the certainty of His madness in view of this war and my destiny in it, as well as my sincerity in reproving Him for it. With or without morphine, I'm almost indifferent to death, but His punishment if I'm innocent terrifies me. Even though you may not believe it, even more than honor I respect justice . . . "

"Yours or someone else's?"

"Justice! Why do you bring that up now? Don't interrupt me or soon I won't know what I'm saying. Look, a man who dared to call

God crazy in full and absolute knowledge of his own impending death must be a lunatic. Each day I look into my eyes in the mirror when I shave, and I tell myself: 'Valdés, you're crazy, no doubt about it. When the hour of judgment comes, and it's very soon now, and God looks at you the way you look at yourself in this mirror, you'll have only one defense . . . '"

"Telling him you were insane when you accused Him of madness."

"Exactly. Then I conclude: 'Any intelligent person in whom I confided my intention would find himself obliged to prove it.' Very well, you're that person. Assure me that I've lost my mind and I'll die at peace with my conscience."

"I don't know whether your God is or isn't deranged, because there's no doubt we're talking about different gods."

"There can be only one because His power is indivisible!"

"In any case, I wonder if yours won't ask for an explanation from the people you shot and allowed to be murdered instead of condemning you for calling Him crazy. In the final analysis, you're dying now and men won't be able to demand liabilities from you for those crimes. For His part God, yours or mine, must put justice above honor just as you do."

"I'm not responsible for the death of anyone. Is it possible you haven't understood anything? It was nothing but the will of God that decreed some shootings and permitted so many crimes. Because I didn't understand such anomalous designs, I called Him crazy and I must be the crazy one for calling Him that. If I contend this at the trial, I'll merely be stating the truth."

"No, Commander Valdés, you won't tell the truth because you agree and all your actions can be explained logically, beginning with an initial resentment: that of a man as dissatisfied with himself as he is with the world around him."

The creature of flesh speaks wearily now. He seems about to collapse like an empty suit, and one might say he holds himself upright only by leaning his palm against me deep inside. In the center of my soul, his hand is as cold as a dead man's.

"I thought you'd make an effort to understand me!"

"I understand you very well. Perhaps in a certain sense we're not as different as your God and mine are. You're as afraid of dying as I was. Afraid you'll cease to be without having been more than the executioner of Granada. Let's end this farce once and for all. Return me to the room that serves as my cell, or do whatever you want with me. But don't ask me to call you crazy because you're not, and God, the God of either one of us, knows it as well as we do."

"Is this your final word?"

"If I thought calling you crazy would save my life, I'd tell you that your God will exempt you from judgment because He believes you're insane. In any event, lying wouldn't change my fate."

"My dear sir, you too have my final word," he replies, hurt and angry, but not looking up. "I told you I'd talk to Sevilla about releasing you tomorrow, and tomorrow you'll be free."

"Valdés, I don't doubt your word or your sanity. In any case, you made a confession to me and I owe you another. We're both part of a drama whose reasons and outcome transcend us because it has already happened before, in a time and a world that are very remote yet identical to ours. You're Castilian, judging by your accent, and perhaps you can't fathom what I'm trying to tell you, but any Gypsy or Andalusian Civil Guard would understand me perfectly. When I left Madrid for Granada, a friend accompanied me to the South Station. With a certain insistence that was not exaggerated, for he also appeared in the cast of our show, he asked me to stay in Madrid where he could protect or hide me. I felt tempted to do as he asked but was struck immediately by the certainty that there could be no discrepancies with what had previously been foretold and staged. I came to Granada, knowing that here I would be arrested even though I tried to hide."

"I'm very tired." He sighs, shrugging his thin shoulders. "I don't think I really understood everything you said, but I can't accept your fatalism. If it were true, the staging of our drama would never end, and the war would keep repeating another identical war that occurred earlier. It makes no sense."

"That's what you say, though I didn't expect you to understand. You're too rational, and you'll never be able to hide that from the eyes of God."

He crossed his arms on the desk and presses his forehead between elbow and wrist. His hair, combed with a part, is thinning in the middle of his head, and long white strands, all very recent, cover his temples with ash.

"I can't stay awake anymore," he murmurs. "What happens now in the play, according to your premonitions? Do you grab my pistol and shoot me while I doze off? That's what I'd do if I were you."

"I don't, and we can't change our roles. In the final analysis, we're as different as our gods."

"Then call the soldier standing guard and ask to be returned to your cell," he whispers with difficulty, his words enveloped in sleep. "It won't be for long. Tomorrow you'll go back to the Rosales family's house. Tell the soldiers to wake me in half an hour." It becomes more and more difficult to understand him, but I'd swear that suddenly, as he was sinking into sleep, he mumbles: "You've cheated me. You refused to think I was crazy and you refused to shoot me. My regards to Pepe Rosales."

"All right," the man of flesh agrees, perhaps disconcerted. "I suppose from now on I ought to be grateful to you for the favor of my life. But I'm not sure I've received it. When I left Madrid, I thought every step I took had been foreseen. Now I'm not sure about anything. Couldn't we have moved away from what had been arranged without realizing it? Couldn't we have insisted on improvising an outcome very different from the only one possible?"

He doesn't argue or respond. Dozing face down on the desk, he slips into sleep like a stone rolling down a hill. Occasionally his back shudders beneath his tunic and he stifles an unconscious groan. Then he is completely motionless, and one might say he falls, fully dressed, to the bottom of an invisible ocean.

Look at him look at him look at him as you saw him so frequently on the stage of this theater of yours in hell Look even if you don't want to see him again and very unwillingly think of him so often Look at the man of flesh in me the one who stopped being afraid in the Civilian Government building when Valdés pleaded with him to think he was crazy Yes look at the man of flesh in me who came with me to the bottom of this spiral Look at him and don't cover your face with handkerchiefs In the elegy to Ignacio Sánchez Mejías he also asked that his face be left bare and uncovered so one might peer into his eyes as one peers into the hard air or the eyes of the anonymous corpse in a thirteen-line-poem that was the premonition of everything you see now Look at him and don't become lost in oblique memories or verses like tangents because at that dawn everything concluded on earth absolutely everything for you man of flesh for me who am your right or your wrong side your heads or your tails and for the poems we conceived of and signed with my name You'll never know whether Ruiz Alonso denounced you or not Whether he was confessing the truth or telling a lie when he said he had carried out the orders of Lieutenant Colonel Velasco the man without a face and almost without a name who appears and disappears in this tragedy of yours as if he had not existed You'll never know whether Valdés called Sevilla as he had promised ("My dear sir, you too have my final word. I told you I'd talk to Sevilla about releasing you tomorrow, and tomorrow you'll be free") to tell them of your release You'll never know whether Sevilla replied that he ought to kill you right away who knows why for being a red a queer a poet a Mason a Gypsy a Jew a friend of Fernando de los Ríos for having voted for the Popular Front for having asked for the freedom of Prestes or as Ruiz Alonso said to Miguel Rosales simply for having done more harm with the pen than others do with a pistol In any case and though you can't explain it to yourself with any certainty you have the retrospective presentiment that Valdés told the truth at least in part In any case never again never no never again because everything concludes now With kicks and rifle butts they open the door to the room that serves as your cell The one with the boy's eyes and another soldier identical to him as alike as the same image in two facing mirrors burst into your cell throw you face first against the wall and tie your hands behind your back with an esparto rope that cuts off the circulation in your wrists You shout that the governor will not tolerate this abuse that the governor has sworn yes sworn to release you tomorrow and one of them you don't whether it was the one who tried to hit you with his rifle ("How do you dare, wretch? In my presence!") or the other one slaps you across the mouth Your palate and tongue taste of blood man of flesh before you feel the mordant bitterness of the blow The blood tastes of India ink and shards of broken glass on frost Two identical laughs welcome your scream of pain and panic Now you would like to be Ignacio even if you're only my right or my wrong side my heads or my tails man of flesh To be Ignacio yes because he grew up defying death ("If a broken body has to enter my house, let it be mine and not my son's") though he would grovel and yield in your presence like a wounded bull With shoves and kicks they take you along the corridor the stairs the lobby while you (*Je ne suis un péderaste! Je suis une tapette!* "I'm not a pederast! I'm a fairy!") cry and pray and they disregard you Outside the strangely cold night waits for you in the middle of an August filled with indifferent crickets You fall to your knees and beg that please in the name of God they return you to your cell and allow you to speak with the governor You repeat that you had prayed for the triumph of the military and are prepared to give everything for their cause including your life A Buick as black as daybreak is waiting parked at the curb and they drag you to the car open one of the rear doors and throw you onto the upholstered seat Suddenly with the unexpected ease with which you change time or persons in dreams you think that if you hadn't refused to drink or eat in the Civilian Government building you'd urinate now with fear and you congratulate yourself for being so prudent In the Buick are two men with their hands tied behind their backs One beside you and the other facing you on one of the folding seats Beside him on the next extra backless seat you recognize Juan Trescastro In the front are two Assault Guards one at the wheel and the other armed with a Mauser that he holds dejected or asleep Trescastro also has a pistol in his hand though now he seems to have dropped it on his lap The prisoner facing you squints when he looks at you and says your name Then he asks whether you're the writer You nod and he tells you in a quiet, calm voice "I'm Paco Galadí This friend beside you is Joaquín Arcollas though we all call him Cabezas a comrade from the bull-ring a banderillero like me They're murdering us without a trial because we're Anarchists and were armed when they arrested us" Cabezas excuses himself for having to look at you over his shoulder since his hands are tied behind him Then as if you were at a picnic instead of going to your deaths he continues "I met Ignacio Sánchez Mejías and almost fought in his cuadrilla When he learned I came from Granada he told me you were a good friend of his and were a genius at writing modern ballads" "All right just shut up once and for all!" growls Trescastro "This isn't a festival" Galadí laughs at him "They're going to kill us and tortured us almost to death What else can an untalented rich kid like you who belongs to Gil Robles do to us? When you suffer this much blows don't hurt anymore and bullets will be a blessing "Olé!" Cabezas agrees "Very well put! Even tied up we're stronger than you!" The truth is that Trescastro falls silent turns around and at a signal from him the police officer starts the car You go up Calle Duquesa and cross the Calle del Gran Capitán Gradually you leave behind a Granada deserted and silent under curfew Above you the stars flicker and ignite before they go out with the first lights If anyone is watching all of you from one of those remote worlds he would feel as indifferent to your fate as you would be to the ants crushed under your feet Yet if an ant said to you "I think I feel I'm mortal just as you are" would you destroy it as they're going to destroy you now? Granada is behind you and you enter the countryside It smells of orange blossoms and mint Frogs sing in a pond A shooting star crosses the windshield Suddenly you're absolutely convinced you're living a farce In spite of all appearances to the contrary these people aren't going to murder you The presence of Trescastro a very well-known member of Popular Action supports your unexpected certainty You see him again in the Rosales family's courtyard while Ruiz Alonso had a snack of biscuits and café con leche with the napkin tied around his neck and spilling down the front of his blue coverall like a bib looking at him with a mixture of embarrassment and contempt This man wasn't born to kill anybody He does no more than go along on arrests like yours protected by the Assault Guards posted even on the roofs just as certain people must have watched autos-de-fé even though they didn't have an executioner's calling He's with you in the Buick to prevent this mockery of an execution from becoming reality It's all a cruel comedy staged by Valdés for your benefit At the last moment when these police officers pretend to be ready to kill you with a bullet to the back of the head Trescastro will stay their hand like the angel of the Lord and order them to take you back to the Civilian Government offices offering absurd reasons Orders received at the last moment following his call to the governor from a farmhouse telephone or simply the Dostoevskian revelation that it was all arranged as a sinister game with the three of you Galadí Cabezas and you as inadvertent protagonists "The mercy of the governor is infinite and this time he decided to give all of you the gift of life though you will spend the rest of it in prison contemplating behind bars the most devout and very military flowering of the new Spain that your revolutionary liberal Marxist Masonic and Judaizing baseness attempted to prevent under orders from Russia" In the Civilian Government build-

ing they'll take you to Valdés again You'll find him paler and more
ashen than ever more corroded by insomnia and lack of sleep like
two acids He does have cancer and is going to die very soon Precisely
for that reason the savage burlesque to which he subjected you must
cheer him in a particular way "You're a man of the theater" he'll say
not looking you in the eye as usual "give me your opinion of my
little farce and its direction Do you or do you not believe now that
I'm insane and my derangement will be the best proof of my innocence in God's judgment?" Perhaps they'll carry their monstrous-
ness even further and kill Galadí and Cabezas ("They're murdering
us without a trial because we're Anarchists and were armed when
they arrested us") exempt you and return you to Valdés In that case
it's also possible you won't even understand his questions those of a
dying man obsessed with proving his insanity because you yourself
have become a raving madman after this sarcastic Calvary when
they grant you your life as a taunt The shooting star extinguished
and having passed the frog pond we cross a small bridge Then the
moon outlines olive groves on both sides of the highway "Where are
we going?" Cabezas asks aloud looking at the countryside and not
addressing anyone "This is the bridge over the Beiro" Galadí replies
while Trescastro and the Assault Guards say nothing "We're going
toward the town of Víznar where my mother came from God rest
her soul Granada is south of us now" He's cut off by a chorus of
barks beyond the river and the olive grove Gradually you recognize
the places that the night obscured in your memory The palace of
Archbishop Don Juan Manuel de Moscoso y Peralta is in Víznar A
few days after Fernando Villalón summoned the souls of dead dogs
to the horror of Rafael María Teresa and you the three of them came
with you to Granada and you took them to Víznar along this road to
admire that eighteenth-century building If in the South Station you
were convinced that present past and future eventually fused in a
higher reality here you had no presentiment of the tragedy and the
joke that together oblige you to live now You remember very well

that before the massive door studded with large nails and then in the porticoed courtyard of the palace you told them that Moscoso y Peralta Archbishop of Granada was the child of American-born Spaniards from Arequipa A nephew of his you said to the astonished surprise of María Teresa and Rafael Mariano Tristán de Moscoso had a daughter out of wedlock with a French aristocrat who had fled the Revolution That girl Flora Tristán would be the grandmother of Paul Gauguin and a sentence of hers "Workers of the world, unite! You have nothing to lose but your chains!" was plagiarized with great success by Engels and Marx in the *Communist Manifesto* Fernando Villalón was silent his eyes and broad humanity gathered in as if he were totally absentminded and at the same time found himself very far from all of you In a kind of aside while Rafael was taking pictures of María Teresa in the palace garden you asked him what was going on behind his interminable silences He placed his palm on his chest and said "Do you remember the dead dogs whose barks you heard in the grove when I summoned them? Now I hear all of them howling here in the middle of my chest" "How much longer to Víznar?" Cabezas asks Galadí his voice touched by a slight tremor "Not far We're almost there If it weren't so late we'd have seen the lights a while back" The Buick stops at the door of the palace Trescastro gets out and for a few moments seems to hesitate between speaking to the Assault Guards or proceeding in silence He leaves finally without opening his lips At the entrance to the building he speaks with a sentry posted there and then the large studded door closes behind him Then the Guards both turn toward you at the same time as if moved by a single spring "We aren't volunteers and never would've done anything like this" murmurs the one with the musket "They forced us because we're suspected of being for the Republic" Like Valdés his accent is from Old Castile Perhaps he's from Logroño or maybe La Montaña The other one nods "I always pray to become a raging lunatic I'd prefer it to this" Galadí spits at his feet "A real man would shoot himself before shooting a defense-

less person in the back" "Olé" Cabezas agrees "Well said and absolutely right!" "We're both married and I have two young kids" the
Guard who's driving replies "I can't abandon them and leave them
stranded Try to understand" "I have a little girl and I'll die at peace
with my conscience because I know that one day she'll see liber-
tarian communism in this country" "Olé! Olé! I have a son and
hope he can forgive you because you're dogs and dogs don't know
what they're doing" You would like to tell them that tonight nobody
will kill anybody because the moment for the crime hasn't arrived
yet Perhaps it was last night and will come again tomorrow but it will
never be this morning There are prescribed times for the murder of
innocents and other times chosen for satanic carnivals to the greater
glory of a man whose only hope is to be seen as insane in the eyes of
God But your voice strangles in your throat like a river of ash Your
heart beats so fiercely in your throat you're afraid it will burst like a
pomegranate or shrink into the blood that burns your soul as if it
were lava ("To die or not to die. That is the question. The bullring is
a theater Shakespeare would've understood perfectly") said Sánchez Mejías when someone asked him to describe bullfighting precisely and succinctly To die or not to die Back when la Argentinita
thought she had been abandoned by her lover she called one afternoon to ask you to her house got rid of the maid the cook and the old
woman who ironed She was alone with you and stated that she
didn't want to live convinced as she was she had lost Ignacio You
tried to comfort her with old lies that bored and debased you when
you repeated them when suddenly she embraced you kissed you on
the mouth and said she was going to bed with you my boy this
afternoon That she had always desired you in a distant but persistent
way like those ideas that assault you several times every year in the
half sleep of a summer siesta or when you make up your eyes in the
dressing-room mirror while you feel very alone far from home and
outside the snow of New York or Paris is falling Yes desired since
the days of the failed premiere of *The Butterfly's Curse* when you

weren't much more than a little nobody so innocent and so serious with those Moorish eyes of yours and that blue shawl She asked you straight out if you'd ever been with a woman and you said no with a gesture saying only with men not adding that you had loved one and bought the rest She replied that you shouldn't be ashamed of what she called your inclinations because one comes as one is to this vale of tears and you were as responsible for coming out queer as you were for being born for in neither case were you asked if you wanted to be a macho man or simply be since the ideal my boy would be if they didn't bother to have us or at least didn't do it without our permission when we suffer afterward the way we do Then as now it was impossible for you to reply because the words burned like embers before turning into dust into nothing and your heart seemed to split open with each beat or turn into porous worn stone like the fossilized birds trapped in amber before man walked the earth that you saw once in Edem Mills the night before the aurora borealis You couldn't tell her you loved her more than your own life though it was true but could never go to bed with her or any woman because in the shredded depths of your being you would have felt you were committing incest with your own mother You fled down the stairs with the words petrified behind your palate and pursued by the shouts of la Argentinita That night she called you again to reiterate her dejection and despair far from Ignacio but never tried to comment on what occurred in her house or what never happened there that afternoon And now the doors of the palace open and Trescastro returns holding his pistol but with a hurried step and bowed head as if he had just received orders to put an end to this farce or been reprimanded for his part in so absurd a burlesque He gets into the Buick and slams the door shut The car pulls away and on the left the olive trees continue but thick pine groves stand on the other side of the highway You feel lost because you'd never left Víznar through this countryside Never until this incredible dawn The sound of water on the side of the olive groves disconcerts you but Galadí as if reading your forehead says "It's the Ainadamar irrigation channel that comes from Fuente Grande" and Cabezas observes in the most indifferent tone "It sounds full even though it wasn't a very rainy winter" "I told you once to shut up" Trescastro repeats without looking at us "Hell no!" shouts Galadí "The one who ought to shut up is you so you can kill us once and for all if you have the balls to do it!" Trescastro lowers his eyes and his gaze is lost in his lap where he still holds the forgotten pistol At each curve in the road his knees push against yours They're round and hard like the knobs that indicate the landings on staircases Suddenly as if two hands pulled away the stray clouds the full moon appears in the sky It whitens the irrigation channel and Cabezas's smooth face The water restores the scent of jasmines and morning glories Nothing however is excessive in this countryside A sense of suitable calm governs heaven and earth though they seem to burn in white-hot fire on all four sides In no time the same measured prudence will constrain even a monster like Trescastro He'll put the pistol in his pocket and give the order to return to the Civilian Government building ("The mercy of the governor is infinite and this time he decided to give you the gift of life . . . ") Even a satanic farce like the one devised to destroy three defenseless creatures by pushing them to the brink of eternity only to hold them back at the edge of the abyss must respect certain limits ("even though you'll spend the rest of it in prison contemplating through the bars the most pious and very military flowering . . . ") You know that between one person and another love extends spider's threads that would shine like the light of this moon if they were visible When death separates them it leaves something like a thread of blood at the loose end of each strand You're convinced you won't die because the spider web between you and your mother in the Huerta de San Vicente is unbreakable The same moon turns different trees white you'd almost say now altering a line of Neruda's You were a boy in the Huerta before you had carnal knowledge of man and fled la Argentinita before you came across the witches of Albaicín before you found in open pianos wordless romanzas sleeping since autumns crossed with stagecoaches and old mirrors before discovering your power to create another universe precisely constructed of words with their Route to Santiago their Gypsy pilgrims their homosexual saints covered in lace their honeysuckle and knives from Albacete long before Alberti dazzled you by saying that blazing feathers fell to earth and a bird could be killed by a lily Before Before Before You were a sleepwalking boy and in the Huerta de San Vicente Without waking you another full moon carried you to those fields illuminated by the open window of your bedroom You were aware of living asleep and also of walking through a dream that was a world of platinum The fountain in the courtyard where a sobbing fish twisted sounded the way the Ainadamar irrigation channel sounds tonight while other morning glories and other jasmines identical to these merged their scents in the motionless air You thought you'd pass among smiling dead people barely outlined in the radiance who would open a path for you as the multitude of murderers stepped aside now happy to know it will be the lot of all of you to go on living You reached the fishpond filled with water lilies and went into the water naked You lost your footing and drowned without waking slipping into a more profound dream where the world resplendent with moonlight turned all to gold Old gold next to hammered copper Gold of wheat fields stirred by the wind Innocent gold of virgin decks of cards Gold of wedding rings lost beneath the lilies Gold of thirteen coins stamped with your profile and your mother's as if you were a king and a queen Gold of cut lemons that many years later would be reborn intact in your poem on the arrest of Antoñito el Camborio Gold of another sun the reflection of the one in the sky at the bottom of the water You were going to the center of that fire when an arm plunged into the water took you by the hand and returned you to the air as in a parody of that miracle this dawn Trescastro will give all of you the gift of existence It was your mother naked and sleepwalking too holding on to you by the spider web of threads that would be silver if love were visible She held you to her breasts and the two of you remained there sobbing very quietly so as not to awaken yourselves Today you have the retrospective certainty of having foreseen on that night in the pond that you weren't going to die because the silvery net though invisible joined you to life as now it binds you again to the person who will give you your being The Buick stops at a building beside the road It is a two-story villa with three doors and several French windows "I know that place" Galadí exclaims "They call the house the Colony because in the summer school children would come here to the country I suppose nowadays you use it as a slaughterhouse" he concludes turning toward Trescastro He doesn't answer gets out of the car and slams the door with a dry sound Then what happened at the archbishop's palace is repeated almost point for point Trescastro talks with two men who guard the Colony and one of them opens the door with no great courtesy "Now or never" Galadí says to the Assault Guards "Start the car and the four of us can get the hell away from here" They look at each other and seem to hesitate for long moments They probably aren't involved in Valdés's scheme because the driver shakes his head sadly "Don't torture us like this I already told you my friend is married and I am too with two children All we'd need is to let you run away or escape with you!" "It's impossible" the one with the Mauser agrees "Don't torment us any more In no time they'd catch us and finish off all of us" "Drop it Galadí" advises Cabezas "You'd convince a couple of vipers sooner than these wretches Beg their pardon for having wounded their delicate sensibilities and let's hope they give us the coup de grâce as if we never offended them" "You're right" says Galadí resigned "This one's kids must be sons of a bitch on their father's side" The Guards pretend not to have heard them and Galadí faces you "I admire you because without being made for danger like this you bear it with so much dignity Cabezas and I are different because we're banderilleros In the bullring you get used to seeing death close up and in the end you almost forget about it In time being butted and knocked down scares you more than the chance of a fatal goring" "It's true" Cabezas agrees "The señor bears everything with more dignity than we do because he responds to them with his contempt and his silence We ought to do the same" Then he turns toward you and says "Don't worry this will take only an instant if our police friends know how to do their job and are used to killing the right way I was with Granero's cuadrilla in the twenty-second year of this century when the bull Pocapena gored him in Madrid You see how things are Granero who was a señor too like you and even had studied the violin he played it like an angel and seemed begging your pardon a queer Nobody ever heard him talk about women or saw him looking at them If they were mentioned in his presence he'd blush like a novice But in the bullring he was the toughest man in the world With more control over himself and the bull than Joselito and courage colder and more measured than Sánchez Mejías's He had the death he deserved in two seconds with no time to suffer Poca-pena caught him in the thigh and tossed him against the barrier He gored him there three times and in one sank his horn into his eye and split open his brain He was unconscious when we picked him up but dead when he went into the infirmary" You wanted to tell them that death is the only thing there's no need to fear in this sinister burlesque to the greater glory of the governor's presumed derangement ("You're too rational and you'll never be able to hide it from the eyes of God") But your voice is still petrified in your throat Vestiges of words from other times before the disaster before the God who'll judge Valdés scorched Sodom and Gomorrah with the fire of His wrath to ravage this land of the unthinking and the rabble where only the executioners preserve their sanity to the greater mockery of all the victims Words like reason moral virtue justice dignity ("The señor bears everything with more dignity than we do because he only responds to them with his contempt and his si-lence") honor fellow man nation religion law progress culture revolution which here took on a meaning completely different from and opposed to the one they have in any other country An entire vocabulary devised for dealings among human beings fossilized now in your throat transformed into outlines of scorpions spiders vipers extinct species of fish To tell them we won't lose our lives but may lose our reason in this ordeal To tell them that perhaps starting tomorrow the three of us will be exhibited in a glass cage as specimens of perfect madmen by the grace of Valdés in this land where good sense is the exclusive inalienable privilege of murderers But your voice has been silenced perhaps forever As in those nightmares where your legs sink up to the knees in a desert that holds all of you and prevents you from walking to a mirror in order to throw you into a chasm that first stifles your shouts between the walls of a pit and then crushes them between its teeth or at the back of its tongue As for the rest they don't seem to expect answers from you either as if they could read in your eyes exactly the opposite of everything you're thinking and feeling ("I admire you because without being made for danger like this you bear it with so much dignity") Can the inability to understand one another while they breathe in this world be the fate of all men? You say this to yourself in your mute despair And now the main door of the Colony opens again and Trescastro returns with the pistol in his pocket Another man his hands tied behind him like the three of you comes limping beside him He's stout broad-shouldered the front of his head is almost bald and he's well into his fifties As he approaches and in the headlights of the Buick you see that his shirt is stained with blood on the front and his lips are disfigured as if blows to his teeth had split them "Slide toward Cabezas this guy has to fit in next to you" Trescastro says to you now in a tone that's almost polite The newcomer struggles to obey him after you've moved over next to Cabezas He tries to get into the car sideways but all his efforts are in vain He has an artificial leg his own perhaps amputated above the knee and he can't flex it to bend over "I can't get in if you don't untie me" he states in a very serene tone not addressing anyone personally and as if he had called on heaven to witness his inability "Try it again" Trescastro insists "I've already tried and it's impossible" the timbre of his voice is almost as strong as his shoulders even though a strange whistle like that of someone not yet accustomed to expressing himself with broken incisors slipped among his words Trescastro hesitates but takes a penknife from his pocket and cuts the cords that bind the stranger His hands tremble when he closes the blade that gleams like a fish in the moonlight and puts away the knife Instinctively he moves a few steps away from the crippled man who has the advantage over him in height and heft The Assault Guards are still inattentive their backs turned as if this new act in your tragedy were none of their concern The man with the beaten face and well-separated temples rubs his wrists for a long time without Trescastro hurrying him or interrupting Standing sideways at the car door he takes the prosthesis by the knee and extends its rigidity into the air Then he slips into the Buick and sits beside me while with both hands he bends his artificial leg, which squeaks like very hard recently broken chalk on a blackboard or a very old iron key in an unoiled lock From his seat his hip pressing against yours he calls to Trescastro with a mocking attitude and offers him the empty jump seat next to Galadí's "Let his highness the executioner make himself comfortable among his victims and friends" Trescastro obeys more terrified now than any of us With a handkerchief he wipes his brow and cheeks and gestures to the Guard to start the engine The car growls and groans like a wounded animal then finally engages shaking us all with an abrupt jolt "What's happening now?" Trescastro asks anxiously The Guard at the wheel shrugs "I don't know This Buick is very old It could be the carburetor and the steering Everything at the same time" "All right all right Go ahead and no breakdowns" he insists peremptorily as if it were in his power or the driver's to prevent them The man with the metal leg smiles and shakes his head "His highness the executioner reminds me of King

Canute determined to stop the waves" he says to Galadí Then he introduces himself "Dióscoro Galindo González teacher in Pulianas" Joaquín Arcollas answers for everyone and it surprises you that Galadí doesn't He tells him in a quiet voice everything his friend explained to you earlier and says who you are The teacher from Pulianas moves his head which was next to yours back a little and greets you almost joyfully "I had the kids in my little school read your *Poem of the Cante Jondo* Naturally most wouldn't have been able to buy it but I typed out the poems and had them memorize many of them Why did they arrest you?" He smiles painfully with his swollen lips and adds "I would have liked to meet you under different circumstances and with more time ahead of us" Again it is Cabezas who must think it his duty to answer for the three of them "Galadí here and yours truly were arrested as dangerous Anarchists We are and very proud of it I don't know why they're going to kill the señor I suppose because of his prestige since fascism hates the poor and the talented" "Four days ago at about ten at night a couple of armed Falangistas not entirely unexpected appeared at my house in Pulianas" says Dióscoro Galindo González without paying too much attention to him "Through the window we saw two more who never came to the house waiting for them in a car parked by the door The first two introduced themselves very politely by the way and requested permission to search the house as they had been ordered to by the Civilian Government I had no choice and gave it to them and you'll forgive the obligatory irony but I added that they wouldn't find anything interesting in the house of a poor public school teacher Then one of them asked me if after the February elections and the victory of the Popular Front people hadn't paraded past my house shouting 'Long live the teacher and death to Barreras!' I said all of that was certainly true even though I wasn't responsible for what people yell on the sidewalks I didn't say that in the electoral campaign I had spoken in public in favor of the Popular Front because they didn't ask me that Gentlemen I was always a republican but never had a calling to be a hero or a martyr only a pedagogue If I confess all this in the presence of our honored executioners it's because in for a thousand pesetas or a hundred 'you can take my life from me but nothing else' as Señor Calvo Sotelo said gallantly in Congress before he was assassinated I was always respectful of the opinions and above all the dignity of my adversaries" You alone know that tonight no one will die that Galindo González is the last inadvertent actor in the farce conceived by Valdés with you in the lead But behind the back of the civilian governor and his cancer another burlesque no less unexpected with the same cast and the Buick as the stage begins to be acted before your eyes While Galadí so assertive earlier is absorbed in his own silence and Trescastro who shares with you the knowledge of the truth seems to waste away in the semidarkness of the night's full moon over the irrigation channel as if through a bitter mistake he foresees that in the end he'll be the one who is really shot dead Cabezas forgets about his imminent murder though he believes it inevitable and takes a lively interest in the story of the teacher from Pulianas "And who was the Barreras they were shouting 'death to' in front of your house sir?" he asks Galindo González "Probably the man who denounced me though that's another long story I'll have to summarize for you in a few words Eduardo Barreras was also the secretary of the Council of Pulianas and the political boss of the town When I came there two years ago he gave me a house that was little more than a stable I went to protest to the Civilian Governor himself and the steps I had taken were reported in *El Ideal*, which took my side though the paper is right-wing After all that the only thing I obtained was Barreras's Hagarene hatred for in the end sick of sending petitions on papers with seals I rented the apartment they came to search four nights ago" "That's when they arrested you?" Cabezas persists "No son not then Since apparently we're proceeding with our drive I'll explain everything in the order it happened When they finished their search the Falangistas told me they really hadn't found anything compromising and would state that in their report They added that if nobody came to arrest me in the next forty-eight hours I could consider myself a free man I remember that as they were leaving one of them asked me what my political thinking was just talking you understand I replied that these details were very private and I didn't believe it was my obligation to reveal them to anyone because what counts is a man's conduct and not his thoughts Though you won't believe it he said I was right" "And what about the forty-eight-hour time limit?" "It expired two nights later But fifty-four hours after the search other Falangistas came to my house this time with no courtesy or manners and arrested me with slaps in the face and shoves I'll spare you the rest because you must know it on your own and my teeth and shirt speak for themselves After the beatings the tortures and the interrogations I had the honor to pass into the presence of Commander Valdés himself the new civilian governor of Granada the Beautiful He spoke to me for only a few moments to ask me again how I thought politically and I repeated what I had said to the Falangista in my house He replied that in any case it didn't matter to him very much because in the city and the province all the teachers were reds Which was an idiotic point of view but a point of view though I didn't have the guts to tell him so It's the one act of my life I regret now" Suddenly and at the end of that speech the car coughs groans and stops coming out of a curve "Why did you stop" Trescastro yells at the driver The Assault Guard shrugs again "I didn't stop This heap is a wreck After we left the Colony it just gave out" "Try to fix it We're not going to stay here forever" The two Assault Guards get out and the one with the rifle leans it against one of the trees at the side of the road Another feline spark crosses Galadí's eyes but he immediately buries himself again in his withdrawn passivity Trescastro opens the door puts one foot on the ground as if preparing to flee when left alone with us Galindo González forces a weary smile "King Canute is afraid of us Sooner or later he'll get down on his knees and beg our pardon like executioners in the movies" Trescastro looks away and tests the ground with his foot but doesn't respond "What are you afraid of King Canute? That I'll strangle you with my bare hands?" the teacher from Pulianas continues "The truth is I could because as a young man I bent a coin with my fingers and the tip of an arrow with my palms Do it in the blink of an eye Before your henchman from the Assault Guard can reach his Mauser and shoot me But I'm not going to try I know that here we all have the stink of gunpowder on us including you Canute because one day you'll pay for our murders and probably many others in front of a firing squad In the long run I'd only shorten your trip to hell I renounce so high an honor because in spite of my verbosity I don't want to shorten my life by even a few minutes I told you before I'm not a hero and not a martyr either Just a republican like any other and a public school teacher rather sparing of speech though you may not believe that" "Olé and how well you speak for someone sparing of speech!" Cabezas says in praise Then incapable of resisting an easy joke he adds "If they let you speak Don Dióscoro they won't hang you" "They won't hang any of us because Canute here and his henchmen are decent civilized people" the teacher replies quickly "I'll bet you anything they finish us off with a single very fast bullet right in the back of the neck" He gestures with his right hand as if to erase for an instant the presence of everyone except me and turning with difficulty on his artificial leg he faces me "It's curious to speak of betting at moments like this when all I have in life is my life and all I leave to the world is reduced to my two sons who are men now and very capable of looking after themselves I never was a dreamer in any sense of the word and couldn't have imagined a crisis like this If I'd foreseen it I think I would've behaved differently though I don't know how Now I understand those French nobles Michelet talks about who on their last night and almost in the shadow of the guillotine gambled passionately with money they no longer had and goods they had lost" He smiles and nods at his own thoughts "That's beside the point It's regrettable we should meet here considering how much I would've liked to talk with you about poetry and so many other things It's a shame there's no other world where we could discuss them all we liked with immortality ahead of us"

Dióscoro Galindo González must now be in a theater along this spiral if he hasn't been acquitted and sleeps in peace in nothingness because the kingdom of heaven must be made up of people like him However and even though he figures in the cast of the drama you watch from your orchestra seat it is yours and has you as an obligatory protagonist I too would have liked to ask you at this precise moment as I see you again with your hands tied in the Buick between Cabezas and the teacher from Pulianas while Galadí darkens in his self-absorption Trescastro hides his face from all your eyes and the two Assault Guards make an effort to repair the car all beneath the same distant moon what you are thinking my man of flesh the one they killed at a dawn more distant than this moon whose fictitious image is represented on your stage Ask you man to man very privately and just between us whether you really imagine that all this is the parody of a crime devised by Valdés or whether in some remote chamber deep inside you that you share with me you didn't realize without admitting it to yourself that before you knew it they would slaughter all of you as if you were cattle For my part and in retrospect I'm certain that if you insist on believing that all of it is the mockery of a murderer determined to be thought of as crazy your deception is nothing but a desperate means of freeing yourself from madness and safeguarding the privilege of dying honorably and in accordance with reason instead of giving in to the contained panic that would drive you insane Dying like an enlightened man who would climb up to the gallows indifferent to his fate and convinced the same lucid laws will one day govern the history of men and the stars in the sky Dying as a Lavoisier would for example even though you were the surrealist poet who spoke of the frozen honey spilled by the moon of fever of the sea with its immense face of a sky turned into an elephant of swallows that soak in blood of a heart in the shape of a shoe and a glove of smoke in a landscape of rusted keys And now one of the Guards not the driver the other one with the Mauser picks up his rifle distractedly and with lowered head approaches Trescastro who is still testing the ground with his foot as if preparing to run from all of you "It's no use" he tells him "We can't fix the car" "What does that mean? Why can't you fix it?" Trescastro asks impatiently "You need a mechanic here and my friend and I aren't mechanics" "Try again" "I already told you it was no use" The police officer wipes his palm on his hip "It could be a minor thing or something very serious Whatever it is we don't know about it" "What do I do now?" "That's up to you You give the orders" Exasperated Trescastro gets out of the car You think or want to believe that he would like to prolong the farce In a moment you tell yourself everything will have ended shamefully for those pretending to be our executioners Trescastro will give the order to return on foot to the Colony Down the highway and following the course of the irrigation channel you'll retrace your steps in single file like a chain gang One police officer at the head and the other behind you with Trescastro rounding out the party Or perhaps there is another variant at the end of this incomplete monstrous tragedy Perhaps he orders one of the Guards probably the driver to return to the Colony and have them send another car that will take us to Granada ("The mercy of the governor is infinite and this time he decided to give you the gift of life") Meanwhile day will have dawned and the night sounds will cease What chirps what warbles what sips nectar will follow what slithers what gnaws and what ambushes Only the sound of the irrigation channel from Ainadamar will remain identical to itself disregarded by men and their crimes or perhaps the moon similarly detached transformed into the hazy image of itself will contemplate you from the blue sky Now Trescastro turns around and grasps the pistol in his shaking hand He hurries to the open car door with wide open eyes and quivering lips to shout at Galadí "Get out right now!" Galadí's voice after his silence of the last few hours or for the agonizing eternity we have just lived through sounds very different Heartrending it roughens breaks or sinks into the chasms of his panic "Me? Are you calling me?" "Who else you bastard? Get out now! That's an order!" Galadí shrinks into his seat and gradually seems to hide his head between his shoulders His teeth chatter and he trembles like quicksilver "Out! Out!" barks Trescastro "Paco! Paco! At least let them see us die like men! Let them see us die the way we always lived!" shouts Cabezas Dióscoro Galindo González closes his eyes and murmurs something no one understands A prayer or a blasphemy Perhaps both things at the same time "Paco! Paco! Don't let them ever make fun of how we died! Paco my brother Paco of my soul! Don't give in now! Don't give up!" Cabezas's efforts are so great the veins in his throat swell up so much one would say he's about to break the cords that secure his arms In despair over the complete surrender of Galadí who does not even seem to hear him he confronts Trescastro "You son of a bitch kill me first and I'll show you how to die when it's your turn! Kill me first! I beg you!" "This isn't the time for shouting Cabezas" Dióscoro Galindo González says suddenly not opening his eyes and Cabezas in his excitement is not able to hear him "Dying like men isn't doing it with shouts but with self-respect" "Out! Out! Out for the last fucking time!" Trescastro is still bellowing bouncing up and down like one possessed holding the pistol in his hand Shaped like a hook Galadí keeps shrinking in his seat not saying a word In the moonlight his eyes blaze just above his chest When Trescastro tries to grab him by the shirt he kicks out and forces him to retreat "Paco! Paco! Don't give in don't surrender! Don't let them ever say we were afraid when it was time to die!" "Dying like men isn't doing it with shouts but with self-respect" "Shove self-respect up your ass" replies Cabezas sobbing openly "We were like brothers! We were like brothers!" You man of flesh my other self inside me you feel an absolute serenity that confuses and disconcerts you Everything was theater as you foresaw but in the end it was reduced to a drama where you really die as you do in the bullring ("Do you know what Pepe-Hillo replied when he was fat, old, and suffering from gout and was advised to stop fighting the bulls: I'LL LEAVE HERE ON FOOT, OUT THE MAIN GATE, HOLDING MY GUTS IN MY HANDS") Death is the final demand of a completed performance Its unexpected presence and the barbarity of the killing about to happen terrify and astonish you less than your own insensitivity bordering on indifference Upon seeing yourself on the stage in hell when your ghost returned to the night of the crime you don't understand the reasons for your inertia at the most irrevocable of moments Perhaps you decided that everything was nothing and nothing is known about nothing Perhaps as the man of the theater you were you thought any role has unexpected demands in rehearsals that become unavoidable at the moment of the definitive performance Perhaps you eventually had a presentiment that immortality was nothing but another drama the one of the staging of all memories in anticipation of the end of your insomnia Suddenly Trescastro signals to the driver The Assault Guard takes Galadí by the knees and drags him out of the car "Kill me first! Kill me first!" the other banderillero's shouting persists Dióscoro Galindo González gives up trying to persuade him and shakes his head again taking refuge in himself while he mumbles the prayers of a nonbeliever "Never Paco! Never never never!" (I'LL WALK OUT OF HERE, THROUGH THE MAIN GATE, HOLDING MY GUTS IN MY HANDS) Galadí his hands tied rolls on the ground to Trescastro's feet For a moment his screams silence all of you and drown out the sound of the irrigation channel "Encarna! Encarnita my daughter! Encarna my love don't abandon me! Encarna baby don't leave your father! Give me some of the life I gave you when you were conceived!" Then the other police officer ("We're not volunteers and we never would have offered to do this") puts the butt of the Mauser to his shoulder and fires

A mute wind, like the one that seemed to shake Galadí in the Buick, carried him to the theater that anticipated Sandro Vasari's memories. On the stage of the bronze monarchs, impassive gulls resting on their shoulders beneath the Baltic sky, the triumph of *la ragione nuda e chiara* on an afternoon resembling the afternoon of Corpus Christi, and the interview between Vasari and Ruiz Alonso in Madrid, there emerged now the street of an unknown city that his recollections of 1928 or 1929 guessed was North American.

On a corner a cement post like the ones marking bus stops in the New York of his youth, where he had seen the line of unemployed beside Saint Patrick's, then witnessed the aurora borealis above the Edem Mills lake surrounded by bulrushes spattered with tiny snail shells, he made out the name of the street at its intersection with a deserted avenue: BRIARWOOD DRIVE.

A gray car drove along BRIARWOOD DRIVE and stopped before a house that had a small sloping front garden with azaleas in bloom. Someone blew the horn, and Sandro Vasari, taking long strides, came down from the porch, while a stranger holding a leather briefcase under his arm got out of the car. The two men stopped to greet each other at the foot of a myrtle tree. Sandro was half a head taller than his visitor, and both seemed the same age. Looking at them in the middle of the proscenium, he told himself they were probably close to half a century old, more or less, and thought, instinctively and inexplicably, that they could both be his sons if he hadn't been killed that dawn on the Ainadamar road with Galadí, Cabezas, and Dióscoro Galindo González, the public school teacher from Pulianas. At that moment his death felt not like someone else's, as it had on other occasions along the spiral of hell, but very distant and committed by people he could neither pardon nor despise, because on one hand they knew perfectly well what they were doing, and on the other he never wanted to consider them his enemies. He did a fast accounting of the past and decided that his sole vanity, a degree lower than his pride, was refusing to tell Valdés he was crazy.

On the glass-enclosed porch with open curtains, which perhaps in the days of another owner and a different generation might have been a conservatory, a small blond woman of uncertain, undetectable age, greeted the newcomer by extending her hand. He kissed her on both cheeks, but she turned her face to avoid returning his kisses. Looking at them, he thought that at one time she had hated and feared the man.

"Marina," he said to her, "I suppose you won't think now that I've been dreaming you and Sandro since the day I introduced the two of you at the university. How many years has it been? Perhaps thirty-five or more."

"No. Now I'm finally convinced of my own existence," she replied with no hesitation but no great satisfaction either. "Sandro and someone who died a long time ago filled me with that certainty." She looked at the high clouds that gave the sky the tonality of slate, of the roof on a French house recently washed by rain. "The snow will begin soon."

"It doesn't look it," Sandro Vasari observed.

"It doesn't look it, but the first snow will start soon."

Sandro invited them to sit on the porch. Three or four low bookcases filled with books in disorder seemed to have been placed haphazardly. They sat at an iron table painted black, and Marina served herself and Sandro coffee. She offered the recent arrival cognac in a very large tulip-shaped glass. An aroma of extremely old wooden barrels and aged wines aerated by the winds of time seemed to spread over the orchestra seats. He recalled the two cognacs he'd had with Martínez Nadal in Puerta de Hierro on his last day in Madrid, while the vans of the Assault Guards drove down Princesa and newsboys hawked papers. (" . . . I moved writing for the theater, mine included, naturally, ahead by several generations. Perhaps entire centuries, though it may be hard for you to believe.")

"Once, near your house, Sandro and I saw the characters from *Blind Man's Bluff* dancing in the snow," Marina said now in an abstracted tone. "When they disappeared, the title of another work by Goya was left on the snowy grass: *Raging Absurdity.*"

The two men pretended to ignore the comment, though she expressed it in a tone of absolute veracity. On a round table covered by a red cloth, he could see a strange gray device topped by a kind of visor. Sandro Vasari pointed at it with a vague gesture and then said:

"When I interviewed Ruiz Alonso, in Madrid, he suspected I was hiding a tape recorder. He asked me whether I intended to write a book about the death of the poet, and I said I wanted only to write a dream. It was the truth."

"In any case you achieved your goal." The stranger took from the leather briefcase a stack of onionskin sheets, typed and hurriedly bound in cardboard. He left it on the table, leaning his open palm on the napkins. "I read your original and thought it was very acceptable. You ought to publish it."

"I won't," Sandro Vasari obstinately shook his head, "though I'm not sorry I wrote it."

"Why would you be sorry? Why don't you want to publish it? I'm not trying to play devil's advocate, but I admit it needs a good job of editing. I pointed out in the margin some passages you might rewrite. It's the final pass of the pumice stone that Ortega thought indispensable for rounding out not only the form but also the content of any original. It all comes down to a few days of work before or after I take the book to a publisher."

"You can take it to whomever you please and say it's yours, if you like, to speed up publication. I give it to you gladly because I renounced the original though I don't regret having written it, as I said before."

"I don't understand anything. You want to publish the book as if it were mine? How could you imagine I'd lend myself to that?"

"It'll be better if we forget about it," Marina interrupted. "Let's talk about something else."

"Absolutely not," replied Sandro Vasari and then, in a different tone to the visitor: "If you don't publish the book, neither will I. I'll keep it, unsigned, in some drawer, and there my happy heirs, who-ever they may be, will find it. They may even come to believe then that the original was yours. Which means you don't help anything by refusing to accept it."

"The snow's coming earlier than we thought," said Marina. "In this part of the country, the first snowfalls melt right away. They disappear in two days and are white tinged with pink, like the color of old coral and conch shells."

From his orchestra seat in hell, he looked at her silently. Though her appearance might have been arrested at some very distant point in the past, and the years passed without disturbing her small fea-tures, he thought he could confirm her an age as similar to Sandro's or their visitor's. ("Marina, I suppose you won't think now that I've been dreaming you and Sandro since the day I introduced the two of you at the university.") Neither of them seemed to have heard his comment, as if in the theaters along the spiral unnoticed asides were possible. For a moment he forgot about them, and Sandro Vasari's dream that later became a book about his own life and his stay in hell, to enjoy contemplating Marina. The pink, perishable white-ness of the first snows on BRIARWOOD DRIVE was merely an inevita-ble analogy or an obligatory identification with her brittle fragility.

"Fine," the visitor seemed to give in. "Let's hear the secret of so peculiar a decision. Or perhaps you'd prefer Marina to tell me about it, assuming she shares it with you. In any event, I'm all ears."

"The secret is simple even if telling it turns out to be difficult," replied Sandro Vasari, resting his palm for a moment on one of the stranger's knees. "I'll translate it into a fable or a parable, as Gerardo

Diego would write elegies in the shape of a hare. Imagine three people like us in their first year at the university. One of them, let's say the one most similar to a ridiculously rejuvenated image of you, introduces the other two, reinvigorated caricatures of Marina and me, in the courtyard of the School of Arts and Letters. If you'll forgive the interruption, and to shorten the fable for you, from now on I'll call the protagonists by our names. Do you follow?"

"At least I suppose I do. Go on."

"The next part you know better than anyone and I'll summarize it, pushing together what happened over many years. Marina and Sandro become lovers in a little house you rent to them beneath the Vallcarca bridge, not very far from the place where Don Antonio Machado y Ruiz, part of the cast of the manuscript that so far you refuse to accept, lived during his last months in Barcelona. As they say in the movies, any similarity to reality is purely coincidental."

"Understood. Continue."

"Marina always has the feeling that someone is watching her through an antique mirror when she and Sandro make love in their bedroom at the Vallcarca Bridge. It's the start of a long process that I'll move forward and conclude right here, in which she'll come to believe that she and Sandro are nothing but characters in a permanently unfinished book of yours. Earlier, much earlier, in the dispensable history of the university under Franco and the years following the Second World War, Marina aborts Sandro's child at the hands of a sweet old woman on Calle Montcada whose address, naturally, you give them. What no one knows then is that after this difficulty, Marina can have no more children."

"Let's move on to the second act."

"Between one act and another many years go by, during which Marina and Sandro stop seeing each other. She marries a gentleman as dispensable as the protohistory of which she continues to be an oblique product. Sandro goes to the Indies of Eisenhower, marries twice, divorces twice. He has two children by his second wife, all of whom die in a car accident though he suffers no injuries. Then he begins a long process of alcoholization that he will virtuously cure though he is never cured of the cure, which he pays for with a good part of his talent. Earlier and as a result of a trip to Spain to confirm that the damn country has never existed and is simply an absurdity dreamed by Goya Lucientes, he meets Marina again at the house of someone who bears your name. I have no choice but to specify that the lovers begin to live in mortal sin and the dispensable gentleman married to Marina discreetly disappears, while the Caudillo of all Spain dies in installments at the Clinic de la Paz. I'll spare you another interpolated history, like the tale of the Recklessly Curious Man, about a book proposed to Sandro Vasari by someone who bears your name, which Sandro never writes because you do it yourself, I mean to say, your double in my fable."

"I believe I've read all that somewhere."

"Perhaps in the catechism of Father Ripalda."

"That's very possible. What's the hidden side of the fable?"

"Marina should tell you that but I don't know if she'll want to." He saw Sandro turn toward the woman with a deferential expression he had not noticed before on the Italian's face marked by a long scar on the cheek. "Darling, you can enlighten us with the final outlandish lines of our story."

"Friday at the latest, the entire street will be covered with snow," said Marina. Looking at her in the indecisive light of dusk that gradually descended to the stage, he thought he saw a Piero della Francesca. One of the women painted in the Church of San Francesco, in Arezzo, or in the *Diptych of Federigo da Montefeltro and Battista Sforza* in the Uffizi. "At midmorning on Sunday, the silence will melt it."

"Fine. I'll do it," Sandro continued, fairly nervous now. "No one knows anyone else, as Señor Goya Lucientes says so well in one of his printed Caprices. You and I didn't know that Marina had studied music, to great advantage, before and after her brief passage through the university. At least I didn't find out until I finished the original you've brought me now. I gave it to her to read and she gave it back with no comment. A few days later, she asked me to buy her a piano."

"A piano?"

"Exactly. A Wurlitzer we chose together, on which I spent my modest savings. Only then, when she had the piano, did she reveal her purpose. She wanted to compose a sonata inspired by the original of my book."

"A sonata." The newcomer shook his head as if making an effort to comprehend the real meaning of the word. "I don't really understand . . ."

"Perhaps I expressed myself badly. More than being inspired by what I had written, the sonata would be its translation into musical terms. Perhaps you remember that the book is divided into four parts, THE SPIRAL, THE ARREST, DESTINY, and THE TRIAL. The sonata would also have four, though the titles wouldn't necessarily coincide or end with the death of Galadí at the hands of the Assault Guard."

"Then how can you two call it a translation?"

"Heavenly bliss must be made up of people like you," Sandro Vasari said with a smile. "Did you ever stop to notice that music not only has its own language but also its inalienable meaning? Demanding textual coincidence would be asking myth simply to repeat history."

"In any case, perhaps there's only myth, and history doesn't exist."

"Precisely, precisely. Perhaps you're not as foolish as I thought. In the same way, my book ceases to exist as soon as Marina transforms it into a sonata. She worked on her composition for an entire year, and you have to judge the result for yourself. Are you ready, or do you prefer to wait until tomorrow?"

"You can begin whenever you like."

Neither one bothered to consult Marina. From his orchestra seat he told himself that she seemed to have vanished from the minds of both men, as if unavoidable forces had sacrificed her to her own unpublished music. At the same time he thought that only a dead pederast could notice that kind of negligence. Immediately all that there was of man in him, even in hell, led him to forget about Marina while Sandro turned on the tape recorder (" . . . defamed me in writing and in printed books. That Englishman or Irishman, the same one who surreptitiously collected everything I said on a . . . What did he say it was called? . . . Yes, that's it, on a tape recorder"). The first chords did not fail to disconcert him. For reasons he could not explain, contemplating the woman who resembled those of Piero, he did not expect music as descriptive as the sounds that took him by surprise. The sonata opened with the evocation of a no-man's land covering the entire world, as if the planet, empty or abandoned by life, turned silently in infinite space. Suddenly that aboriginal time, initiated in so vast and desolate a manner, was concretized into a sign isolated in the midst of solitudes. A grave as lost as a tomb in Antarctica. A grave, however, that was his, in the unpopulated land of ice and wilderness. The theme of that music confused him as much as the mode. It would have suited the ending of an elegy and reminded him of the last part of his lament for Sánchez Mejías, perhaps his best poem, conceived precisely as a sonata in four movements, but he felt it was too obvious and solemn for the start of a piano piece. He opened and closed an oblique parenthesis to recall the phrase he had once written to Gerardo Diego: " . . . we're mad about bad music." But this was not reprehensible music from any more or less social, historical concept of the arts, and therefore he was not obliged to praise it to himself. Only to follow it with complete interest, though its execution was fairly poor. Deficient, typical of someone in whom ideas raced faster than hands and whose fingers had been away from the keyboard for a long time. The elegy transformed suddenly into a sustained shout of hope and counteracted his own weeping for the death of Ignacio

Sánchez Mejías, where only his voice and a gentle wind in the olive trees sounded to recall the bullfighter, his present body, his absent soul. Here, on the other hand, existence was affirmed in all its vigor, repeating and defining itself by means of interminable death, in terms very similar to his. ("Any instant of my fleeting, impetuous life, any of these moments, present now and impossible on the stage of the theater, is preferable to immortality in hell.") The spiral, which according to Sandro Vasari was the title of the sonata's first movement, shattered into fragments before the burning experience of all memory. His in the restaurant in Madrid, reconciling with Ignacio. ("Come on, man, tell me what you'll have and how the bulls will be this summer.") An imagined Julius Caesar's in the radiance of the aurora borealis, reciting arrogant blank couplets like: "Better first in a village / than second in Rome." Martínez Nadal's saying goodbye to him on the step of the Andalucía express and then walking away along the platform, unaware that their last encounter on earth had concluded there. The man of flesh inside him, asking Valdés whether both of them would set aside everything that had been arranged, whether they weren't insisting in vain on improvising an impossible outcome. If Sandro Vasari said he had divided the book he wrote about him, or the dream that inspired him, into four parts: THE SPIRAL, THE ARREST, DESTINY, THE TRIAL, the music cut across everything the words divided and Marina expounded almost from the first her entire purpose: to reduce to an irreducible unity the history of a poet. The first movement ended in a kind of fugue, a rapid declaration of principles with his name as counterpoint. The story, the music affirmed, would embrace not only existence but death. The other face of life as a function of eternity and even the irrevocable destiny that preceded the birth of man on earth. An academic question, perhaps unnecessary because it was so obvious, underscored the purpose of the entire sonata in its formal aspect. Would it be possible to incorporate into his immortality and mortal biography presentiments like the one he had in the

South Station when, like a good Andalusian, he believed his steps measured and prescribed since a time before all times? Almost without transition the sonata entered its second part with an analogous theme and different counterpoint. While the second established constant references to lines and citations from his dramatic work, the first returned his calvary in Granada and the Rosales family's house to the present. Its execution was also cleaner and perhaps excessively skilled for someone accustomed to the labored awkwardness of the first part. He thought of two Marinas existing together, and created the image of Piero della Francesca's women, the one who conceived the unnamed sonata and the one the music demanded for its realization and performance. Between the two of them, and in another no-man's land like the one he sometimes thought separated him from the man of flesh, a third Marina wandered: the plaintive, fragile creature who looked at the heavens as if they were a mirror and apparently had seen the characters of Goya's *Blind Man's Bluff* dancing on the snows of yesteryear. He forgot about Marina, or her three images disappeared, in the counterpoint's literary evocations. Antoñito el Camborio, "Camborio with the strong mane," was arrested by five Civil Guards, leaving behind him a river of lemons. The same Camborio was knifed to death, murmuring words lost in a gush of blood. A dead Ignacio Sánchez Mejías climbed the steps in an empty bullring, searching in vain for his lost body. Invisible bells tolled each afternoon in Granada for a child. The moon went across the sky holding another child by the hand like his mother, sleepwalking, rescued him from the water where he sank, asleep. A hyacinth light illuminated the keyboard and his right hand, while his father contemplated him in the semi-darkness of the Huerta de San Vicente. From the top of railings bathed in the brilliance of the stars, the shadow of a girl inclined over a cistern, while he repeated in silence the words he said to himself so often on the spiral of hell: "I thought the dead were blind, like the ghost of the Gypsy girl in one of my poems who, poured into the reservoir in the garden, did not see things when they were looking at her." Another woman ran through her house as if mad, pursued by a grief that would be black if it were visible. An identical sorrow assailed a horseman riding through magnetic mountains, on a sea crossed by thirteen ships. A lover declared he hadn't wanted to fall in love, as if love were the result of will and not passion. To fulfill his obligation to himself and not the woman who had given herself to him, to behave like the man he was, he gave her a satin sewing basket before he left her. An ironic note, some rhythms that changed when repeated, revealed his own mordancy toward that poem. Universally known for its piercing eroticism, it had been written by someone who perhaps had never gone to bed with or desired a woman. ("Then like now it was impossible for you to reply because the words burned like embers before turning into dust into nothing and your heart seemed to crack open at each beat or turn into porous, worn stone like those birds trapped in amber before man walked the earth . . . ") The third movement altered the brilliant tonalities of the second. At least at first one might say it was painted entirely in sepia and gold, like the murals by Sert in the Vic Cathedral that Dalí had forced him to admire against his will. So sudden a change confounded him again, even though by then he thought himself accustomed to the sonata's variations. The visitor murmured something about how interconnected he judged the music and the third part of the unpublished book to be. Sandro obliged him to be quiet with an impatient gesture. At that instant he understood that the composition did not refer precisely to him, alive or dead, but to one of his hypothetical phantoms or hallucinations. In other words, to the first of his doubles who had appeared in hell. ("Boy, this isn't hell and we're not dead. I know hell very well to my misfortune and I can assure you it's on earth. Do you know where we really are?") The ill-tempered old man said he dreamed him in a sepia nightmare on the top floor on Calle de Angulo, where he had spent close to half a century in hiding. He had taken refuge there to avoid being arrested, but then the hiding place turned into a voluntary prison made to the measure of his pride. In his judgment, very well expressed in the somewhat mocking rhetoric of the music, the real penitentiary or authentic cemetery was his unfortunate country that in vain thought itself free after the death of a dictator and the attempted metamorphosis of one regime into another. (" . . . reconsider and recall the time when I taught you what an hendecasyllable was. Now it's up to me to show you who and where we are.") In spite of a repeated note like the dripping of a fountain in spring onto the ice of the past winter, the old man continued his derisive denial. "You're not me but my imprisoned dream," the dialoguing water sang softly, as in some of Machado's poems. "You're merely my delirium because in so many years, constantly hidden in the Rosales family's house, you didn't write a single line; you didn't outline one piece for the theater. I, so fearful, would not have renounced being who I am only to save my hidden life." With the thaw, the fountain transformed into a stream and then a river that pulled the ghost underwater. The current carried away the flailing and shouting of a Punchinello in the *commedia dell'arte*. It reduced him to its own image by bouncing him against polished stones. Then to the shade of its shade. Afterward to nothingness. Solemn chords made Don Antonio Machado pass across the sky, his lapels sprinkled with cigarette ash, his green thermos pressed to his chest. ("I like poetry and music.") Machado disappeared and the water stopped at a beach of golden sand. His other self in his delirium, the one who stayed in Madrid when he said he had left for Granada and then passed through France to the United States at the end of a war he considered lost, stood on the shore with his arms crossed behind him. He was the strongest of the three, as the music stated while the river was lost in its bed as if it had never existed. He assumed his latent manhood with the woman whose gaze resembled Melibea's; he turned down the Nobel Prize in Literature because he thought it the vanity of vanities, and acknowledged that his life as a university professor in America was a hell to which he submitted willingly and not without lucid irony. Yet he was as much an impostor as the old man hiding on Calle de Angulo. Implacably, the music alluded to his skeptical competence and sarcastic disdain in contrast to the fragile condition of the true poet, in whom something of the boy he had been persisted, until they decided to murder him in his own Granada. If he had lived a hundred years, the same innocence would have endured inside him and in that no-man's-land that distanced him at times from the man of flesh. The third movement ran into the fourth, joining in something like parallel whirlpools, where as soon as he dreamed any of his three ghosts they were the three dreamed by Sandro Vasari. Then the last part of the sonata opened with a trial, in part solemn and in part almost festive, as if Antoñito el Camborio and Ignacio Sánchez Mejías accused him of considering them dead in two of his poems. Characterized in broad strokes, Valdés, Ruiz Alonso, Trescastro, and the Assault Guards appeared. He didn't acquit them or tell himself to forgive them. In the voice he had learned to recognize as his in the sonata, he simply stated that he pitied them since he, or the innocent with whom he had always lived, couldn't have endured the death of another person in his heart or his gut. Immediately all his executioners disappeared because, after all, as the music was not afraid to affirm, the immortality of those poor souls was part of his own. Just as his memory among men was due in part to the arrest and death of Antonio el Camborio. As if the memory of that character in two of his poems could determine Marina's music retrospectively and transfix eternity itself on a slant, the sonata repeated phrases and allusions from many other poems of his, poured like a rain of gold over a limitless area. A horseman rode toward Córdoba, knowing he'd never reach the promised city because death would come out to meet him. From the towers of Córdoba, identifying at the same time the man's end and his purpose, death watched him like a lover who would then come down to wait for him at the gates and along the inaccessible walls. The amputated hands of Saint Eulalia still clasped each other, like decapitated prayers. Narrow streams, rushing like water buffalo, charged with silver horns the naked boys swimming. The prematurely aged silence of his dead profile foretold during a summer filled with red fish, flushed like a crocodile. In the absence of another dead man, the clock and the wind sounded together, as in a line of Machado's that perhaps had inspired his though he couldn't remember it now, the bell in the tribunal building struck one above sleeping Soria. The moon descended to the forge looking for a boy and her fragrant skirt was made of illuminated tuberoses in the summer night. Death transformed Ignacio Sánchez Mejías on the bier and turned him into a dark minotaur. His coffin borne by a carriage descended slowly along the streets of Madrid on the way to Atocha Station. A landscape of nascent America, with sibilant railroads, fences covered by advertisements, and land gutted by coal mines contemplated the passing of Walt Whitman, dressed in corduroy, his beard covered by butterflies. Not far away, in another landscape of a cubist stage prepared for a ritual or a ballet, Amnon raped his half-sister Tamar, and their father, King David, cut the strings of his harp. The rain of gold having fallen to earth, the music seemed to become quiet and recede toward silence along the path of the first solitudes, those that populated only his lonely grave. The gold poured from the heavens dimmed gradually, as fire beetles and lightning bugs disappear at dawn. A single light, gold like a flame at its very center, began to burn on his grave. At that point he expected the end of the sonata, unwilling to confess to himself his disenchantment with a rather conventional ending. That is to say, a few chords tapering off until they disappear, in the way a bright, sonorous stream empties its last threads of water into a shoreless lake never discovered by man. But Marina surprised him again, sustaining this movement of the sonata until she had elevated it to a new dimension. The golden light in the silent solitudes stopped being the one on his grave and became his alert consciousness burning in hell. He was surrounded now not by the spiral and infinite eternity (assuming the spiral wasn't infinite eternity patiently awaiting the last dead person for the last theater) but by his own unfathomable, interminable unconscious that held every reference alluded to in Sandro Vasari's book. There, inhabiting him and redeeming himself in the poet, Sandro himself, his nameless visitor, his executioners, his parents, his friends whom he always loved, his lovers whom he never loved, the landscapes of his soul and his childhood, the vertical perspectives of Madrid and New York ("Gas in every apartment," *Brother, can you spare a dime*), Dalí's Cadaqués and Maqueda Castle with Alberti and María Teresa, *La Gare Saint Lazare* and the South Station, Machaquito and Vicente Pastor, the flashy young men and women on the platforms, la Argentinita and Esperancita Rosales, the dogs summoned by Villalón and Dióscoro Galindo González, Galadí and Cabezas, Martínez Nadal and the Morla Lynches, *The Public* and *Lament,* his ghosts in hell and his midmorning visitors, the old unemployed actor, Isidro Máiquez and Medioculo, swift-footed Achilles and José Antonio Primo de Rivera laughing at Ruiz Alonso, his dreams and all the dreams of the living and the dead, the gold slipper and the house shoes of Doña Juana the Mad. There, finally, Marina herself sharing with him that entire world with no bottom and no shores, as a queen would with the king, her husband.

"Do you understand now why I can't publish the original you've returned to me?" Sandro asked the stranger as he turned off the tape recorder.

"Yes, yes, I believe I understand."

"An unknown destiny, about which I am totally ignorant except for the fact that it transcended me, obliged me to write this book, born of a dream, so that Marina would compose her sonata. I was a means, not an end, and since the sonata is finished, my novel, we'll call it that in order to call it something, represents absolutely nothing."

"But that's no reason to destroy it."

"Perhaps not. Some bad habits of vanity oblige me to agree with you about this not especially transcendent detail. Which is why I'd like it to be published under your name and dedicated to Marina and me. You won't refuse, will you?"

"And suppose I do?"

"Then I'd burn it in the fireplace when the first snow falls. The one Marina announced would come very soon."

Marina didn't seem to be listening to them. Bent over, arms extended, her hands were crossed between her knees. Her hair fell over her forehead and cheeks, hiding her face, as if she were a penitent forgetful of the faults she had committed or preparing to atone for others she hadn't committed yet. One would say she was as distant from the woman who composed the piano sonata as if one of them had never existed.

"All right," the visitor conceded. "I'll do as you wish and publish the original as mine." He picked up the bound typed sheets and slipped them into his leather briefcase, then closed it carefully. He noticed his hands. They were identical to Sandro Vasari's.

"You won't forget to dedicate the book to us when it's published," Sandro insisted.

"No, I won't forget."

"Can we count on it?"

"You can count on it." The stranger shrugged.

"I feel much better now," Sandro replied. His irony was painful and indecisive, as if gliding along the edge of a barber's razor.

"I don't." The other man shook his head. "In a way I understand or would like to understand your reasons for not publishing the work under your own name. On the other hand . . . "

"On the other hand . . . "

"I'd like to know what you'll do with your sonata, Marina. Did both of you decide to destroy it too?"

He didn't seem to dare look at her, as if he didn't expect an answer from her either. Marina lifted her head and made a vague gesture as she looked at him with her gray eyes. Then she began to hum, almost mumbling, a strange melody completely unlike the sonata.

"Destroying it or publishing it would be two faces of the same aberration," Sandro replied. "The sonata is ours and will live with us as long as we live. If you'll forgive the obligatory rhetoric of the circumstance."

"You're forgiven, even though I don't understand you."

"I assumed that too, because you never understood us, though Marina came to believe we lacked existence outside your dreams and your books."

"Sometimes I still think that," murmured Marina.

"I already told you my original was nothing more or less than an inadvertent way for her to compose the sonata," Sandro continued, addressing the stranger without listening to her. "Soon after you realize what has happened, you'll become aware of an erudite consequence. It's logical and in a sense inevitable that Marina should write this music, as it is also reasonable she would need my manuscript to conceive it. Said another way, and this time so you'll understand us, the sonata is the child of flesh and blood we'll never be able to have."

"That occurred to me and I had to reject it. On one hand it sounds like a prosopopoeia, on the other it's too reasonable. The prosopopoeia is an affectation and therefore doesn't tally with the truth. The excess of reason is no more and no less . . . " He hesitated a few moments and then repeated in a loud voice, " . . . no more and no less than madness."

"It's true!" Sandro confirmed, struggling to contain his excitement. "It's true! Don't you see?"

"Sincerely, I don't."

"Then listen to me. Marina is sick and her illness has a name not recorded in treatises on the soul because it bears your own surname. Perhaps you're correct when you claim she suffers from an excess of reason or filthy logic, as Unamuno would say. You governed our lives from the day you chose to introduce us at the university while monarchists and Falangistas, two species that are almost extinct today, were bludgeoning one another in front of Don Juan's first statement against Franco, which was tacked on the bulletin board. I, always prone to reticence, recounted to you in detail, and in spite of myself, our moments of love in the bedroom beneath the Vallcarca Bridge . . . "

"Nobody forced you to reveal anything," the new arrival observed with a note of impatience at the back of his voice. "This is all absurd, Sandro, even if it is true."

"Perhaps there's nothing more absurd than truth itself. Marina came to believe that someone, perhaps you, was watching us from behind the mirror that the years had turned ashen black. I'd say that what happened was different and of course more inexplicable. In a way I'll never understand, because thank God I'm not a writer or a dramatist, before my revelations you already knew everything I was going to tell you, including the fact of my confession."

"*The act of love is identical to the act of lust,* says Graham Greene in one of his exemplary novels. Even a blind man like Borges would add that any couple in the act of love, or of simple pleasure, is every couple in any of those acts."

"I care very little about what those old hypocrites say. I'll save you another recounting of the abortion on Montcada Street, though I can't hide from you that even then I thought it had been anticipated by your mediocre fantasy, with the two of us acting as protagonists. We'll forget many years to return to those of the death throes and passing of the Caudillo Franco, when you reunited Marina and me and commissioned me to write a book on the life and painting of Goya."

"Now you'll say I did it knowing you wouldn't write it."

"You did it knowing I wouldn't write it, though naturally you did publish another book about my inability to finish mine."

"Sandro, I'm more a master of both your destinies than I am of my own."

"Possibly you're less the master of your own than of ours because you too submit to another's will without knowing it. The fact is I don't care, because ever since that distant day when you joined the three of us in the courtyard of Arts and Letters, the case is ours only as it relates to me. Shall I go on?"

"If you like."

"After I forgot about Goya, I dreamed about our murdered poet in hell, talked to Ruiz Alonso, and wrote this book, which I did finish and therefore give to you. Because it is all mine from beginning to end." He rested his palm on the briefcase that contained the original, close to the hand of his visitor. From his orchestra seat, he was surprised again at the similarity between the hands of the two men. "I won't hide from you that at times, as I was writing, I suspected I was your puppet again, your Doppelgänger with a different face. I told myself then: ' . . . Marina's right. He dreams I'm struggling to move this book forward. It never would've occurred to me to begin it, since I never had any great interest in the poetry of that unfortunate man, though it's still applauded in lecture halls, on stages, and profusely printed in textbooks so many years after his death.'"

"Why did you finish it then?"

"Inadvertently, so that Marina would compose her music. I think I told you this before. When I heard the entire sonata, after having listened to fragments, not paying much attention, I understood it was our child and our freedom because you had lost all power over us. For the first time we counted on something of ours created behind your back. Something that would free us forever and transform us into our own and only reason for being."

"How should I interpret all this?"

"However you choose. Perhaps as a love story. Notice that now I'm the one who reveals to you our present and immediate past and not the reverse. We lived a circumstance diametrically opposed to that of my confessions, following the afternoons beneath the Vall-carca Bridge. When in a way I knew you knew, with no need to play the voyeur behind the mirror. Now I also know that whatever happens, it will be for the best and we'll never see one another again."

From the orchestra seats, he thought he detected on stage the silence of the denouement, as unforeseen as it was irrevocable. At the same time and in one of those sudden vacillations he was as prone to in hell as on earth, he thought that perhaps, in spite of what had been said by Sandro Vasari, the performance of other people's memories would go on endlessly. So that the appearance of their sudden end was due only to a sudden fatigue that unexpectedly began to overwhelm him. Yet on stage he saw the stranger stand and pick up the briefcase that held the original.

"I suppose you'll invite me to leave."

"There's no hurry at all," Sandro replied, still sitting and spreading his arms in an imprecise gesture. "I didn't ask you to go and in fact you can stay as long as you like, because you've already lost all power over us. I said only that we'd never see one another again."

"You may be right. Are you really prepared to renounce your book?"

"I turn it over to you gladly and won't change my mind."

"Very well." He rested a palm on Marina's shoulder. She hesitated a few moments and then quickly caressed that hand, as if it were a statue's.

"I'll walk with you to the end of the garden," said Sandro Vasari, while the stranger shrugged. "Don't get lost in the labyrinth of streets when you leave this neighborhood, and hurry. You don't want to get caught by snow on the highway."

They went down together to the myrtle hedge along the sloping lawn and he observed that not once did Marina turn to look at them. Suddenly the sky began to darken and an absolute silence, with no wind and no birds, descended over the street. They couldn't hear the grass growing, covered with dark spots of autumn, but their steps made a noise when they walked on it.

"All right, then. I suppose we say goodbye forever here."

"We say goodbye forever here," Sandro Vasari agreed. "Good luck with your book."

"I'll dedicate it to you and Marina."

"You don't have to, but do as you like."

"I will in any case."

The man Sandro accused of having ruled their lives, as if they were dreamed puppets, opened the car door, tossed the briefcase on one of the upholstered seats, and closed the door again. In that quiet the slam sounded like a pistol shot, while Marina shivered and for the first time turned to look at them. Across the street, in some of the houses also separated by small sloping gardens, lights began to go on. One would say they went on by themselves, as if each afternoon they punctually held a vigil for the absence of persons who had gone away, or were very distant, in a world populated only by Sandro, Marina, and the visitor. From his orchestra seat, he thought in a very quiet voice: "Soon it will be autumn on earth."

"When you get to the end of Briarwood, turn right. Then, after the first light, take the street immediately to the left," Sandro Vasari explained.

"I know, I know. Don't worry."

"I'm not worried at all. But as I told you, this is a labyrinth."

"They say the only way to get out of a labyrinth is to always go left."

"Perhaps that was true in other times and different latitudes. These days in this country, it isn't."

The stranger smiled when he opened the other car door. For an instant, while Marina looked at them and the clouds seemed to rise in the sky, they shook hands with the coldness of two strangers. Then, in a sudden, mutual impulse, before the stranger got into his car and Sandro walked back to the house, they embraced closely. Afterward, the car drove off toward the labyrinth.

The proscenium went dark and there was nothing on stage. Recalling that embrace, he thought of the one between Don Quixote and Cardenio at their first meeting in the Sierra Morena, at the end of Chapter XXIII of the First Part. When he read it in his adolescence, he hesitated about the vocation that had already been planned, telling himself he could never write anything as beautiful and as true. Now, dead though not tired and on the spiral of hell, he admitted willingly to not having written it, while a sudden fatigue was taking possession of him. Some shepherds had told the knight the tale of Cardenio, driven mad by love, who runs almost naked over the rugged terrain, sometimes very sane and other times quite deranged. As soon as chance arranges the meeting of the two madmen (the Ragged or Bad-looking One and the Sad One), Don Quixote descends from Rocinante, approaches that other stranger, and holds him to his chest. Cardenio, perhaps the less demented of the two, moves him back a little and looks into his eyes to see if he recognizes him. Or perhaps to determine whether in those eyes he can detect himself, with the correct and essential clarity that knowing oneself alive demands. Years later he told Dalí in Cadaqués that he had never read anything more profound and didn't believe anything more profound had ever been written. Cardenio sees himself in Don Quixote as Don Quixote sees himself in Cardenio. Each of the two men is the fellow and mirror of the other: his confessor, his image, and his witness. At the same time and even though centuries have to pass for anyone to become aware of it, Cardenio is also Cervantes embracing the most successful and universal of his creations only to come upon himself in his eyes. No, he had never written anything like it in a fairly extensive work given the few years he walked the earth. No, and he didn't lament it either. That was simply the way it was and with the unexpected fatigue came a serene resignation. In any case and somewhat in spite of himself, he admitted that Cervantes had determined his life as a writer (since the idea of never writing was very fleeting), in the same way that so long after his death, he had led Sandro Vasari and through him Marina to create the book and the sonata. Having that kind of influence, after years or after centuries, on strangers like them was the sole and the true immortality. But he did not proceed with that trend of thinking because an infinite exhaustion prevented it as he slowly slipped toward the center of himself, where waiting for him were peace, sleep, and a very dark light resembling nothingness.

Yale University Press books may be purchased in quantity for educational, business, or promotional use. For information, please e-mail sales.press@yale.edu (U.S. office) or sales@yaleup.co.uk (U.K. office).

Set in Electra and Nobel types by Keystone Typesetting, Inc.
Printed in the United States of America.

A catalogue record for this book is available from the British Library.

This paper meets the requirements of ANSI/NISO Z39.48-1992 (Permanence of Paper).

CARLOS ROJAS is a novelist, an art historian, and since the age of fifty a creator of visual works of art. He was born in Barcelona and came to the United State as a young man. In 1960 he joined the faculty of Emory University, where he is now Charles Howard Candler Professor of Spanish Emeritus. He has received numerous important Spanish literary prizes, including the Premio Nadal. He lives in Atlanta.

EDITH GROSSMAN has translated into English many works by major Latin American and Peninsular writers, garnering an array of awards and honors.